THE NEW YORK TIMES BESTSELLER BY THE AUTHOR OF THE CAT WHO SAW STARS

Lilian Jackson Braun

The Cat Who Played Brahms

The captivating series featuring Mystery's most extraordinary detective team

JOVE

$6.99 U.S.
$9.99 CAN

THE CRITICS ARE PURRING OVER
THE CAT WHO SERIES!

"BRAUN OFFERS SOME OF THE MOST WITTY, ORIGINAL FARE IN THE GENRE."
—NEW YORK DAILY NEWS

"GLORIOUS CAPERS...PURR-FECTLY WONDERFUL!"
—INSIDE BOOKS

"THOROUGHLY DELIGHTFUL...SHEER READING ENJOYMENT."
—DETROIT FREE PRESS

"WHIMSICAL AND WONDERFUL...A DELIGHT FROM START TO FINISH. A MUST!"
—SHERIDAN (OR.) SUN

"READ THESE BOOKS IF YOU WANT TO FORGET YOUR TROUBLES!"
—FT. MYERS BEACH BULLETIN

"THE MIX OF CRIME AND CATS [IS] CATNIP TO READERS WHO LIKE BOTH."
—CHICAGO SUN-TIMES

Read ALL the CAT WHO mysteries!

THE CAT WHO COULD READ BACKWARDS: The world of modern art is a mystery to many—but for Jim Qwilleran and Koko it's a mystery of another sort . . .

THE CAT WHO ATE DANISH MODERN: Qwill isn't thrilled about covering interior design for *The Daily Fluxion*. Little does he know that a murderer has designs on a woman featured in one of his stories . . .

THE CAT WHO TURNED ON AND OFF: Qwill and Koko are joined by Yum Yum as they try to solve a murder in an antique shop . . .

THE CAT WHO SAW RED: Qwill starts his diet—*and* a new gourmet column for the *Fluxion*. It isn't easy—but it's not as hard as solving a murder case!

THE CAT WHO PLAYED BRAHMS: Fishing at a secluded cabin, Qwill hooks on to a mystery—and Koko develops a strange fondness for classical music . . .

THE CAT WHO PLAYED POST OFFICE: Koko and Yum Yum turn into fat cats when Qwill inherits millions. But amid the caviar and champagne, Koko starts sniffing clues to a murder!

THE CAT WHO HAD 14 TALES: A delightful collection of feline mystery fiction from the creator of Koko and Yum Yum!

*TURN THE PAGE FOR MORE
CAT WHODUNITS . . .*

THE CAT WHO KNEW SHAKESPEARE: The local newspaper publisher has perished in an accident—or is it murder? This is the question. . . .

THE CAT WHO SNIFFED GLUE: After a rich banker and his wife are killed, Koko develops an odd appetite for glue. To solve the murder, Qwill has to figure out why. . . .

THE CAT WHO WENT UNDERGROUND: Qwill and the cats head for their Moose County log cabin for a relaxing summer—but when a handyman disappears, Koko must dig up the buried motive for a sinister crime. . . .

THE CAT WHO TALKED TO GHOSTS: Qwill and Koko try to solve a haunting mystery in a historic farmhouse.

THE CAT WHO LIVED HIGH: A glamorous art dealer was killed in Qwill's high-rise apartment—and he and the cats are about to reach new heights in detection as they try to find out whodunit. . . .

THE CAT WHO KNEW A CARDINAL: The director of the local Shakespeare production dies in Qwill's orchard—and the stage is set for a puzzling mystery!

THE CAT WHO MOVED A MOUNTAIN: Qwill moves to a new home in the beautiful Potato Mountains. But when a dispute between local residents and developers boils over into a murder case, he has to keep his eyes open to find the culprit!

THE CAT WHO WASN'T THERE: Qwill's on his way to Scotland—and on his way to solving another purrplexing mystery!

THE CAT WHO WENT INTO THE CLOSET: Qwill's moved into a mansion . . . and it has fifty closets for Koko to investigate! But among the junk, Koko finds a clue—and now Quill's unearthing some surprising skeletons. . . .

THE CAT WHO CAME TO BREAKFAST: Qwill and the cats face a puzzle when peaceful Breakfast Island is turned upside-down by real-estate developers, controversy—and murder . . .

THE CAT WHO BLEW THE WHISTLE: An old steam locomotive has been restored, causing excitement in Moose County. But a mysterious murder brings the fun to a screeching halt—and Qwill and Koko are tracking down the culprit. . . .

THE CAT WHO SAID CHEESE: At the Great Food Explo, scheduled events include a bake-off, a cheese tasting, and a restaurant opening. Unscheduled events include mystery and murder. . . .

THE CAT WHO TAILED A THIEF: A rash of petty thievery—and death of a wealthy young woman—leaves a trail of clues as elusive as a cat burglar. . . .

THE CAT WHO SANG FOR THE BIRDS: Spring comes to Moose County—and a young cat's fancy turns to crime solving . . .

THE CAT WHO SAW STARS: UFOs in Mooseville? When a backpacker disappears, Qwill investigates a rumored "abduction"—with the help of his own little aliens. . . .

THE CAT WHO ROBBED A BANK: As the Highland Games approach, Qwill has a lot of mysteries to sort out—not the least of which is Koko's sudden interest in photographs, pennies, and paper towels. . . .

THE CAT WHO SMELLED A RAT
Available from Jove Books

Jove titles by Lilian Jackson Braun

THE CAT WHO SMELLED A RAT
THE CAT WHO ROBBED A BANK
THE CAT WHO COULD READ BACKWARDS
THE CAT WHO ATE DANISH MODERN
THE CAT WHO TURNED ON AND OFF
THE CAT WHO SAW RED
THE CAT WHO PLAYED BRAHMS
THE CAT WHO PLAYED POST OFFICE
THE CAT WHO KNEW SHAKESPEARE
THE CAT WHO SNIFFED GLUE
THE CAT WHO WENT UNDERGROUND
THE CAT WHO TALKED TO GHOSTS
THE CAT WHO LIVED HIGH
THE CAT WHO KNEW A CARDINAL
THE CAT WHO MOVED A MOUNTAIN
THE CAT WHO WASN'T THERE
THE CAT WHO WENT INTO THE CLOSET
THE CAT WHO CAME TO BREAKFAST
THE CAT WHO BLEW THE WHISTLE
THE CAT WHO SAID CHEESE
THE CAT WHO TAILED A THIEF
THE CAT WHO SANG FOR THE BIRDS
THE CAT WHO SAW STARS

THE CAT WHO HAD 14 TALES
(short story collection)

The Cat Who Played Brahms

Lilian Jackson Braun

JOVE BOOKS, NEW YORK

THE CAT WHO PLAYED BRAHMS

A Jove Book / published by arrangement with the author

PRINTING HISTORY
Jove edition / June 1987

Copyright © 1987 by Lilian Jackson Braun.

Visit our website at
www.penguinputnam.com

ISBN: 0-515-09050-6

A JOVE BOOK®
Jove Books are published by
The Berkley Publishing Group, a division of Penguin Putnam Inc.,
375 Hudson Street, New York, New York 10014.
JOVE and the "J" design are trademarks
belonging to Penguin Putnam Inc.

PRINTED IN THE UNITED STATES OF AMERICA

40   39   38   37   36   35   34   33   32   31

ONE

For Jim Qwilleran, veteran journalist, it was one of the most appalling moments of his career. Years before, as a war correspondent, he had been strafed on the beaches; as a crime reporter he had been a target of the Mob. Now he was writing restaurant reviews for a midwestern newspaper, the *Daily Fluxion,* and he was not prepared for the shocking situation at the Press Club.

The day had started well enough. He had eaten a good breakfast at his boarding house: a wedge of honeydew melon, an omelette *fines herbes* with sautéed chicken livers, cheese popovers, and three

1

cups of coffee. He planned to lunch with his old friend Arch Riker at the Press Club, their favorite haunt.

At twelve noon Qwilleran bounded up the steps of the grimy limestone fortress that had once been the county jail but now dispensed food and drink to the working press. As he approached the ancient nail-studded portal, he sensed that something was wrong. He smelled fresh varnish! His sharp ear detected that the massive door no longer creaked on its hinges! He stepped into the lobby and gasped. The murky, smoky ambience that he loved so well was now all freshness and sparkle.

Qwilleran was aware that the Press Club had been closed for two weeks for something called annual housekeeping, but no one had hinted at this metamorphosis. It had happened while he had been out of town on assignment.

His luxuriant pepper-and-salt moustache was rampant with rage, and he pounded it into submission with his fist. Instead of the old paneled walls, black with numberless coats of cheap varnish, the lobby was wallpapered with something resembling his grandmother's tablecloths. Instead of the scarred plank floor rippled with a century of wear, there was wall-to-wall carpet over thick rug padding. Instead of fluorescent tubes glaring on the domed ceiling, there was a chandelier of polished brass. Even the familiar mustiness was missing, replaced by a chemical smell of newness.

Gulping down his shock and dismay, the newsman dashed into the bar, where he always lunched in a far dark corner. There he found more of the same: creamy walls, soft lighting, hanging baskets of plastic plants, and mirrors. *Mirrors!* Qwilleran shuddered.

Arch Riker, his editor at the *Daily Fluxion*, was sitting at the usual table with his usual glass of Scotch, but the scarred wooden table had been sanded and varnished, and there were white paper placemats with scalloped edges. The waitress was there promptly with Qwilleran's usual glass of tomato juice, but she was not wearing her usual skimpy white uniform with frilly handkerchief in the breast pocket. All the waitresses were now dressed as French maids in chic black outfits with white aprons and ruffled caps.

"Arch! What happened?" Qwilleran demanded. "I don't believe what I'm seeing!" He lowered his substantial bulk into a chair and groaned.

"Well, the club has lots of women members now," Riker explained calmly, "and they got themselves appointed to the housekeeping committee so they could clean the place up. It's called reversible renovation. Next year's housekeeping committee can rip out the wallpaper and carpet and go back to the original filth and decrepitude. . . ."

"You sound as if you like it. Traitor!"

"We have to swing with the times," Riker said with the bored equanimity of an editor who has seen it all. "Look at the menu and decide what you want to eat. I've got a meeting at one-thirty. I'm going to order the lamb curry."

"I've lost my appetite," Qwilleran said, his disgruntled expression accentuated by the downcurve of his moustache. He waved an arm at the surrounding scene. "The place has lost all its character. It even smells phony." He raised his nose and sniffed. "Synthetic! Probably carcinogenic!"

"You're getting to have a nose like a bloodhound, Qwill. No one else has complained about the smell."

"And another thing," Qwilleran said with belligerence. "I don't like what's happening at the *Fluxion* either."

"What do you mean?"

"First they assigned all those women to the copy desk in the City Room and switched all those men to the Women's Department. Then they gave us unisex restrooms. Then they moved in all those new desks in green and orange and blue. It looks like a circus! They they took away my typewriter and gave me a video display terminal that gives me a headache."

Riker said in his soothing tone: "You never forgot those old movies, Qwill. You still want reporters to type with their hats on and poke the keys with two fingers."

Qwilleran slumped in his chair. "Look here, Arch. I've been trying to make up my mind about something, and now I've made a decision. I've got three weeks of vacation coming and two weeks of comp time. I want to add some leave-of-absence and go away for three months."

"You've gotta be kidding."

"I'm tired of writing flattering hogwash about restaurants that advertise in the *Fluxion*. I want to go up north and get away from city hype and city pollution and city noise and city crime."

"Are you all right, Qwill?" Riker asked with alarm. "You're not sick or something, are you?"

"Is it abnormal to want to breathe a little fresh air?"

"It'll kill you! You're a city boy, Qwill. So am I. We were both brought up on carbon monoxide and smoke and all that dirt that blows around Chicago. I'm your oldest friend, and I say: *Don't do it!* You're just getting on your feet financially, and . . ." (he lowered his voice) "Percy is thinking about a great new assignment for you."

Qwilleran grunted. He knew all about the managing editor's great new assignments. Four of them had come his way in the last few years, and every one of them was an insult to a former war correspondent and prize-winning crime reporter. "What is it this time?" he mumbled. "Obituaries? Household hints?"

Riker smiled smugly before saying in a whisper: "Investigative reporting! You can call your own shots. Expose political graft, corporate fraud, environmental violations, government spending, anything you dig up."

Qwilleran touched his moustache gingerly and

stared across the table at his editor. Investigative reporting was something he had wanted to do long before it became the media rage. Yet his sensitive upper lip—the source of his best hunches—was sending him signals. "Maybe next fall. Right now I want to spend the summer where people don't lock their doors or take the car keys out of the ignition."

"The job may not be open next fall. We've found out the *Morning Rampage* is hunting for an investigative reporter, and Percy wants to beat them to the gun. You know how he is. You're taking a big gamble if you're not here to grab it when it's offered to you."

The waitress returned to serve Riker another Scotch and take their lunch order. "You're looking thin," she said to Qwilleran. "What'll you have? Half-pound burger with fries, double malt, and apple pie?"

He threw her a grouchy look. "I'm not hungry."

"Order a TLT," she suggested. "You can eat the lettuce and tomato and take the turkey home to Koko. I'll bring you a doggie bag."

Qwilleran's Siamese cat was a celebrity at the Press Club. Koko's portrait hung in the lobby along with Pulitzer Prize winners, and he was probably the only cat in the history of journalism who had his own press card signed by the chief of police. Although Qwilleran's suspicious nature and inquisitive mind had brought a few criminals to justice, it was commonly understood at the Press Club that the brains behind his success belonged to a feline of outstanding intelligence and sensory perception. Koko always seemed to sniff or scratch in the right place at the right time.

The two newsmen applied themselves to the lamb curry and the turkey sandwich in silence, indicating deep thought. Finally Riker asked: "Where would you go if you took the summer off?"

"I'd take a little place on the lake, about four hundred miles north. Near Mooseville."

"That far away? What would you do with the cats?"

"Take them along."

"You don't have a car. And there are no taxis in the north woods."

"I could put a downpayment on a car—a used car, of course."

"Of course," said Riker, knowing his friend's reputation for thriftiness. "And I suppose the feline genius will get a driver's license."

"Koko? I wouldn't be surprised. He's getting interested in pushbuttons, knobs, dials, levers—anything mechanical."

"But what would you *do,* Qwill, in a place like Mooseville? You don't fish. You don't sail. The lake up there is too cold for swimming. It's frozen ice in winter and melted ice in summer."

"Don't worry, Arch. I've got plans. I've got a great idea for a book. I'd like to try writing a novel—with lots of sex and violence. All the good stuff."

Riker could only stare and search his mind for

more objections. "It would cost you a bundle. Do you realize the rent they're getting for summer cottages?"

"Actually," Qwilleran said with a note of triumph, "it won't cost me a cent. I've got an old aunt up there, and she has a cabin I can use."

"You never told me about any old aunt."

"She's not really a relative. She was a friend of my mother's, and I called her Aunt Fanny when I was a kid. We lost touch, but she saw my byline in the *Fluxion* and wrote to me. We've been corresponding ever since. . . . Speaking of bylines, my name was spelled wrong in yesterday's paper."

"I know, I know," Riker said. "We have a new copy editor, and no one told her about that ridiculous *W*. We caught it in the second edition."

The waitress brought the coffee—a brew as black as the sooty varnish concealed by the new wallpaper—and Riker studied his cup in search of clues to Qwilleran's aberrant behavior. "How about your friend? The one who eats health foods. What does she think about your sudden insanity?"

"Rosemary? She's in favor of fresh air, exercise, all that jazz."

"You haven't been smoking your pipe lately. Is that her idea?"

"Are you implying I never have any ideas of my own? What happened, I realized how much trouble it is to buy tobacco, fill a pipe, tamp it, light it, relight it two or three times, knock out the ashes, empty the ashtray, clean the pipe . . ."

"You're getting old," Riker said.

After lunch the restaurant reviewer went back to his olive-green desk with matching telephone and VDT, and the feature editor attended the meeting of assistant editors, sub-editors, group editors, divisional editors, managing editors, and executive editors.

Qwilleran was pleased that his announcement had jarred Riker's professional cool. Admittedly the editor's questions had dented his resolve. How would he react to three months of the simple life after a lifetime of urban chaos? It was true he planned to do some writing during the summer, but how many hours a day can one sit at a typewriter? There would be no lunches at the Press Club, no telephone calls, no evenings with friends, no gourmet dinners, no big league ballgames, no Rosemary.

Nevertheless, he needed a change. He was disenchanted with the *Fluxion,* and the offer of a lakeside hideaway for the entire season appealed to his thrifty nature.

On the other hand, Aunt Fanny had mentioned nothing about comforts and conveniences. Qwilleran liked an extra-long bed, deep lounge chairs, good reading lamps, a decent refrigerator, plenty of hot water, and trouble-free plumbing. He would undoubtedly miss the amenities of Maus Haus, the glamorous boarding house where he occupied a luxury apartment. He would miss the Robert Maus standard of elegant dining and the camaraderie of the other tenants, especially Rosemary.

The green telephone on his desk buzzed, and he answered it absent-mindedly.

"Qwill, have you heard the news?" It was Rosemary's velvet voice, but it had the high pitch of alarm.

"What's happened?" There had been two homicides at Maus Haus in the last year, but the murderer was now behind bars, and the residents had settled down to pleasurable living and a sense of security.

"Robert is selling the building," Rosemary said plaintively, "and we've all got to move out."

"Why is he selling? Everything was going so well."

"Someone made him a wonderful offer for the property. You know he's always wanted to give up his law practice and open a fine restaurant. He says this is his chance. It's prime real estate, and a developer wants to build a high-rise apartment house."

"That's really bad news," Qwilleran agreed. "Robert has spoiled us all with his Châteaubriand and his lobster thermidor and his artichoke hearts Florentine. Why don't you come over to Number Six when you get home? We'll talk about it."

"I'll bring a bottle. Chill the glasses," Rosemary said. "We just got a shipment of pomegranate juice." She was part-owner of a specialty food store called Helthy-Welthy, a coy spelling that Qwilleran found obnoxious.

He replaced the receiver thoughtfully. The bad news had been a message from the fates, telling him to go north. He left the office early that afternoon with a small bag of turkey from the Press Club and a tape measure from the Blue Dragon antique shop.

The River Road bus dropped him at a used car lot, and he went directly to a row of small fuel-efficient automobiles. Methodically he moved from one vehicle to the next, opening the door and measuring the floor space behind the driver's seat.

A salesman who had been watching the performance sauntered into the picture. "Interested in a compact?"

"It all depends," Qwilleran mumbled with his head buried in the back seat. He made a mental note: *twelve by fifteen.*

"Looking for any particular model?"

"No." The drive-shaft seemed to be the problem. *Thirteen by fifteen.*

"You want automatic or stick?"

"Doesn't matter," Qwilleran said as he busied himself with the tape measure again. *Thirteen by sixteen.* After years of driving company cars from newspaper garages, he could drive anything; his selectivity had been numbed.

The salesman was studying the heavy drooping moustache and the mournful eyes. "I know you," he finally said. "Your picture's in the *Fluxion* all the time. You write about restaurants. My cousin has a pizza place in Happy View Woods."

Qwilleran grunted from the innards of a four-door.

"I'd like to show you a job that just came in. We

haven't even cleaned it up yet. Last year's model—only two thousand miles. Came from an estate."

Qwilleran followed him into the garage. There stood a green two-door, not yet sprayed with New Car Scent. He ducked into the back seat with his tape measure. Then he moved the driver's seat back to accomodate his long legs and measured again. *Fourteen by sixteen.* "Perfect," he said, "although I might have to cut off the handles. How much?"

"Come in the office and we'll work out a deal," the salesman said.

The newsman drove the green car around the block and noted that it lurched, bounced, chugged, and rattled less than any company car he had ever driven. And the price was right. He made a down-payment, signed some papers, and drove home to Maus Haus.

As he expected, there was a letter in his mailbox from Robert Maus, written on the man's legal stationery. It explained with the utmost compunction that the property heretofore known as Maus Haus had been purveyed, after due deliberation, to a syndicate of out-of-town investors who would be pursuing extensive plans requiring, it was regretted, the eviction of present tenants at a date not later than September 1.

Qwilleran, who had torn the envelope open on the spot, shrugged and climbed the stairs to his apartment on the balcony. As he unlocked the door to Number Six he was accompanied by a delicate essence of turkey that should have brought two hungry Siamese to meet him, prancing in leggy circles and figure eights, crowing and wailing in a discordant duet of anticipation. Instead, the two ingrates sat motionless on the white bearskin rug in a conspiracy of silence. Qwilleran knew why. They sensed an upheaval in the status quo. Although Koko and his accomplice Yum Yum were experts at devising surprises of their own, they resented changes originated by others. At Maus Haus they were perfectly satisfied with the wide sunny windowsill, the continuous entertainment provided by neighborhood pigeons, and the luxury of a bearskin rug.

"Okay, you guys," Qwilleran said. "I know you don't like to move, but wait till you see where we're going! I wish we could take the rug but it doesn't belong to us."

Koko, whose full name was Kao K'o-Kung, had the dignity of an Oriental potentate. He sat regally tall with disapproval in every whisker. Both he and Yum Yum were aware of how magnificent they looked on the fluffy white rug. They had the classic Siamese coloring and conformation: blue eyes in a dark brown mask, pale fawn-colored fur of a quality that made mink look second-rate, elegantly long brown legs, and a graceful whip of a tail.

The man chopped the turkey for them. "C'mon and get it! They sliced it off an actual turkey this time." The two Siamese maintained their frigid reserve.

A moment later Qwilleran raised his nose. He identified a familiar perfume, and soon Rosemary knocked on the door. He greeted her with a kiss that was more than a perfunctory social peck. The Siamese sat in stony immobility.

Pomegranate juice was poured over ice with a dash of club soda, and a toast was drunk to the condemned building in memory of everything that had happened there.

"It was a way of life we'll never forget," Qwilleran said.

"It was a dream," Rosemary added.

"And occasionally a nightmare."

"I suppose you'll accept your aunt's offer now. Will the *Fluxion* let you go?"

"Oh sure. They may not let me come back, but they'll let me go. Have you made any plans?"

"I may return to Canada," Rosemary said. "Max wants to open a natural food restaurant in Toronto, and if I can sell my interest in Helthy-Welthy I might go into partnership with him."

Qwilleran huffed into his moustache. Max Sorrel! That womanizer! He said: "I was hoping you'd come up north and spend some time with me."

"I'd love it if I don't get involved in Toronto. How will you get up there?"

"I bought a car today. The cats and I will drive up to Pickax City to say hello to Aunt Fanny and then go on up to the lake. I haven't seen her for forty years. Judging from her correspondence she's a character. Her letters are cross-written."

Rosemary looked puzzled.

"My mother used to do cross-writing. She'd hand-write a page in the usual way, then turn the paper sideways and write across the original lines."

"What for? To save paper?"

"Who knows? Maybe to preserve privacy. It isn't easy to read. . . . She's not my real aunt," he went on. "Fanny and my mother were doughnut girls in World War I. Then Fanny had a career of some kind—never married. When she retired she went back to Pickax City."

"I never heard of the place."

"It used to be mining country. Her family made their fortune in the mines."

"Will you write to me, Qwill dearest?"

"I'll write—often. I'll miss you, Rosemary."

"Tell me all about Aunt Fanny after you meet her."

"She calls herself Francesca now. She doesn't like to be called Aunt Fanny. She says it makes her feel like an old woman."

"How old is she?"

"She'll be ninety next month."

TWO

Qwilleran packed the green car for the trek north: two suitcases, his typewriter, the thirteen-pound dictionary, five hundred sheets of typing paper, and two boxes of books. Because Koko refused to eat any commercial product intended for cats, there were twenty-four cans of boned chicken, red salmon, corned beef, solid pack white tuna, cocktail shrimp, and Alaska crabmeat. On the back seat was the blue cushion favored by the Siamese, and on the floor was an oval roasting pan with the handles sawed off in order to fit between the drive-shaft and the rocker-panel. It contained an inch-thick layer of kitty gravel. This was the cats' commode. After their previous commode of hand-painted tole had rusted out, Robert Maus had donated the roasting pan from his well-stocked kitchen.

The furniture in Qwilleran's apartment belonged to an earlier tenant, and his few personal possessions—such as the antique scale and a cast-iron coat of arms—were now stored for the summer in Arch Riker's basement. Thus unencumbered, the newsman started for the north country with a light heart.

His passengers in the back seat reacted otherwise. The little female howled in strident tones whenever the car turned a corner, rounded a curve, crossed a bridge, passed under a viaduct, encountered a truck, or exceeded fifty miles an hour. Koko scolded her and bit her hind leg, adding snarls and hisses to the orchestrated uproar. Qwilleran drove with clenched jaw, enduring the stares and glares of motorists who passed him, their fretful horn-honking and hostile tailgating.

The route passed through a string of suburbs and then the winding roads of horse country. Beyond that came cooler temperatures, taller pine trees, deer-crossing signs, and more pickup trucks. Pickax City was still a hundred miles ahead when Qwilleran's jangled nerves convinced him to stop for the night. The travelers checked into a tourist camp, where rickety cabins of pre-motel vintage were isolated in a wooded area. All three of them were in a state of exhaustion, and Koko and Yum Yum immediately fell asleep in the exact center of the bed.

The next day's journey was marked by fewer protests from the back seat. The temperature dropped still further, and deer-crossings became elk-crossings. The highway gradually ascended into hilly country and then plunged into a valley to become the main thoroughfare of Pickax City. Here majestic old houses reflecting the wealth of the mining and lumbering pioneers lined both sides of Main Street, which divided in the center of town and circled a little park. Facing the park were several impressive buildings: a nineteenth century courthouse, a library with the columns of a Greek temple, two churches, and a stately residence with a polished brass house number that was Aunt Fanny's.

It was a large square mansion of fieldstone, with a carriage house in the rear. A blue pickup truck stood in the driveway, and a gardener was working on the shrubs. He stared pointedly at Qwilleran with an expression the newsman could not identify. In the front door there was an old-fashioned mail slot framed in brass and engraved with the family name: Klingenschoen.

The little old lady who answered the doorbell was undoubtedly Aunt Fanny: a vigorous eighty-nine, tiny but taut with energy. Her white, powdery, wrinkled face wore two slashes of orange lipstick and glasses that magnified her eyes. She gazed at her visitor and, after focusing through the thick lenses, flung her arms wide in a dramatic gesture of welcome. Then from that little woman came a deep chesty growl:

"Bless my soul! How you have grown!"

"I should hope so," Qwilleran said genially. "The last time you saw me I was seven years old. How are you, Francesca? You're looking great!"

Her exotic name was in keeping with her flamboyant garb: an orange satin tunic embroidered with peacocks and worn over slim black trousers. A scarf, also orange, was tied around her head and knotted on top in a way that added height to her four-feet-three.

"Come in, come in," she growled pleasantly. "My, how glad I am to see you! . . . Yes, you look just like your picture in the *Fluxion*. If only your dear mother could see you now, rest her soul. She would *adore* your moustache. Are you ready for a cup of coffee? I know you journalists drink a lot of coffee. We'll have it in the sun parlor."

Aunt Fanny led the way through a high-ceilinged hallway with a grand staircase, past a formal drawing room and ornate dining room, past a paneled library and a breakfast room smothered in chintz, into an airy room with French windows, wicker furniture, and ancient rubber plants.

In her chesty voice she said: "I have some *divine* cinnamon buns. Tom picked them up from the bakery this morning. You *adored* cinnamon buns when you were a little boy."

While Qwilleran relaxed on a wicker settee his hostess trotted away in little black Chinese slippers, disappearing into a distant part of the house, continuing a monologue that he could only halfhear. She returned carrying a large tray.

Qwilleran sprang to his feet. "Here, let me take that, Francesca."

"Thank you, dear," she barked. "You were always such a thoughtful little boy. Now you must put cream in your coffee. Tom picked it up from the dairy farm this morning. You don't get cream like this in the city, my dear."

Qwilleran preferred his coffee black, but he accepted cream, and as he bit into a doughy cinnamon bun his gaze wandered to the French windows. The gardener was leaning on his rake and peering into the room.

"Now you're going to stay for lunch," Aunt Fanny said from the depths of a huge wicker rocking chair that swallowed her tiny figure. "Tom will go to the butcher to pick up a steak. Do you like porterhouse or Delmonico? We have a *marvelous* butcher. Would you like a baked potato with sour cream?"

"No! No! Thank you, Francesca, but I have two nervous animals in the car, and I want to get them up to the cabin as soon as possible. I appreciate the invitation, but I'll have to take a rain check."

"Or maybe you'd prefer pork chops," Aunt Fanny went on. "I'll make you a big salad. What kind of dressing do you like? We'll have crêpes suzette for dessert, I always made them for gentlemen callers when I was in college."

Qwilleran thought: Is she deaf? Or doesn't she

bother to listen? The trick is to get her attention. *"Aunt Fanny!"* he shouted.

She looked startled at the name and the tone. "Yes, dear?"

"After we're settled," he said in a normal voice, "I'll come back and have lunch with you, or you can drive up to the lake and I'll take you to dinner. Do you have transportation, Francesca?"

"Yes, of course! Tom drives me. I lost my license a few years ago after a little accident. The chief of police was a *very* disagreeable person, but we got rid of him, and now we have a *charming* man. He named his youngest daughter after me . . ."

"Aunt Fanny!"

"Yes, dear?"

"Will you tell me how to reach the cabin?"

"Of course. It's very easy. Go north to the lake and turn left. Watch for the ruins of a stone chimney; that's all that's left of an old log schoolhouse. Then you'll see the letter *K* on a post. Turn into the gravel driveway and follow it through the woods. That's all my property. The wild cherries and sugarplums should be in blossom now. Mooseville is only three miles further on. You can drive into town for restaurants and shopping. They have a *charming* postmistress, but don't get any ideas! She's married . . ."

"Aunt Fanny!"

"Yes, dear?"

"Do I need a key?"

"Goodness, no! I don't believe I've ever seen a key

to the place. It's just a little old log cabin with two bunkrooms, but you'll be comfortable. It will be nice and quiet for writing. It was *too* quiet for my taste. I was in clubwork in New Jersey, you know, and I had *scads* of people around all the time. I'm so happy you're writing a book, dear. What is the title? Your dear mother would be so proud of you."

Qwilleran was travel-weary and eager to reach his destination. It required all his wiles to disengage himself from Aunt Fanny's overwhelming hospitality. As he left the house the gardener was doing something to the bed of tulips around the front steps. The man stared, and Qwilleran gave him a mock salute.

His passengers celebrated his return with howls of indignation, and Yum Yum's protests continued as a matter of principle even though there were no turns, bridges, viaducts, or large trucks. The highway ran through desolate country, some of it devastated by forest fires; skeletons of ravaged trees were frozen in a grotesque dance. Behind a sign advertising *Hot Pasties,* a restaurant had collapsed and was overgrown with weeds. Traffic was sparse, mostly pickup trucks whose drivers waved a greeting to the green two-door. The sites of defunct mines—the Dimsdale, the Big B, the Goodwinter—were marked by signs warning *Danger—Keep Out.* There was no Klingenschoen mine, Qwilleran noticed. He tuned in a local station on the car radio and turned it off in a hurry.

So Aunt Fanny had been a clubwoman! He could

visualize her bustling about at afternoon teas, chairing committees, wearing flowered hats, being elected Madame President, presiding at conventions, organizing charity balls.

His ruminations were interrupted by a glance in the rearview mirror. He was being followed by a blue pickup truck. Qwilleran reduced his speed, and the truck slowed accordingly. The game continued for several miles until he was distracted by the appearance of a farm with several low sheds. Their rooftops as well as the farmyard itself were in constant motion—a bronze-colored mass, heaving and rippling. "Turkeys!" he said to his passengers. "You're going to live near a turkey farm, you lucky guys."

When he glanced again in the rearview mirror the blue pickup was nowhere to be seen.

Farther on he passed a large cultivated estate—well-kept lawns and flower beds behind a high ornamental fence. Set far back on the property were large buildings of an institutional nature.

The highway ascended a hill. Immediately two heads were raised in the back seat. Two noses sniffed the first hint of water, still a mile away. Irritable yowls changed to excited yips. Then the lake itself came into view, an endless stretch of placid blue water stretching to meet an incredibly blue sky.

"We're almost there!" Qwilleran told his restless passengers.

The route now followed the shoreline, sometimes close to the beach, sometimes dipping back into the woods. It passed a rustic gate guarding the private road to the Top o' the Dunes Club. Half a mile beyond was the crumbling chimney of the old schoolhouse—and the letter *K* on a post. Qwilleran turned into a gravel driveway that snaked through a forest of evergreens and oaks. Occasional sunlit clearings were filled with wild flowers, tree stumps, and fragrant flowering shrubs. He wished Rosemary were with him; she noticed everything and appreciated everything. After climbing over a succession of sandy dunes the driveway ended in a clearing with a sudden view of the lake, dotted with sailboats far out near the horizon.

There, perched on top of the highest dune and dwarfed by hundred-foot pine trees, was the picturesque cabin that would be his home for the summer. Its logs and chinking were dark with age. A screened porch overlooking the lake promised quiet hours of thought and relaxation. A massive fieldstone chimney and an ample woodpile suggested lazy evenings with a good book in front of a blazing fire.

The entrance to the cabin was through a second screened porch facing the woods and the clearing that served as parking lot. As Qwilleran approached it a squirrel ran up a tree, looked down at him, and scolded. Flurries of little yellow birds darted and twittered. On top of the woodpile a tiny brown animal sat up, cocked its head, and looked at the man inquiringly.

Qwilleran shook his head in disbelief. All these

mysterious pleasures of nature, this peaceful country scene—they were his for three months.

A ship's bell in gleaming brass hung at the entrance to the porch. Its dangling rope tempted him to ring it for sheer joy. As he walked toward it, something slimy and alive dropped off a tree onto his head. And what was that hole in the screened door? Jagged edges bent inward as if someone had thrown a bowling ball through the wire mesh. He pressed the thumb latch of the door and stepped cautiously onto the porch. He saw a grass rug and weatherproof furniture and antique farm implements hanging on the back wall—and something else. There was a slight movement in a far corner. A beady eye glistened. A large bird with a menacing beak perched on the back of a chair, its rapacious claws gripping the vinyl upholstery: A hawk? It must be a hawk, Qwilleran thought. It was his first encounter with a bird of prey, and he was glad he had left the Siamese in the car; the bird might be injured—and vicious. Powerful force had been necessary to crash through that screen, and the piercing eyes were far from friendly.

The implements hanging on the wall included a primitive wooden pitchfork, and Qwilleran reached for it in slow motion. Quietly he opened the screen door and wedged it. Cautiously he circled behind the bird, waving the pitchfork, and the hawk shot out through the doorway.

Quilleran blew a sigh of relief into his moustache. Welcome to the country, he said to himself.

Although the cabin was small, the interior gave an impression of spaciousness. An open ceiling of knotty pine soared to almost twenty feet at the peak, supported by trusses of peeled log. The walls also were exposed logs, whitewashed. Above the fieldstone fireplace there was a moose head with a great spread of antlers, flanked by a pickax and a lumberjack's crosscut saw with two-inch teeth.

Qwilleran's keen sense of smell picked up a strange odor. Dead animal? Bad plumbing? Forgotten garbage? He opened doors and windows and checked the premises. Everything was shipshape, and soon the cross-ventilation brought in the freshness of the lake and the perfume of wild cherry blossoms. Next he examined the window screens to be sure they were secure. Koko and Yum Yum were apartment cats, never allowed to roam outdoors, and he was taking no chances. He looked for trap doors, loose boards, and other secret exits.

Only then did he bring the Siamese into the cabin. They advanced warily, their bellies and tails low, their whiskers back, their ears monitoring noises inaudible to humans. But by the time the luggage was brought in from the car, Yum Yum was somewhere overhead leaping happily from beam to beam while Koko sat imperiously on the moose head, surveying his new domain with approval. The moose—with his long snout, flared nostrils, and underslung mouth—bore this indignity with sour resignation.

Qwilleran's approval of the cabin was equally enthusiastic. He noted the latest type of telephone on the bar, a microwave oven, a whirlpool bath, and several shelves of books. The latest issues of status magazines were on the coffee table, and someone had left a Brahms concerto in the cassette slot of the stereo. There was no television, but that was unimportant; Qwilleran was addicted to the print media.

He opened a can of boned chicken for his companions and then drove into Mooseville for his own dinner. Mooseville was a resort village stretched out along the lakeshore. On one side of Main Street were piers and boats and the Northern Lights Hotel. Across the street were commercial establishments housed largely in buildings of log construction. Even the church was built of logs.

At the hotel Qwilleran had mediocre pork chops, a soggy baked potato, and overcooked green beans served by a friendly blonde waitress who said her name was Darlene. She recognized him from his picture in the *Daily Fluxion* and insisted on serving second helpings of everything. At the office he had frequently questioned the wisdom of publishing the restaurant-reviewer's photograph, but it was *Fluxion* policy to print headshots of columnists, and at the *Fluxion,* policy was policy.

It was not only Qwilleran's moustache that made him conspicuous at the Northern Lights Hotel. In the roomful of plaid shirts, jeans, and windbreakers his tweed sports coat and knit tie were jarringly out-of-key. Immediately after the gelatinous blueberry pie he went to the General Store and bought jeans, sports shirts, deck shoes . . . *and* a visored cap.

Every man in Mooseville wore one. There were baseball caps, nautical caps, hunting caps, beer caps, and caps with emblems advertising tractors, fertilizer, and feed. Qwilleran chose hunter orange, hoping it would prove an effective disguise.

The drug store carried both the *Daily Fluxion* and its competitor, the *Morning Rampage,* as well as the local paper. He bought a *Fluxion* and a *Pickax Picayune* and headed back to the cabin.

On the way he was stopped by a police roadblock, but a polite trooper said: "Go right ahead, Mr. Qwilleran. Are you going to write about the Mooseville restaurants?"

"No, I'm on vacation. What's happening here, officer?"

"Just routine war games," the trooper joked. "We have to keep in practice. Enjoy your vacation, Mr. Qwilleran."

It was June. The days were long in the city and even longer in the north country. Qwilleran was weary and kept looking at his watch and checking the sun, which was reluctant to set. He slipped down the side of the dune to inspect the shore and the temperature of the water. It was icy, as Riker had warned. The lake was calm, making the softest splash when it lapped the beach, and the only sound was the humming of mosquitoes. By the time Qwilleran scrambled frantically up the hill he was chased by a winged horde. They quickly found the hole in the screen and funneled into the porch.

He dashed into the cabin, slammed the door, and made a hurried phone call to Pickax.

"Good evening," said a pleasant voice.

"Francesca, just want you to know we arrived safely." Qwilleran talked fast, hoping to get his message across before her attention wandered. "The cabin is terrific, but we have a problem. A hawk crashed through the screen and left a big hole. I shooed him off the porch, but he had messed up the rug and furniture."

Aunt Fanny took the news calmly. "Now don't you worry about it, dear," she growled sweetly. "Tom will be there tomorrow to fix the screen and clean the porch. No problem at all. He enjoys doing it. Tom is a jewel. I don't know what I'd do without him. How are the mosquitoes? I'll have Tom get you some insect spray. You'll need it for spiders and hornets, too. Let me know if the ants invade the cabin; they're very possessive. Don't kill any ladybugs, dear. It's bad luck, you know. Would you like a few more cassettes for the stereo? I have some *marvelous* Chicago jazz. Do you like opera? Sorry there's no television, but I think it's a waste of time in the summer, and you won't miss it while you're busy writing your book."

After the conversation with Madame President, Qwilleran tried the cassette player. He punched two buttons and got the Double Concerto with excellent fidelity. He had once dated a girl who listened to nothing but Brahms, and he would never forget good old Opus 102.

The sun finally slipped into the lake, flooding the water and sky with pink and orange, and he was ready for sleep. The Siamese were abnormally quiet. Usually they indulged in a final romp before lights-out. But where were they now? Not on the moose head or the beams overhead. Not on their blue cushion that he had placed on top of the refrigerator. Not on the pair of white linen sofas that angled around the fireplace. Not on the beds in either of the bunkrooms.

Qwilleran called to them. There was no answer. They were too busy watching. Crouched on a windowsill in the south bunkroom they stared out at something in the dusk. The property had been left in a wild state, and the view offered nothing but the sand dune, underbrush, and evergreens. A few yards from the cabin there was a depression in the sand, however—roughly rectangular. It looked like a sunken grave. The Siamese had noticed it immediately; they always detected anything unusual.

"Jump down," Qwilleran said to them. "I've got to close the window for the night."

He chose the north bunkroom for himself because it overlooked the lake, but—tired though he was—he could not sleep. He thought about the grave. What could be buried there? Should he report it to Aunt Fanny? Or should he just start digging? There was a toolshed on the property, and there would be shovels.

He tossed for hours. It was so dark! There were no street lights, no neon signs, no habitations, no moon, no glow from any nearby civilization—just total blackness. And it was so quiet! No rustling of trees, no howling of wind, no crashing of waves, no hum of traffic on the distant highway—just total silence. Qwilleran lay still and listened to his heart beating.

Then through his pillow he heard an irregular *thud-thud-thud.* He sat up and listened carefully. The thudding had stopped, but he could hear voices—a man's voice and a woman's laughter. He looked out the window into the blackness and saw two flashlights bobbing on the beach at the foot of the dune, bound in an easterly direction. He lay down again, and with his ear to the pillow he heard *thud-thud-thud.* It had to be footsteps on the packed sand. The sound gradually faded away.

It was well after midnight. He wondered about the prowlers on the beach. He wondered about the grave. And then there was a crackling in the under-brush—someone climbing a tree—footsteps on the roof, clomping toward the chimney.

Qwilleran leaped out of his bunk, bellowing some curse he had learned in North Africa. He turned on lights. He shouted at the cats, who flew around the cabin in a frenzy. He punched buttons on the cassette player. Brahms again! He banged pots and pans in the kitchen. . . . The footsteps hurried back across the roof; there was scrambling in the under-brush, and then all was quiet.

Qwilleran sat up reading for the rest of the night until the sun rose and the birds began their dawn chirruping, tweeting, cawing, and skreeking.

THREE

Mooseville, Tuesday

Dear Arch,

If I get any mail that looks personal, please forward it c/o General Delivery. Will appreciate. We arrived yesterday, and I'm a wreck. The cats yelled for four hundred miles and drove me crazy. What's more, I bought a car to fit their sandbox, and they didn't use it once! They waited till we got to where we were going. Siamese! Who can figure them out?

This is beautiful country, but I didn't sleep a wink last night. I'm suffering from culture shock.

Fortunately Mooseville gets the outstate edition of the *Fluxion*. The *Pickax Picayune* is just a chicken-dinner newspaper.

Qwill

Looking haggard, but buoyed by the excitement of a new environment, Qwilleran drove into Mooseville for breakfast. On the way he was stopped by another roadblock. This time a friendly character in a moose costume handed him a *Welcome to Mooseville* brochure and urged him to visit the tourist information booth on Main Street.

At the bank Qwilleran opened a checking account. Although the log building was imitation antique, he could detect the characteristic aroma of fresh money. The teller was a sunburned blonde named Jennifer, almost unbearably friendly, who remarked that the weather was super and she hoped he was going fishing or sailing.

At the post office he was greeted by a young woman with long golden hair and a dazzling smile. "Isn't this gorgeous weather?" she said. "I wonder how long it will last. They say there's a storm brewing. What can I do for you? I'm Lori, the postmistress."

"My name is Jim Qwilleran," he told her, "and I'll be staying at the Klingenschoen cabin for three months. My mail will come addressed to General Delivery."

"Yes, I know," she said. "Ms. Klingenschoen informed us. You can have rural delivery if you want to put up a mailbox."

Precisely at that moment Qwilleran's nostrils were assaulted by the foulest odor he had ever encountered. He looked startled, mumbled "no thanks," and bolted from the building, feeling sick. Other postal patrons who had been licking stamps or unlocking numbered mailboxes made their exit quietly but swiftly. Qwilleran stood on the sidewalk gulping fresh air; the others walked away without comment or any visible reaction to the experience. There was no explanation that he could imagine. In fact, there were many unexplained occurrences in this north country.

For example, everywhere he went he seemed to be haunted by a blue pickup truck. There was one parked in front of the post office, its truck-bed empty except for a rolled tarpaulin. There was another in front of the bank, hauling shovels and a wheelbarrow. On the highway the driver of a blue truck had tooted his horn and waved. And the truck that had followed him on the Pickax Road the night before was blue.

Tugging the visor of his orange cap down over his eyes he approached a log cabin with a freshly painted sign: *Information Center—Tourist Development Association*. The interior had the pungent odor of new wood.

Behind a desk piled with travel folders sat a pale young man with a very black beard and a healthy head of black hair. Qwilleran realized that his own graying hair and pepper-and-salt moustache had once been equally black. He asked: "Is this where tourists come to be developed?"

The young man shrugged apologetically. "I told them it should be *tourism*. But who was I to advise the Chamber of Commerce? I was only a history teacher looking for a summer job. Isn't this great weather? What can I do for you? My name is Roger. You don't need to tell me who you are. I read the paper."

"The *Daily Fluxion* seems to have a big circulation up here," Qwilleran said. "The *Fluxion* was almost sold out at the drug store yesterday, but they still had a big stack of the *Morning Rampage*."

"Right," said Roger. "We're boycotting the *Rampage*. Their travel editor did a write-up on Mooseville and called it Mosquitoville."

"You have to admit they're plentiful. And large."

Roger glanced aside guiltily and said in a lowered voice: "If you think the mosquitoes are bad, wait till you meet the deer flies. This is off-the-record, of course. We don't talk about deer flies. It's not exactly good for tourism. Are you here to write about our restaurants?"

"No, I'm on vacation. I'll be around for three months. Is there a barber in town?"

"Bob's Chop Shop at the Cannery Mall. Men's and women's hair styling." Roger handed Qwilleran another copy of the Mooseville brochure. "Are you a fisherman?"

"I can think of things I'd rather do."

"Deep-sea fishing is a great experience. You'd enjoy it. You can charter a boat at the municipal pier and go out for a day or half a day. They supply the gear, take you where the fish are biting, even tell you how to hold the rod. And they guarantee you'll come back with a few big ones."

"Anything else to do around here?"

"There's the museum; it's big on shipwreck history. The flower gardens at the state prison are spectacular, and the prison gift shop has some good leather items. You can see bears scrounging at the village dump, or you can hunt for agates on the beach."

Qwilleran was studying the brochure. "What's this about a historic cemetery?"

"It's not much," Roger admitted. "It's a nineteenth century burial ground, abandoned for the last fifty years. Sort of vandalized. If I were you, I'd take a fishing trip."

"What are these pasties everyone advertises?"

"It's like a turnover filled with meat and potatoes and turnips. Pasties are traditional up here. The miners used to carry pasties in their lunch buckets."

"Where's a good place to try one?"

"Hats-off or hats-on?"

"What?"

"What I mean—we have some restaurants with a little class, like the hotel dining room, and we have the other kind—casual—where the guys eat with their hats on. For a good hats-off place you could try a little bistro at the Cannery Mall, called the Nasty Pasty. A bit of perverse humor, I guess. The tourists like it."

Qwilleran said he would prefer real north country atmosphere.

"Right. So here's what you want to do: Drive west along the shore for about a mile. You'll see a big electric sign that says FOO. The *D* dropped off about three years ago. It's a dump, but they're famous for pasties, and it's strictly hats-on."

"One more question." Qwilleran touched his moustache tentatively, as he did when a situation was bothering him. "How come there are so many blue pickup trucks in this neck of the woods?"

"I don't know. I never really noticed." Roger jumped up and went to the side window overlooking the parking lot of the Shipwreck Tavern. "You're right. There are two blue pickups in the lot. . . . But there's also a red one, and a dirty green, and a sort of yellow."

"And here comes another blue one," Qwilleran persisted. It was the truck with the shovels. The agile little man who jumped out of the driver's seat wore overalls and a visored cap and a faceful of untrimmed gray whiskers.

"That's old Sam the gravedigger. He's got a lot of bounce, hasn't he? He's over eighty and puts away a pint of whiskey every day—except Sunday."

"You mean you still dig graves by hand?"

"Right. Sam's been digging graves and other things all his life. Keeps him young. . . . Look at that sky. We're in for a storm."

"Thanks for the information," Qwilleran said. "I think I'll go and try the pasties." He glanced at his wrist. "What time is it? I left my watch at the cabin."

"That's normal. When guys come up here, the first thing they do—they forget to wear their watches. Then they stop shaving. Then they start eating with their hats on."

Qwilleran drove west until he saw an electric sign flashing its message futilely in the sunshine: FOO . . . FOO . . . FOO. The parking lot was filled with pickups and vans. No blue. He thought: Why am I getting paranoid about blue pickups? The answer was a familiar uneasiness on his upper lip.

The restaurant was a two-story building in need of paint and shingles and nails. A ventilator expelled fumes of fried fish and smoking hamburgers. Inside, the tables were filled, and red, green, blue, and yellow caps could be seen dimly through the haze of cigarette smoke. Country music on the radio could not compete with the hubbub of loud talk and laughter.

Qwilleran took a stool at the counter not far from a customer with a sheriff's department patch on his sleeve and a stiff-brimmed hat on his head.

The cook shuffled out of the kitchen and said to the deputy: "We're in for a big one."

The brimmed hat nodded.

"Another roadblock last night?"

Two nods.

"Find anything?"

The hat waggled from side to side.

"We all know where the buggers go."

Another nod.

"But no evidence."

The hat registered negative.

The waitress was standing in front of Qwilleran, waiting wordlessly for his order.

"A couple of pasties," he said.

"To go?"

"No. To eat here."

"Two?"

Qwilleran found himself nodding an affirmative.

"You want I should hold one back and keep it hot till you eat the first one?"

"No, thanks. That won't be necessary."

The conversation at the tables concerned fishing exclusively, with much speculation about an approaching storm. The movement of the lake, the color of the sky, the behavior of the seagulls, the formation of the clouds, the feel of the wind—all these factors convinced veteran fishermen that a storm was coming, despite predictions on the local radio station.

When Qwilleran's two pasties arrived they completely filled two large oval platters. Each of the crusty turnovers was a foot wide and three inches thick. He surveyed the feast. "I need a fork," he said.

"Just pick 'em up," the waitress said and disappeared into the kitchen.

Roger was right. The pasties were filled with meat and potatoes and plenty of turnip, which ranked with parsnip at the bottom of Qwilleran's list of edibles. He chomped halfway through the first pasty, lubricating each dry mouthful with gulps of weak coffee, then asked to have the remaining artifacts wrapped to take home. He paid his check glumly, receiving his change in dollar bills that smelled of cigar smoke.

The cashier, a heavy woman in snugly fitting pants and a Mooseville T-shirt, leered at his orange cap and said: "All ready for Halloween, Clyde?"

Glancing at her blimplike figure he thought of an apt retort but curbed his impulse.

He returned home with one and a half pasties in soggy waxed paper and discovered some new developments. The damaged screen in the porch door had been replaced, and the hawk-spotted furnishings had been cleaned. There was a can of insect spray in the kitchen. Additional cassettes were stacked on the stereo cabinet. And his watch was missing. He clearly remembered placing it on a bathroom shelf before showering. Now it was gone. It was an expensive timepiece, presented to him by the Antique Dealers' Association at a testimonial dinner.

With mystification and annoyance muddling his head he sat down to think. Koko rubbed against his ankles, and Yum Yum jumped upon his knee. He stroked her fur absently as he reviewed the last twenty-four hours.

First there was the sunken grave; the cats were still mesmerized and kept returning to their vantage point in the guest-room window. Next there were the footsteps on the roof; the intruder was heading for the chimney when frightened away by light and noise. This morning there had been the incredible odor at the post office. And why did Roger discourage him from visiting the old cemetery? The Chamber of Commerce brochure recommended it to history buffs, photographers, and artists interested in making rubbings of nineteenth century tombstones.

And now his watch had been stolen. He had another he could use, but the missing watch was gold and had pleasant associations. Would Aunt Fanny's trusted employee attempt a theft so easily traceable? Perhaps he had a light-fingered helper; after all, a lot of work had been accomplished in a very short time.

Qwilleran's reverie was interrupted by the sound of a vehicle moving slowly up the driveway, tires crunching on gravel. It had the purring motor of an expensive car.

The cats were alerted. Koko marched to the south porch to inspect the new arrival. Yum Yum hid under one of the sofas.

The man who stepped out of the car was an alarming sight in this northern wilderness. He wore a business suit, obviously tailor-made, and a white shirt with a proper striped tie. There was a hint of cologne, a conservative scent. His long thin face was somber.

"I presume you are Miss Klingenschoen's nephew," he said when Qwilleran advanced. "I'm her attorney . . ."

"Is anything wrong?" Qwilleran cut in quickly, alarmed by the funereal tone.

"No, no, no, no. I had business in the vicinity and merely stopped to introduce myself. I'm Alexander Goodwinter."

"Come in, come in. My name is Qwilleran. Jim Qwilleran."

"So I am aware. Spelled with a *W*," the attorney said. "I read the *Daily Fluxion*. We all read the *Fluxion* up here, chiefly to convince ourselves that we're fortunate to live four hundred miles away. When we refer to the metropolitan area as Down Below, we are thinking not only of geography." He seeemd entirely at ease in the cabin, seating himself on Yum Yum's sofa and crossing his knees comfortably. "I believe a storm is imminent. They can be quite violent up here."

The newsman had learned that any conversation in the north country opened with comments on the weather, almost as a matter of etiquette. "Yes," he said with a declamatory flourish, "the texture of the lake and the lambency of the wind are rather ominous." When the attorney gave him a wary look, Qwilleran quickly added: "I'd offer you a drink, but I haven't had a chance to stock up. We arrived only yesterday."

"So Fanny informed me. We are pleased to have one of her relatives nearby. She is so very much alone—the last of the Klingenschoens."

"We're not . . . really . . . relatives," Qwilleran said with a slight lapse of concentration. He could see Yum Yum's nose emerging stealthily under the skirt of the sofa, not far from the attorney's foot. "She and my mother were friends, and I was encouraged to call her Aunt Fanny. Now she disclaims the title."

"Fanny is her legal name," Goodwinter said. "She was Fanny when she left Pickax to attend Vassar or Wellesley or whatever, and she was Francesca when she returned forty years later." He chuckled. "I find the name Francesca Klingenschoen a charming incongruity. Our firm has handled her family's legal affairs for three generations. Now my sister and I are the sole partners, and Fanny retains Penelope to handle her tax work and lawsuits and real estate transactions. We have been urging her to sell this place. Anyone who owns shore property has a gold mine, you may be aware. Fanny should liquidate some of her holdings to expedite—ah—future arrangements. She is, after all, nearing ninety. No doubt you will be seeing her during the summer?"

"Yes, she promised to come up for lunch, and I have a rain check on a steak dinner in Pickax."

"Ah, yes, we all know Fanny's steak dinners," Goodwinter said with a humorous grimace. "She promises steak, but when the time comes she serves scrambled eggs. One forgives her eccentricities because of her—ah—*energetic* involvement in the community. It was Fanny who virtually blackmailed the city fathers of Pickax into installing new sewers, repairing the sidewalks, and solving the parking problem. A very—ah—*determined* woman."

Yum Yum's entire head was now visible, and one paw was coming into view.

The attorney went on: "My sister and I are hoping you will break bread with us before long. She reads your column religiously and quotes you as if you were Shakespeare."

"I appreciate the invitation," Qwilleran said, "but it remains to be seen how sociable I will be this summer. I'm doing some writing." He waved his hand toward the dining table across the room, littered with books, typewriter, paper, pens, and pencils. As he did so, he noticed Yum Yum's paw reaching slowly and cautiously toward the attorney's shoelace.

"I applaud your intentions," Goodwinter said. "The muse must be served. But please remember: the latchstring is out at the Goodwinter residence." After a small cough he added: "Did you find Fanny looking—ah—*well* when you visited her?"

"Remarkably well! Very active and spirited for a woman of her age. Only one problem: It's hard to get her attention."

"Her hearing is excellent, according to her doctor. But she seems preoccupied most of the time—in a world of her own, so to speak." The attorney coughed again. "To be perfectly frank—and I speak to you in confidence—we have been wondering if Fanny is—ah—drinking a little."

"Some doctors recommend a daily nip for the elderly."

"Ah, well . . . the truth of the matter is . . . the druggist informs me she has been buying a considerable amount of liquor lately. A bottle of good sherry used to take care of her needs for two months, I am told, but the houseman who does her shopping has been picking up hard liquor two or three times a week."

"He's probably drinking it himself," Qwilleran said.

"We doubt that. Tom has been under close observation since coming to Pickax to work for Fanny, and all reports are good. He's a simple soul but dependable—a competent handyman and careful driver. The local bar-owners assure me that Tom never drinks more than one or two beers."

"What kind of liquor is he buying?"

"Rye, gin, Scotch. No particular label. And only a pint at a time. You might keep this confidential matter in mind when you see Fanny. We all consider her a community treasure and feel a sense of responsibility. Incidentally, if she asks your advice, you might suggest selling the large house in Pickax and moving into smaller quarters. She has had a few fainting spells recently—or so she describes them. You can see why we are all concerned about this gallant little lady. We don't want anything to happen to her."

When the attorney had said goodbye and had tied

his shoelace and had driven away, Koko and Yum Yum gave Qwilleran the hungry eye. He scooped the filling from half a pasty, mashed it into a gray paste, warmed it slightly, and spread it on what looked like a handmade raku plate. The Siamese approached the food in slow motion, sniffed it incredulously, walked around it in an effort to discover its purpose, withdrew in disdain, and looked at Qwilleran in silent rebuke, shaking their front paws in a gesture of loathing.

"So much for pasties," he said as he opened a can of red salmon.

An evening chill was descending and he tried to light a fire. There were twigs and old newspapers in a copper coal scuttle, split logs in the wood basket, and long matches in a brass holder, but the paper was damp and the matches only glowed feebly before expiring. He made three attempts and then gave up.

After the nerve-wracking drive from Down Below and two sleepless nights, he was weary. He was also disoriented by the sudden change from concrete sidewalks to sand dunes, and by odd situations he did not understand.

He went to the row of windows overlooking the lake—a hundred miles of water with Canada on the opposite shore. It shaded from silver to turquoise to deep blue. How Rosemary would enjoy this view! As he tried to imagine it through her eyes he heard an eerie whistling in the tops of the tallest pines. There was no breeze—only the soft shrill hissing. At the same time, the Siamese—who should have been drowsy after their feast of salmon—began prowling restlessly. Yum Yum emitted ear-splitting howls for no apparent reason, and Koko butted his head belligerently against the legs of tables and chairs.

Within minutes the lake changed to steel gray dotted with whitecaps. Then a high wind rushed in without warning. The whitecaps became breakers crashing in maelstroms of foam. When the tall pines started to sway, the maples and birches were already bending like beach grass. Suddenly rain hit the windows with the staccato racket of machine gun fire. The gale howled; the surf pounded the shore; tree limbs snapped off and plunged to the ground.

For the first time since his arrival Qwilleran felt really comfortable. He relaxed. The peace and quiet had been insufferable; he was used to noise and turmoil. It would be a good night to sleep.

First he had an urge to write to Rosemary. He put a sheet of paper in the typewriter and immediately ripped it out. It would be more appropriate to write with the gold pen she had given him for his birthday.

Rummaging among the jumble on his writing table he found yellow pencils, thick black *Fluxion* pencils, cheap ballpoints, and an old red jumbo fountain pen that had belonged to his mother. The sleek gold pen from Rosemary was missing.

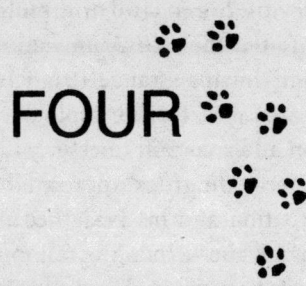

FOUR

Qwilleran slept well, lulled by the savage tumult outdoors. He was awakened shortly after dawn by the opening chords of the Brahms Double Concerto. The cassette was still in the player, and Koko was sitting alongside it, looking pleased with himself. He had placed one paw on the "power" button, activating a little red light, and another on "play."

The storm was over, although the trees could be heard dripping on the roof. The wind had subsided, and the lake had flattened to a sheet of silver. Everywhere there was the good wet smell of the woods after heavy rain. The birds were rejoicing.

Even before he rolled out of bed Qwilleran's thoughts went to the stolen pen and the stolen watch. Should he report the theft to Aunt Fanny? Should he confront Tom? In this strange new environment he felt it was a case of foreign diplomacy, requiring circumspection and a certain finesse.

Koko was the first to hear the truck approaching. His ears snapped to attention and his body became taut. Then Qwilleran heard the droning of a motor coming up the hilly, winding drive. He pulled on some clothes hastily while Koko raced to the door and demanded access to the porch, his official checkpoint for arriving visitors. Qwilleran's tingling moustache told him it would be a blue truck, and the message was correct. A stocky little old man was taking a shovel from the truck-bed.

"Hey, what's going on here?" Qwilleran demanded. He recognized the gravedigger from the parking lot of the Shipwreck Tavern.

"Gotta dig you up," said Old Sam, heading for the grave on the east side of the cabin.

"What for?" Qwilleran slammed the porch door and raced after him.

"Big George be comin' soon."

"Who told you to come here?"

"Big George." Old Sam was digging furiously. "Sand be heavy after the storm."

Qwilleran spluttered in a search for words. "What—who—look here! You can't dig up this property unless you have authorization."

"Ask Big George. He be the boss." Sand was flying out of the shallow hole, which was becoming more precisely rectangular. Soon the shovel hit a concrete slab. "There she be!" After a few more swings with the shovel Old Sam climbed out of the hole, just as a large dirty tank truck lumbered into the clearing that served as a parking lot.

Qwilleran strode to the clearing and confronted the driver. "Are you Big George?"

"No, I'm Dave," said the man mildly, as he unreeled a large hose. "Big George is the truck. The lady in Pickax—she called last night. Told us to get out here on the double. Are you choked up?"

"Am I *what?*"

"When she calls, we jump. No foolin' around with that lady. Should've pumped you out last summer, I guess."

"Pumped what?"

"The septic tank. We had to get Old Sam outa bed this morning, hangover and all. He digs; we pump. No room for the back-hoe in here. Too heavily wooded. You new here? Sam'll come and fill you in later. He doesn't fill all the way; makes it easier next time. Unless you want him to. Then he'll level it off."

Old Sam had driven away, but now a black van appeared in the clearing, driven by a slender young man in a red, white, and blue T-shirt and a tall silk opera hat.

Qwilleran stared at him. "And who are you?"

"Little Henry. You having trouble? The old lady in Pickax said you'd catch on fire any minute. Man, she's a tough baby. Won't take no excuses." He removed his topper and admired it. "This is my trademark. You seen my ads in the *Picayune?*"

"What do you advertise?"

"I'm the only chimney sweep in Moose County. You should be checked every year. . . . Is that your phone ringing?"

Qwilleran rushed back into the cabin. The telephone, which stood on the bar dividing kitchen from dining area, had stopped ringing. Koko had nudged the receiver off the cradle and was sniffing the mouthpiece.

Qwilleran grabbed it. "Hello, hello! *Get down!* Hello?" Koko was fighting for possession of the instrument. "*Get down, dammit!* Hello?"

"Is everything all right, dear?" the deep voice said after a moment's hesitation. "Did the storm do any damage? Don't worry about it; Tom will clean up the yard. You stick to your typewriter. You've got that wonderful book to finish. I know it will be a best-seller. Did you see Big George and Little Henry? I don't want anything to go wrong with the plumbing or the chimney while you're concentrating on your writing. I told them to get out there immediately or I'd have their licenses revoked. You have to be firm with these country people or they go fishing and forget about you. Are you getting enough to eat? I've bought some of those *divine* cinnamon buns to keep in your freezer. Tom will drive me up this morning, and we'll have a pleasant lunch on the porch. I'll bring a picnic basket. Get back to your writing, dear."

Qwilleran turned to Koko. "Madame President is coming. Try to act like a normal cat. Don't answer the phone. Don't play the music. Stay away from the microwave."

When Big George and Little Henry had finished their work, Qwilleran put on his orange cap and drove to Mooseville to mail his letter to Rosemary and to buy supplies. His shopping list was geared to his culinary skills: instant coffee, canned soup, frozen stew. For guests he laid in a supply of liquor and mixes.

In the canned soup section of the supermarket he noticed a black-bearded young man in a yellow cap with a spark-plug emblem. They stared at each other.

"Hi, Mr. Qwilleran."

"Forget the mister. Call me Qwill. Aren't you Roger from the tourist bureau? Roger, George, Sam, Henry, Tom, Dave . . . I've met so many people without surnames, it's like biblical times."

"Mine's a tough one: MacGillivray."

"What! My mother was a Mackintosh!"

"No kidding! Same clan!"

"Your ancestor fought like a lion for Prince Charlie."

"Right! At Culloden in 1746."

"April sixteenth."

Their voices had been rising higher with surprise and pleasure, to the mystification of the other customers. The two men pumped hands and slapped backs.

"I hope that's Scotch broth you're buying," Roger said.

"Why don't we have dinner some night?" Qwilleran suggested. "Preferably not at the FOO."

"How about tonight? My wife's out of town."

"How about the hotel dining room? Hats-off."

Qwilleran returned to the cabin to shower and shave in preparation for the visit of Aunt Fanny and the remarkable Tom—gardener, chaffeur, handyman, errand boy, and petty thief, perhaps. Shortly before noon a long black limousine inched its way around the curves of the drive and emerged triumphantly in the clearing. The driver, dressed in work clothes and a blue visored cap, jumped out and ran around to open the passenger's door.

Out came Indian moccasins with beadwork, then a fringed suede skirt, then a leather jacket with more fringe and beadwork, then Aunt Fanny's powdered face topped with an Indian red turban. Qwilleran noticed that she had well-shaped legs for an octogenarian soon to be a nonagenarian.

"Francesca! Good to see you again!" he exclaimed. "You're looking very . . . very . . . sexy."

"Bless you, my dear," she said in her surprising baritone voice. "Little old ladies are usually called chipper or spry, and I intend to shoot the next fool who does." She reached into her fringed suede handbag and withdrew a small pistol with a gold handle, which she waved with abandon.

"Careful!" Qwilleran gasped.

"Dear me! The storm did a lot of damage. That jack pine is almost bare. We'll have to remove it. . . . Tom, come here to meet the famous Mr. Qwilleran."

The man-of-all-work stepped forward obediently, removing the blue cap that advertised a brand of fertilizer. His age was hard to guess. An old twenty or a young forty? His round scrubbed face and pale blue eyes wore an expression of serene wonder.

"This is Tom," Aunt Fanny said. "Tom, it's all right to shake hands with Mr. Qwilleran; he's a member of the family."

Qwilleran gripped a hand that was strong but unaccustomed to social gestures. "How do you do, Tom. I've heard a lot of good things about you." Thinking of the missing watch and pen he looked inquiringly into the man's eyes, but their open innocent gaze was disarming. "You did a fine job with the porch yesterday, Tom. How did you do so much work in such a short time? Did you have a helper?"

"No," Tom said slowly. "No helper. I like to work. I like to work hard." He spoke in a gentle, musical voice.

Aunt Fanny slipped something into his hand. "Go into Mooseville, Tom, and buy yourself a big pasty and a beer, and come back in two hours. Bring the picnic basket from the car before you leave."

"Tom, do you know what time it is?" Qwilleran asked. "I've lost my watch."

The handyman searched the sky for the sun, hiding in the tall pines. "It's almost twelve o'clock," he said softly.

He drove away in the limousine, and Aunt Fanny said: "I've brought some egg salad sandwiches and a thermos of coffee with that *marvelous* cream. We'll sit on the porch and enjoy the lake. The temperature is perfect. Now where are those intelligent cats I've heard so much about? And where do you do your writing? I must confess, I'm awed by your talent, dear."

As a newsman, Qwilleran was expert at interviewing difficult subjects, but he was defeated by Aunt Fanny. She chattered nonstop about shipwrecks on the lake, bears in the woods, dead fish on the beach, caterpillars in the trees. Questions were ignored or evaded. Madame President was in charge of the conversation.

In desperation Qwilleran finally shouted: *"Aunt Fanny!"* After her startled pause he continued: "What do you know about Tom? Where did you find him? How long has he worked for you? Is he trustworthy? He has access to this cabin when I'm not here. You can't blame me for wanting to know."

"You poor dear," she said. "You have always lived in cities. Life is different in the country. We trust each other. Neighbors walk into your house without knocking. If you're not there and they want to borrow an egg, they help themselves. It's a friendly way of living. Don't worry about Tom. He's a fine young man. He does everything I tell him to do and nothing more."

A bell rang—the clear golden tone of the ship's bell outside the south porch.

"That's Tom," she said. "He's right on time. Isn't he a marvel? You go and talk to him while I powder my nose. This has been such a pleasant visit, my dear."

Qwilleran went into the yard. "Hello, Tom. You're right on time, even without a watch."

"Yes, I don't need a watch," he said quietly, his face beaming with pride. He stroked the brass bell. "This is a nice bell. I polished it yesterday. I like to clean things. I keep the truck and the car very clean."

Qwilleran was fascinated by the singsong inflection of his voice.

"I saw your truck in Pickax. It's blue, isn't it?"

"Yes. I like blue. It's like the sky and the lake. Very pretty. This is a nice cabin. I'll come and clean it for you."

"That's a kind offer, Tom, but don't come unless I call you. I'm writing a book, and I don't like people around when I'm writing."

"I wish I could write. I'd like to write a book. That would be nice."

"Everyone has his own talents," Qwilleran said, "and you have many skills. You should be proud of yourself."

Tom's face glowed with pleasure. "Yes, I can fix anything."

Aunt Fanny appeared, goodbyes were said, and the limousine moved carefully down the drive.

The Siamese, who had been invisible for the last two hours, materialized from nowhere. "You two weren't very sociable," Qwilleran said. "What did you think of Aunt Fanny?"

"YOW!" said Koko, shaking himself vigorously.

Qwilleran remembered offering Aunt Fanny a drink before lunch—a whiskey sour, or a gin and tonic, or a Scotch and soda, or dry sherry. She had declined them all.

Now he had four hours to kill before dining with Roger, and he had no incentive to start page one of chapter one of the book he was supposed to be writing. He might watch the bears at the village dump or visit the prison flower gardens or study shipwreck history at the museum, but it was the abandoned cemetery that tugged at his imagination, even though Roger had advised against it—or perhaps *because* Roger had advised against it.

The Chamber of Commerce brochure gave directions: Go east to Pickax Road and turn south for five miles; enter the cemetery on a dirt road (unmarked) through a cobblestone gate.

The route passed the landscaped grounds that were evidently the prison compound. It passed the turkey farm, and Qwilleran slowed to watch the sea of bronze-feathered backs rippling in the farmyard. Ahead of him a truck was turning out of a side road and heading toward him, one of those ubiquitous blue pickups. As it passed he waved to the driver, but the greeting was not returned. When he reached the cobblestone gate he realized the truck had come from the cemetery.

The access to the graveyard was merely a trail, rutted and muddy after the storm. It meandered through the woods with a clearing here and there, just big enough for a car to pull off and park; there was evidence of picnicking and beer-drinking. Eventually the trail branched in several directions through a meadow dotted with gravestones. Qwilleran followed the set of ruts that appeared to have been recently used.

Where the tire marks stopped he got out of the car and explored the burial ground. It was choked with tall grasses and vines, and he had to tear them away to read the inscriptions on the smaller stones: 1877–1879, 1841–1862, 1856–1859. So many infants were buried there! So many women had died in their twenties! The larger family monuments bore names like Schmidt, Campbell, Trevelyan, Watson.

Trampled grasses suggested a slight path leading behind the Campbell stone, and when he followed it he found signs of recent digging. Dried weeds had been thrown across freshly turned soil, barely concealing the brown plastic lid of a garbage pail. The pail itself, about a twelve-gallon size, was buried in the ground. Qwilleran removed the cover cautiously. The pail was empty.

He returned the hiding place to its previous condition and drove home, wondering who would bury a garbage pail in a cemetery—and why. The only clue was a tremor on his upper lip.

Before going to dinner in Mooseville he prepared a dish of tuna for the Siamese. "Koko, you're not earning your keep," he said. "Strange things are happening, and you haven't come up with a single clue." Koko squeezed his blue eyes languidly. Perhaps the cat's sleuthing days were over. Perhaps he would become nothing but a fussy consumer of expensive food.

At that moment Koko's ears pricked up, and he bounded to the checkpoint. The distant rumble of an approaching vehicle became gradually louder until it sounded like a Russian tank. A red pickup truck was followed by a yellow tractor with a complicated superstructure.

The driver of the truck jumped out and said to Qwilleran: "You got a jack pine that's ready to fall on the house? We got this emergency call from Pickax. Something about the power lines. We're supposed to take the tree down and cut it up."

The tractor extended its skybox; the chain saws whined; three men in visored caps shouted; Yum Yum hid under the sofa; and Qwilleran escaped to Mooseville half an hour before the appointed time for dinner.

The Northern Lights Hotel was a relic from the 1860s when the village was a booming port for shipping lumber and ore. It was the kind of frame building that should have burned down a century ago but was miraculously preserved. In style it was a shoe-box with windows, but a porch had been added at the rear, overlooking the wharves. Qwilleran sat in one of its rustic chairs and indulged in his favorite pastime: eavesdropping.

Two voices nearby were in nagging disagreement. Without seeing the source Qwilleran guessed that the man was fat and red-faced and the woman was scrawny and hard-of-hearing.

"I don't think much of this town," the man said in a gasping, wheezing voice. "There's nothing to do. We could've (gasp) stayed home and sat on the patio. It would've (gasp) been cheaper."

The woman answered in a shrill voice, flat with indifference. "You said you wanted to go fishing. I don't know why. You've always hated it."

"Your brother's been blowing off about the fishing up here for (gasp) six years. I wanted to show him he wasn't the only one (gasp) who could land a trout."

"Then why don't you sign up for a charter boat, the way the man said, and stop bitching?"

"I keep telling you—it's too expensive. Did you see how much they want (gasp) for half a day? I could buy a Caribbean cruise for (gasp) that kind of dough."

Qwilleran had checked the prices himself and thought them rather steep.

"Then let's go home," the woman insisted. "No sense hanging around."

"After driving all this way? Do you know what we've spent on gas (gasp) just to get up here?"

Roger appeared at that moment, wearing a black baseball cap.

"I see you're dressed for evening," Qwilleran said. "You didn't tell me it was formal."

"I collect 'em," Roger explained. "I've got seventeen so far. If you've got any enemies, I should warn you about that orange cap of yours; you'd make a perfect target."

They hung their caps with a dozen others on a row of pegs outside the hotel dining room, then took a side table underneath a large tragic painting of a three-masted schooner sinking in a raging sea.

"Well, we had a perfect day," Qwilleran said, opening with the obligatory weather report. "Sunny. Pleasant breeze. Ideal temperature."

"Yes, but the fog's starting to roll in. By morning you won't be able to see the end of your nose. It's no good for the trolling business."

"If you ask me, Roger, the artwork in this room isn't any good for the trolling business. Every picture on the wall is some kind of disaster at sea. It scares the hell out of me. Besides, the charter boats charge too much—that is, too much for someone like me who isn't really interested in fishing."

"You should try it once," Roger urged. "Trolling is a lot more exciting, you know, than sitting in a rowboat with a worm on a hook."

Qwilleran looked at the menu. "If the lake is full of fish, why isn't there one local product on the menu? Nothing but Nova Scotia halibut, Columbia River salmon, and Boston scrod."

"It's all sport-fishing here. The commercial fisheries down the shore net tons of fish and ship them out."

To Nova Scotia, Massachusetts, and the state of Washington, Qwilleran guessed.

Roger ordered a bourbon and water; Qwilleran, his usual tomato juice. A cranky-looking couple took a table nearby, and he noted smugly that the man was red-faced and obese and the woman wore a hearing aid.

Roger said: "Is that all you drink? I thought newsmen were hard drinkers. I studied journalism before I switched to history ed. . . . Say, you've got me counting blue pickups, and I found out you're right. My wife always says people in northern climates like blue. . . . Do you live alone?"

"Not entirely. I've adopted a couple of despotic Siamese cats. One was orphaned as the result of a murder on my beat. The female was abandoned when she was a kitten. They're both purebred, and the male is smarter than I am."

"I have a hunting dog—Brittany spaniel," Roger said. "Sharon has a Scottie. . . . Were you ever married, Qwill?"

"Once. It wasn't an overwhelming success."

"What happened?"

"She had a nervous breakdown, and I tried to pickle my troubles in alcohol. You ask a lot of questions, Roger. You should have stuck to journalism."

The newsman said it with good humor. He had spent his entire career asking questions, and now he enjoyed being interrogated.

"Would you ever get married again?"

Qwilleran allowed the glimmer of a smile to twitch his moustache. "Three months ago I would have said no; now I'm not so sure." He rubbed the backs of his hands as he spoke; they were beginning to itch. The bartender at the Press Club had predicted he would get hives from drinking so much tomato juice, and perhaps Bruno was right.

The fat man at the next table seemed to be listening, so Qwilleran lowered his voice. "The police set up a roadblock Monday night. What was that all about? There was nothing in the paper or on the radio."

Roger shrugged. "Roadblocks are a social activity up here, like potluck suppers. I think the cops do it once in a while when things get dull."

"Are you telling me there isn't enough crime in Moose County to keep them busy?"

"Not like you have in the city. The conservation guys catch a few poachers, and things get lively at the Shipwreck Tavern on Saturday nights, but the cops spend most of their time chasing accidents— single-car accidents mostly. Someone drives too fast and hits a moose, or kids get a few beers and wrap themselves around a tree. There's a lot of rescue work on the lake, too; the sheriff has two boats and a helicopter."

"No drug problem?"

"Maybe the tourists smoke a few funny cigarettes, but—no problem, really. What I worry about is shipwreck-looting. The lake is full of sunken ships. Some of them went down a hundred years ago, and their cargoes are on public record. The looters have sophisticated diving equipment—cold-water gear, electronic stuff, and all that. There's valuable cargo down there, and they're stripping the wrecks for private gain."

"Isn't that illegal?"

"Not yet. If we had an underwater preserve protected by law it would be a big boost for tourism. It could be used by marine historians, archaeologists, and sport-divers."

"What's holding you back?"

"Money! It would take tens of thousands for an archaeological survey. After that we'd have to lobby for legislation."

Qwilleran said: "It would be a tough law to enforce. You'd need more boats, more helicopters, more personnel."

"Right! And by that time there wouldn't be any sunken cargo to protect."

The men had ordered a second round of drinks, but Qwilleran stopped sipping his TJ. He rubbed his itching hands and wrists surreptitiously under the table.

Roger lowered his voice. "See those two guys sitting near the door? They're wreck-divers. Probably looters."

"How do you know?"

"Everybody knows."

When the food was served, Qwilleran rated it *E* for edible, but the conversation was enlightening. At the end of the meal he remarked to Roger: "Do you think there might be a skunk living under the post office? I went in there yesterday, and the odor drove everyone out of the building."

"Probably some hog farmer picking up his mail," Roger said. "If they come into town in their work-clothes, the whole town clears out. You wouldn't believe the way some of their kids come to school. They're not all like that, of course. One of my hunting partners raises hogs. No problem."

"Another mystery: A hawk flew through a screened door at the cabin and left a big hole. I can't figure it out."

"He was diving for a rabbit or chipmunk," Roger explained, "and he didn't put on the brakes fast enough."

"You think so?"

"Sure! I've seen a hawk carry off a cat. I was hunting once and heard something mewing up in the sky. I looked up, and there was this poor little cat."

Qwilleran thought of Yum Yum and squirmed uncomfortably. There was a moment of silence, and then he said: "A couple of nights ago I heard footsteps on the roof in the middle of the night."

"A raccoon," Roger said. "A raccoon on the roof of a cabin like yours sounds like a Japanese wrestler in space boots. I know! My in-laws have a cottage near you. One year they had a whole family of raccoons in their chimney."

"Do your in-laws give wild parties? I've heard some hysterical laughing late at night."

"That was a loon you heard. It's a crazy bird."

The fog was thickening, and the view from the dining room windows was almost obliterated. Qwilleran said he should get back to the cabin.

"I hope my wife doesn't try driving home tonight," Roger said. "She's been on a buying trip Down Below. She has a little candle and gift shop in the mall. How do you like this money clip? It came from Sharon's shop." He paid his half of the check with bills from a jumbo paper clip that looked like gold.

Qwilleran drove home at twenty miles an hour with the fog swirling in front of the windshield. The private drive up to the cabin was even more hazardous, with tree trunks suddenly appearing where they were not supposed to be. As he parked the car he thought he saw two figures moving away from the cabin, down the slope toward the beach.

"Hello!" he called. "Hello there!" But they disappeared into the fog.

Indoors he first checked the whereabouts of the Siamese. Koko was huddled on the moose head, and Yum Yum cautiously wriggled out from underneath the sofa. Nothing appeared to have been disturbed, but he detected the aroma of pipe tobacco. In the guestroom there was a slight impression in one of the bunks, where the cats took their naps, and one of his brown socks was on the floor. Yum Yum had a passion for his socks. Everything else seemed to be in order.

Then he found a note in the kitchen, scribbled on one of his own typing sheets: "Welcome to the dunes. I'm Roger's mother-in-law. See foil package in your fridge. Thought you might like some roast turkey. Come and see us."

That was all. No name. Qwilleran checked the refrigerator and found a generous supply of sliced turkey breast and chunks of dark meat. As he started chopping a portion of it for the cat's dinner, Yum Yum squealed in anticipation, and Koko pranced back and forth, warbling an aria of tenor yowls and ecstatic gutterals.

Qwilleran watched them eat, but his mind was elsewhere. He liked Roger. Under thirty, with coal-black hair, was a good age to be. But the young man had been remarkably glib on the subject of hawks, loons, raccoons, blue trucks, and police roadblocks. How many of his answers were in the interest of tourism? And if the official brochure encouraged tourists to visit the old cemetery, why did Roger try to discourage it? Did he know something about the pail? And if there was no crime in Moose County, why did Aunt Fanny make a point of carrying a gun?

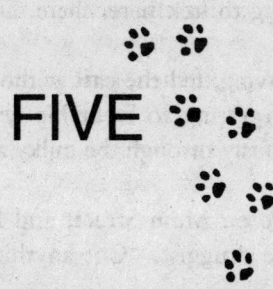

FIVE

Qwilleran was wakened by Yum Yum. She sat on his chest, her blue eyes boring into his forehead, conveying a subliminal message: breakfast. The lake view from the bunkroom windows had been replaced by total whiteness. The fog had settled on the shore like a suffocating blanket. There was no breeze, no sound.

Qwilleran tried to start a blaze in the fireplace to dispel the dampness, using Wednesday's paper and some book matches from the hotel, but nothing worked. His chief concern was the condition of his hands and wrists. The itching was unbearable, and blisters were forming as large as poker chips. Furthermore he was beginning to itch here, there, and everywhere.

He dressed without shaving, fed the cats without ceremony, and—even forgetting to wear his new cap—steered the car nervously through the milky atmosphere.

There was a drug store on Main Street, and he showed his blisters to the druggist. "Got anything for this?"

"Yikes!" said the druggist. "Worse case of poison ivy I've ever seen. You'd better go and get a shot."

"Is there a doctor in town?"

"There's a walk-in clinic in the Cannery Mall. You know the mall? Two miles beyond town—an old fish cannery made into stores and whatnot. In this fog you won't be able to see it, but you'll smell it."

There was hardly a vehicle to be seen on Main Street. Qwilleran hugged the yellow line, watching the odometer, and at the two-mile mark there was no doubt he had reached the Cannery Mall. He angle-parked between two yellow lines and followed the aroma to a bank of plate glass doors opening into an arcade.

The medical clinic, smelling appropriately antiseptic, was deserted except for a plain young woman sitting at a desk. "Is there a doctor here?" he asked.

"I'm the doctor," she replied, glancing at his hands. "Where did you go to get that magnificent case of ivy poisoning?"

"I guess I picked it up in the old cemetery."

"Really? Aren't you a little old for that kind of thing?" She threw him a mischievous glance.

He was too uncomfortable to appreciate badinage. "I was looking at the old gravestones."

"A likely story. Come into the torture chamber, and I'll give you a shot." She also gave him a tube of lotion and some advice: "Keep your hands out of hot water. Avoid warm showers. And stay away from old cemeteries."

Leaving the clinic Qwilleran was in a sulky humor. He thought the doctor should have been less flip and more sympathetic. By the time he inched his car back to town through the fog, however, the medication was working, bringing not only relief but a heady euphoria, and he remembered that the doctor had attractive green eyes and the longest eyelashes he had ever seen.

At the hotel, where he stopped for coffee and eggs, four men at the next table were complaining about the weather. "The boats won't go out in this soup. Let's get a bottle of red-eye and play some cards."

At the table behind him a familiar voice said: "We're not leaving here (gasp) till we go fishing."

A shrill flat voice answered: "Why are you so stubborn? You don't even *like* to fish."

"This is different, I told you. We go out (gasp) on thirty-six-foot trollers and catch maybe twenty-pound trout."

"You said it was too expensive."

"The prices at the main dock are highway robbery, but I found a boat (gasp) that'll take us for fifteen bucks."

Qwilleran's thrifty nature sensed an opportunity, and the combination of the medication and the unnatural atmosphere gave him a feeling of reckless excitement. When the couple left the dining room he followed them. "Excuse me, sir, did I hear you say something about a troller that's less expensive?"

"Sure did! Fifteen bucks for six hours. Split three ways (gasp) that's five bucks apiece. Not bad. Two young fellas (gasp) own the boat. You interested?"

"Is fishing any good in this weather?"

"These young fellas say it doesn't make any difference. By the way," he wheezed, "my name's Whatley—from Cleveland—wholesale hardware." He then introduced his wife, whose manner was frosty, and he volunteered to drive, since he knew the way to the dock. "The boat ties up outside of town. That's why (gasp) it's cheaper. You have to shop around to get a good buy."

The trip to the dock was another slow agonizing crawl through earthbound clouds. At one point the three giant electric letters of the FOO glowed weakly through the mist. Farther on, the Cannery Mall announced itself strongly although the building was invisible. Then there were miles of nothing. Each mile seemed like five. Whatley drove on grimly. No one talked. Qwilleran strained his eyes, peering at the road ahead, expecting to meet a pair of yellow foglights head-on or the sudden taillights of a stalled logging truck.

"How will you know when you get there?" he asked.

"Can't miss it. There's a wreck of a boat (gasp) where we turn off."

When the wreck eventually loomed up out of the mist, Whatley turned down a swampy lane bordering a canal filled with more wrecks.

"I'm sorry I came," Mrs. Whatley announced in her first statement of the day.

Where the lane ended, a rickety wharf extended into the lake, and the three landlubbers groped their way across its rotting planks. The water lapped against the pilings in a liquid whisper, and a hull could be heard creaking against the wharf.

Previously Qwilleran had seen the gleaming white fishing fleet at the municipal pier. Boats with names like *Lady Aurora, Queen of the Lake,* and *Northern Princess* displayed posters boasting of their ship-to-shore radios, fishing sonars, depth-finders, and automatic pilots. So he was not prepared for the *Minnie K.* It was an old gray tub, rough with scabs of peeling paint. Incrustations on the deck and railings brought to mind the visits of seagulls and the intimate parts of dead fish. The two members of the crew, who were present in a vague sort of way, were as shabby as their craft. One boy was about seventeen, Qwilleran guessed, and the other was somewhat younger. Neither had an alertness that would inspire confidence.

There were no greetings or introductions. The boys viewed the passengers with suspicion and, after collecting their money, got the boat hastily under weigh, barking at each other in meaningless syllables.

Qwilleran asked the younger boy how far out they were planning to cruise and received a grunt in reply.

Mrs. Whatley said: "This is disgusting. No wonder they call these things stink-boats."

"Whaddaya want for five bucks?" her husband said. "The *Queen Elizabeth?*"

The passengers found canvas chairs, ragged and stained, and the *Minnie K* moved slowly through the water, creating hardly a ripple. Mr. Whatley dozed from time to time, and his wife opened a paperback book and turned off her hearing aid. For about an hour the boat chugged through the total whiteness in apathy, its fishy emanations blending with exhaust fumes. Then the engine changed its tune to an even lower pitch, and the boys lazily produced the fishing gear: rods with enormous reels, copper lines, and brass spoons.

"What do I do with this thing?" Qwilleran asked. "Where's the bait?"

"The spoon's all you need," Whatley said. "Drop the line over the rail (gasp) and keep moving the rod up and down."

"And then what?"

"When you get a bite, you'll know it. Reel it in."

The *Minnie K* moved through the placid lake with

reluctance. Occasionally the engine died for sheer lack of purpose and started again unwillingly. For an hour Qwilleran waved the fishing rod up and down in a trance induced by the throbbing of the engine and the sense of isolation. The troller was in a tight little world of its own, surrounded by a fog that canceled out everything else. There was no breeze, not even a splash of water against the hull— just the hollow putt-putt of the engine and the distant moan of a foghorn.

Whatley had reeled in his line and, after taking a few swigs from a flask, fell asleep in his canvas chair. His wife never looked up from her book.

Qwilleran was wondering where they were—and why he was there—when the engine stopped with an explosive cough, and the two boys, muttering syllables, jumped down into the hold. The silence became absolute, and the boat was motionless on the glassy lake. It was then that Qwilleran heard voices drifting across the water—men's voices, too far away to be distinguishable. He rested the rod on the railing and listened. The voices were coming closer, arguing, getting louder. There were shouts of anger followed by unintelligible torrents of verbal abuse, then a sharp *crack* like splitting wood . . . grunts . . . sounds of lunging . . . a heavy thump. A few seconds later Qwilleran heard a mighty splash and a light patter of spray on the water's surface.

After that, all was quiet except for a succession of ripples that crossed the surface of the lake and lapped against the *Minnie K*. The fog closed in like cotton batting, and the water turned to milk.

The crew had their heads bent over the contraption that passed for an engine. Whatley slept on, and his wife also dozed. Wonderingly, Qwilleran resumed the senseless motion of the fishing rod, up and down, up and down, in exaggerated arcs. He had lost all sense of time and his watch had been left at home because of his itching wrists.

Thirty minutes passed, or an hour, and then there was a pull on the line, sending vibrations down the rod and into his arms. He shouted!

Whatley waked with a start. "Reel it in! Reel it in!"

At that magic moment, with the roots of his hair tingling, Qwilleran realized the thrill of deep-sea fishing. "Feels like a whale!"

"Not so fast! Keep it steady! Don't stop!" Whatley was gasping for breath, and so was Qwilleran. His hands were shaking. The copper line was endless.

Everyone was watching. The young skipper was leaning over the rail. "Gaff!" he yelled, and the other boy threw him a long-handled iron hook.

"Gotta be fifty pounds!" Qwilleran shouted, straining to reel in the last few yards. He could feel the final surge as the monster rose through the water. "I've got him! I've got him!"

The huge shape had barely surfaced when he lost his grip on the reel.

"Grab it!" cried Whatley, but the reel was spinning wildly. As it began to slow, the skipper pulled pliers from his pocket and cut the line.

"No good," he said. "No good."

"Whaddaya mean?" Whatley screamed at him. "That fish was thirty pounds (gasp) if it was an ounce!"

"No good," the skipper said. He swung himself up to the wheelhouse; the younger boy dropped into the hold, and the engine started.

"This whole deal is a fraud!" Whatley protested.

His wife looked up from her book and yawned.

"I don't know about you people," Qwilleran said, "but I'm ready to call it a day."

The boat picked up speed and headed for what he hoped would be dry land. On the return voyage he slumped in the canvas chair, engrossed in his own thoughts. Whatley had another swig and dozed off.

Qwilleran was no fisherman, but he had seen films of the sport, and this experience was hardly typical. His catch didn't fight like a fish; when it broke the surface it didn't splash like a fish; and it certainly didn't look like a fish.

Back in Mooseville he headed straightway for the tourist bureau. He was not feeling amiable, but first he had to engage in the weather amenities. "You were right about the fog, Roger. How long do you think it will last?"

"It should clear by noon tomorrow."

"Did your wife get home all right?"

"One-thirty this morning. Took her two hours to

drive the last twenty miles. She was a basket case when she finally got in. What have you been doing in this fog, Qwill?"

"I've been trolling."

"What! You're hallucinating. The boats didn't go out today."

"The *Minnie K* went out. We were out for four hours, and that was three hours too many."

Roger reached for a file. "I never heard of the *Minnie K*. And she's not here on the list of registered trollers. Where did you find her?"

"A guest at the hotel lined up the expedition. His name is Whatley."

"Yeah, I know him. Overweight, short of breath. He's been in here three times, complaining. How much did they charge? I assume you didn't catch any fish."

"No, but I caught something else," Qwilleran said. "It didn't behave like a fish, and when I got it to the surface, the skipper cut my line and took off for shore in a hurry. He didn't like the look of it, and neither did I. It looked like the body of a man."

Roger gulped and stroked his black beard. "It was probably an old rubber tire or something like that. It would be hard to tell for sure in the fog. The boaters lash tires to the side of the wharf—to act as bumpers, you know. They can break loose in a storm. We had a big storm Tuesday night . . ."

"Knock it off, Roger. We all know the Chamber of Commerce writes your script. I'd like to report this—this *rubber tire* to the police. Where do I find the sheriff?"

Roger flushed and looked guilty but not contrite. "Behind the log church. The building with a flag."

"By the way, I got a surprise last night," Qwilleran continued in a more genial humor. "Your mother-in-law left some turkey and a note at my cabin, but she didn't sign her name. I don't know how to thank her."

"Oh, she's like that—scatterbrained. But she's nice. Laughs a lot. Her name's Mildred Hanstable, and she lives at Top o' the Dunes, east of you. I should warn you about something. She'll insist on telling your fortune and then expect a donation."

"Isn't that illegal?"

"It's for charity. She's helping to raise money for some kind of heart machine at the Pickax Hospital."

"Count me in," Qwilleran said. "I'll need the machine before this restful vacation is over."

When he returned to the cabin, it was still daylight, filtered through fog. Indoors he smelled vinegar, reminding him of the homemade brass polish used by antique dealers. Sure enough, the brass lantern hanging over the bar was newly polished. Tom had been there in spite of the stipulation; he had been told not to come to the cabin until called. Qwilleran had left his old watch and some loose change on the dresser in the bunkroom, and they were still there. He shrugged.

When he called to his friends, Yum Yum came running from the guest room, but Koko was too busily engaged to respond. He was perched on the moose head, fussing and talking to himself in small musical grunts that originated deep in his snowy chest.

"What are you doing up there?" Qwilleran demanded.

Koko was shifting position on the antlers, standing on his hind legs and reaching up with a front paw as if searching for a toehold. The moose head was mounted on a varnished wooden plaque that was hung on the uneven log wall. Koko was trying to thrust his paw into one of the crevices behind the plaque. After some experimental footwork he finally braced himself well enough to reach the aperture. His paw ventured warily into the opening. Something rattled inside. Koko tried harder, stretched longer, still muttering to himself.

Qwilleran walked closer, and when the prize fell out of the crevice and bounced off the antler, he caught it. "What's this? A cassette!"

It was a blank tape that had been used for home-recording. Side A was inscribed *1930 Favorites* in what appeared to be Aunt Fanny's handwriting. Side B was labeled *More 1930 Favorites*. There was no dust on the clear plastic case.

Qwilleran took the cassette to the stereo and removed the Brahms concerto that had been in the player ever since he arrived. "Wait a minute," he said aloud. "This is not the way I left it." The cassette had been reversed, and the flip side, offering Beethoven, was faceup.

Koko's trophy produced bouncy music: renditions of *My Blue Heaven, Exactly Like You,* and others of the period, all with the dubious fidelity of old 78s. It was a strange collection to hide behind a moose head.

Qwilleran finished listening to Side *A* and then flipped it over. There was more of the same. Then halfway through *Little White Lies,* a voice interrupted—an unprofessional voice—an ordinary man's voice, but forceful. After a brief and surprising message, the music resumed. He rewound the cassette and played it again.

The demanding voice cut in: "Now hear this, my friend. You get busy or you'll be sorry! You know what I'll do! You gotta bring up more stuff. I can't pay off if you don't come up with the loot. And we've gotta make some changes. Things are gettin' hot. You come and see me Saturday, you hear? I'll be at the boat dock after supper."

The tape had been used recently. It was only the day before that Koko had stepped on the buttons and played the Brahms. Someone had been there in the meantime and had either taped the message or listened to it, afterwards replacing the Brahms concerto upside-down. Someone had also stolen a gold watch and a gold pen, but that had happened earlier. Unidentified visitors were walking in and out of the cabin in the casual way that Aunt Fanny found so neighborly.

Someone had undoubtedly climbed on a bar stool to reach the moose head, and Qwilleran checked the four pine stools for footprints, but the varnished surfaces were clean.

Koko was watching intently as Qwilleran tucked the cassette into a dresser drawer. "Koko," the man said, "I don't like this open-door policy. People are using the place like a bus terminal. We've got to find a locksmith. . . . And if you are ever in danger, or if Yum Yum is in danger, you know what to do."

Koko blinked his eyes slowly and wisely.

SIX

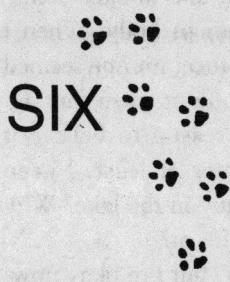

Mooseville, Friday

Dear Arch,

I'm too tight to buy you an anniversary card, but here's wishing you and your beautiful bride a happy twenty-fourth and many more to come. It seems only yesterday that you dropped the wedding ring and I lost your honeymoon tickets.

Well, since coming to Mooseville I've discovered that all civilization is divided into two parts: Up Here and Down Below. We have friendly people up here who read the *Fluxion*—

also mysterious incidents that they try to cover
up. Yesterday I went fishing and hooked something that looked like a human body. When I
reported it to the sheriff's office, no one seemed
particularly concerned. I know it wasn't an ac-
cidental drowning. I have reason to believe it
was homicide—manslaughter at least. I keep
wondering: Who was that guy in the lake? Why
was he there? Who tossed him in?

I got into some poison ivy, but I'm okay now.
And early this morning I thought someone was
stealing my tires, but it was a seagull making a
noise like a car-jack. The eateries up here are
so-so. For a restaurant reviewer it's like being
sent to Siberia.

                                          Qwill

P.S.

Koko has some new tricks—answering the
phone and playing the stereo. In a few years
he'll be working for NASA.

The fog was lifting. From the windows of the
cabin it was possible to see nearby trees and the burial place of the septic tank. Although Old Sam had
filled the depression and leveled it neatly, the cats
had resumed their previous occupation of staring in
that direction.

When the telephone rang on Friday morning
Koko leaped from the windowsill and raced to the
bar. Qwilleran was close behind but not fast enough

to prevent him from dislodging the receiver. It fell to the bar top with a crash.

The man seized it. "Hello? Hello?"

"Oh, *there* you are," said the gravel voice from Pickax. "I was worried about you, dear. I called yesterday and the phone made the most *unusual* noises. When I called back I got a busy signal. I finally told the operator to cut in, and she said the phone was off the hook, so I sent Tom out there to investigate. He said the receiver was lying on the bar—and no one was home. You should be more careful, dear. I suppose you're preoccupied with your book. How is it progressing? Are you still . . ."

"*Aunt Fanny!*"

"Yes, dear?"

"I spent the day in town, and my cat knocked the receiver off. It's a bad habit he's developed. I'm sorry about it. I'll start keeping the phone in the kitchen cupboard, if the cord will reach."

"Be sure to close the windows whenever you go out, dear. A squall can come up suddenly and *deluge* the place. How many chapters of the book have you written? Do you know when it will be published? Tom says the big jack pine has been cut down. He'll be out there tomorrow with a log-splitter. Have you noticed the canoe under the porch? The paddles are in the toolshed. Don't go out in rough weather, dear, and be sure to stay close to shore. Now I won't talk any more because I know you want to get back to your writing. Some day you can write my life story, and we'll both make a *fortune*."

*   *   *

Wearing his orange cap, of which he was getting inordinately fond, Qwilleran drove to Mooseville to mail the letter to Arch. At the post office he sniffed warily but detected only fresh floor wax.

His next stop was the Cannery Mall, where he decided the aroma of smoked fish was not entirely unpleasant after all. At the medical clinic the young doctor was sitting at the reception desk, reading a gourmet magazine. He was right about her green eyes; they sparkled with youth and health and humor.

"Remember me?" he began, doffing his cap. "I'm the patient with the Cemetery Syndrome."

"Glad to see you're not as grouchy as you were yesterday."

"The shot took effect immediately. Do you get many cases like mine?"

"Oh, yes," she said. "Ivy poisoning, second-degree sunburn, infected heel blisters, rabid squirrel bites—all the usual vacation delights."

"Any drownings?"

"The police emergency squad takes care of those. I hope you're not planning to fall in the lake. It's so cold that anyone who falls overboard goes down once and never comes up. At least, that's the conventional wisdom in these parts." She closed her magazine. "Won't you sit down?"

Qwilleran settled into a chair and smoothed his moustache nervously. "I'd like to ask you a question about that shot you gave me. Could it cause hallucinations?"

"Extremely unlikely. Do you have a history of hallucinating?"

"No, but I had an unusual experience after the shot, and no one believes I saw what I saw. I'm beginning to doubt my sanity."

"You may be the one person in ten million who had an abnormal reaction," the doctor said cheerfully. "Congratulations!"

Qwilleran regarded her intently, and she returned his gaze with laughing eyes and fluttering eyelashes.

He said: "Can I sue you for malpractice? Or will you settle for a dinner date?"

"Make it a quick lunch, and I can go right now," she said, consulting her watch. "I never refuse lunch with an interesting *older* man. Do you like pasties?"

"They'd be okay if they had flaky pastry, a little sauce, and less turnip."

"Then you'll *love* the Nasty Pasty. Let's go." She threw off the white coat that covered a Mooseville T-shirt.

The restaurant was small and designed for intimacy, with two rows of booths and accents of fishnet, weathered rope, and stuffed seagulls.

Qwilleran said: "I never thought I'd be consulting a doctor who is female and half my age and easy to look at."

"Better get used to the idea," she said. "We're in plentiful supply. . . . You're in good shape for your age. Do you exercise a lot?"

"Not a great deal," he said, although "not at all"

would have been closer to the truth. "I'm sorry, doctor, but I don't know your name."

"Melinda Goodwinter."

"Related to the attorney?"

"Cousin. Pickax is loaded with Goodwinters. My father is a GP there, and I'm going to join his office in the fall."

"You probably know Fanny Klingenschoen. I'm borrowing her log cabin for the summer."

"Everyone knows Fanny—for better or worse. Maybe I shouldn't say that; she's a remarkable old lady. She says she wants to be my first patient when I start my practice."

"Why do you call her remarkable?"

"Fanny has a unique way of getting what she wants. You know the old county courthouse? It's an architectural gem, but they were ready to tear it down until Fanny went to work and saved it—single-handedly."

Qwilleran touched his moustache. "Let me ask you something, Melinda. This is beautiful country, and the people are friendly, but I have a gnawing suspicion that something is going on that I don't comprehend. Am I supposed to believe that Moose County is some kind of Utopia?"

"We have our problems,," she admitted, "but we don't talk about them—to outsiders. This is not for publication, but there's a tendency up here to resent visitors from Down Below."

"They love the tourists' dollars, but they don't like the tourists, is that right?"

She nodded. "The summer people are too smooth, too self-important, too aggressive, too condescending, too *different*. Present company excepted, naturally."

"You think *we're* different? You're the ones who are *different*," Qwilleran objected. "Life in the city is predictable. I go out on assignment, eat lunch at the Press Club, hurry back to the paper to write the story, have dinner at a good restaurant, get mugged on the way home . . . no surprises!"

"You jest. I've lived in the city, and country is better."

The pasties were a success: flaky, juicy, turnipless and of comfortable size. Qwilleran felt comfortable with Melinda, too, and at one point he smoothed his moustache self-consciously and said: "There's something I'd like to confide in you, if you don't mind."

"Flattered."

"I wouldn't discuss it with anyone else, but since you're a doctor . . ."

"I understand."

"How shall I begin? . . . Do you know anything about cats? They have a sixth sense, you know, and some people think their whiskers are a kind of extrasensory antenna."

"Interesting theory."

"I live with a Siamese, and I swear he's tuned in to some abstruse body of knowledge."

She nodded encouragingly.

Qwilleran lowered his voice. "Sometimes I get unusual vibrations from my moustache, and I perceive things that aren't obvious to other people. And that's not all. In the last year or two my sense of smell has been getting unusually keen—disturbingly keen, in fact. And now my hearing is becoming re-markably acute. A few nights ago someone was walking on the beach a hundred feet away—on the soft sand—and I could hear the footsteps through my pillow: thud thud thud."

"Quite phenomenal," she said.

"Do you think it's abnormal? Is it something I should worry about?"

"They say elephants can hear the footsteps of mice."

"I hope you're not implying that I have large ears."

"Your ears are very well proportioned," Melinda said. "In fact, you're quite an attractive man—for your age."

On the whole Melinda Goodwinter was enjoyable company, although Qwilleran thought she referred to his age too frequently and even asked if he had grandchildren. Nevertheless, he was feeling good as he drove home to the cabin; he thought he might start work on his book, or get some exercise.

The fog had all but disappeared. Intermittent gusts of offshore breeze were pushing it out to sea, and the lake had a glassy calm. Perfect canoeing weather, he decided.

Qwilleran had not been canoeing since he was a twelve-year-old at summer camp, but he thought he remembered how it was done. He found paddles in the toolshed and chose the longest one. It was easy to drag the aluminum canoe down the sandy slope to the beach, but launching it was another matter, involving wet feet and a teetering lunge into a wobbly and uncooperative craft. When he finally seated himself in the stern and glided across the smooth glistening water, he sensed a glorious mix of exhilaration and peace.

He remembered Aunt Fanny's advice and turned the high bow, which rose out of the water considerably, to follow the shore. A moment later a gust of offshore wind caught the bow, and the canoe swiveled around and headed for open water, but its course was quickly corrected when the breeze abated. He paddled past deserted beaches and lonely dunes topped with tall pines. Farther on was the Top o' the Dunes Club, a row of substantial vacation houses. He fancied the occupants watching and envying him. Two of them waved from their porches.

The offshore breeze sprang up again, riffling the water. The bow swung around like a weathervane, and the canoe skimmed in the direction of Canada a hundred miles away. Qwilleran summoned all his remembered skills, but nothing worked until the wind subsided again.

He was now farther from shore than appeared wise, and he tried to turn back, but he was out of the lee of the land, and the offshore gusts were persistent, swiveling the bow and making the canoe unmanageable. He paddled frantically, digging the paddle in the water without plan or purpose, desperately trying to turn the canoe. It only drifted farther out, all the while spinning crazily in water that was becoming choppy.

He had lost control completely. Should he jump overboard and swim for shore and let the canoe go? He was not a competent swimmer, and he remembered the reputation of the icy lake. There was no time to lose. Every second took him farther from shore. He was on the verge of panic.

"Back-paddle!" came a voice riding on the wind. "Back-paddle . . . back-paddle!"

Yes! Of course! That was the trick. He reversed his stroke, and while the bow was still pointed north the canoe made gradual progress toward shore. Once in the lee of the land, he was able to turn the canoe and head for the beach.

A man and a woman were standing on the sand watching him, the man holding a bullhorn. They shouted encouragement, and he beached the canoe at their feet.

"We were really worried about you," the woman said. "I was about to call the helicopter." She laughed nervously.

The man said: "You need a little more practice before you try for the Olympics."

Qwilleran was breathing heavily, but he managed to thank them.

"You must be Mr. Qwilleran," the woman said. She was middle-aged, buxom, and dressed in fashionable resortwear. "I'm Mildred Hanstable,

Roger's mother-in-law, and this is our next-door neighbor, Buford Dunfield."

"Call me Buck," said the neighbor.

"Call me Qwill."

They shook hands.

"You need a drink," Buck said. "Come on up to the house. Mildred, how about you?"

"Thanks, Buck, but I've got a meat loaf in the oven. Stanley is coming to dinner tonight."

"I want to thank you for the turkey," Qwilleran said. "It made great sandwiches. A sandwich is about the extent of my culinary expertise."

Mildred laughed heartily at that and then said: "I don't suppose you found a bracelet at your cabin—a gold chain bracelet?"

"No, but I'll look for it."

"Otherwise it could have dropped off when I was walking on the beach."

"In that case," Buck said, "it's gone forever."

Mildred gave a hollow laugh. "If the waves don't get it, *those girls* will."

The two men climbed the dune to the cottage. Buck was a well-built man with plentiful gray hair and an authoritative manner. He spoke in a powerful voice that went well with a bullhorn. "I'm sure glad to see that fog let up," he said. "How long are you going to be up here?"

"All summer. Do you get fog very often?"

"A bad one? Three or four times a season. We go to Texas in the winter."

The cottage was a modern redwood with a deck

overlooking the lake and glass doors leading into a littered living room.

"Excuse the mess," the host said. "My wife went to Canada with my sister to see some plays about dead kings. The gals go for that kind of stuff. . . . What'll you have? I drink rye, but I've got Scotch and bourbon. Or maybe you'd like a gin and tonic?"

"Just tonic water or ginger ale," Qwilleran said. "I'm off the hard stuff."

"Not a bad idea. I should cut down. Planning on doing any fishing?"

"My fishing is on a par with my canoeing. My chief reason for being here is to find time to write a book."

"Man, if I could write I'd write a best-seller," Buck said. "The things I've seen! I spent twenty-five years in law enforcement Down Below. Took early retirement with a good pension, but I got restless— you know how it is—and took a job in Pickax. Chief of police in a small town! Some experience!" He shook his head. "The respectable citizens were more trouble than the lawbreakers, so I quit. I'm satisfied to take it easy now. I do a little woodworking. See that row of candlesticks? I turn them on my lathe, and Mildred sells them to raise money for the hospital."

"I like the big ones," Qwilleran said. "They look like cathedral candlesticks."

They were sitting at the bar. Buck poured refills and then lighted a pipe, going through the ritual that Qwilleran knew so well. "I've made bigger sticks than that," he said between puffs. "Come on downstairs and see my workshop." He led the way to a room dominated by machinery and sawdust. "I start with one of these four-by-fours and turn it on the lathe. Simple, but the tourists like 'em, and it's for a good cause. Mildred finished one pair in gold and made them look antique. She's a clever woman."

"She does a lot for the hospital, I hear."

"Yeah, she's got crazy ideas for fund-raising. That's all right. It keeps her mind off her troubles."

The pipe smoke was reaching Qwilleran's nostrils, and he remarked: "You get your tobacco from Scotland."

"How did you know? I order it from Down Below."

"I used to smoke the same blend, Groat and Boddle Number Five."

"Exactly! I smoked Auld Clootie Number Three for a long time, but I switched last year."

"I used to alternate between Groat and Boddle and Auld Barleyfumble."

Buck swept the sawdust from the seat of a captain's chair and pushed it toward his guest. "Put it there, my friend."

Qwilleran slid into the chair and enjoyed the wholesome smell of sawdust mixed with his favorite tobacco. "Tell me, Buck. How long did it take you to adjust to living up here?"

"Oh, four or five years."

"Do you lock your doors?"

"We did at first, but after a while we didn't bother."

"It's a lot different from Down Below. The surroundings, the activities, the weather, the customs, the pace, the attitude. I never realized it would be such a drastic change. My chief idea was to get away from pollution and congestion and crime for a while."

"Don't be too sure about that last one," Buck said in a confidential tone.

"What makes you say that?"

"I've made a few observations." The retired policeman threw his guest a meaningful glance.

Qwilleran smoothed his moustache. "Why don't you drop in for a drink this weekend? I'm staying at the Klingenschoen cabin. Ever been there?"

Buck was relighting his pipe. He puffed, shook his head, and puffed again.

"It's on the dune, about a half mile west of here. And I've got a bottle of rye with your name on it."

When Qwilleran paddled the canoe home through shallow water, he was thinking about the man who had saved his life with a bullhorn. Buck had denied ever being at the Klingenschoen cabin, and yet . . . On the evening when Mildred left her gift of turkey, two figures had disappeared into the fog, headed for the beach, and one of them had been smoking Groat and Boddle Number Five.

SEVEN

The muffled bell of the telephone rang several times before Qwilleran roused enough to answer it. The instrument was now housed in a kitchen cupboard, and Koko had not yet devised a means of unlatching the cupboard door.

Qwilleran was not ready for a dose of directives from Madame President before his morning coffee, and he shuffled to the phone reluctantly.

A gentle voice said: "Hello, Qwill dearest. Did I get you out of bed? Guess what! I can drive up to see you if you still want me?"

"Want you! I'm pining away, Rosemary. When can you come? How long can you stay?"

"I should be able to leave the store after lunch today and arrive sometime tomorrow, and I can stay a week unless someone makes a firm offer for Helthy-Welthy. I'm being *very nice* to Max Sorrell, hoping he'll offer cash."

Qwilleran's response was a disapproving grunt.

There was a pause. "Are you there, dearest? Can you hear me?"

"I'm speechless with joy, Rosemary. I sent you the directions to the cabin, didn't I?"

"Yes, I have them."

"Drive carefully."

"I can hardly wait."

"I need you."

He missed Rosemary in more ways than one. He needed a friend who would share his pleasures and problems. He was surrounded by friendly people, yet he was lonely.

He kept saying to the cats: "Wait till she sees the cabin! Wait till she sees the lake! Wait till she meets Aunt Fanny!" His only regret was the fishy odor wafting up from the beach. During the night the lake had deposited a bushel or more of silvery souvenirs, which began to reek in the morning sun.

When he drove into town for breakfast he waved breezy greetings to every passing motorist. Then, fortified by buckwheat flapjacks and lumbercamp syrup, he went in search of the candle shop at Cannery Mall. He detected the thirty-seven different scents even before he saw the sign: *Night's Candles.*

"Are you Sharon MacGillivray?" he asked a young woman who was arranging displays. "I'm Jim Qwilleran."

"Oh, I'm so glad to meet you! I'm Sharon Hanstable," she said, "but I'm married to Roger MacGillivray. I've heard so much about you."

"I like the name of your shop." He thought a moment and then declaimed: " 'Night's candles are burnt out, and jocund day stands tiptoe on the misty mountain.' "

"You're fabulous! No one else has ever noticed that it's a quote."

"Maybe fishermen don't read Shakespeare. How do they feel about scented candles?"

Sharon laughed. "Fortunately we get all kinds of tourists up here, and I carry some jewelry and woodenware and toys as well as candles."

Qwilleran browsed through the narrow aisles of the little shop, his sensitive nose almost overcome by the thirty-seven scents. He said: "Roger has a good-looking money clip. Do you have any more of them?"

"Sorry, they're all gone. People bought them for Father's Day, but I've placed another order."

"How much for the tall wooden candlesticks?"

"Twenty dollars. They're made locally by a retired policeman, and every penny goes to charity. It was my mother's idea."

"I met your mother on the beach yesterday. She's very likable."

Sharon nodded. "Everyone likes Mom, even her students. She teaches in Pickax, you know. We're all teachers, except Dad. He runs the turkey farm on Pickax Road."

"I've seen it. Interesting place."

"Not really." Sharon wrinkled her nose in distaste. "It's smelly and messy. I took care of the poults when I was in high school, and they're so *dumb!* You have to teach domesticated turkeys how to eat and drink. Then they go crazy and kill each other. You have to be a little crazy yourself to raise turkeys. Mom can't stand them. Has she offered to tell your fortune?"

"Not yet," Qwilleran said, "but I've got a few questions I'd like her to answer. And I've got one for you: Where can I find a locksmith?"

"I never heard of a locksmith in Mooseville, but the garage mechanic might be able to help you."

He left the store with a two-foot candlestick and a stubby green candle and drove home inhaling deep draughts of pine scent. When he placed the candlestick on a porch table, Koko sniffed every inch of it. Yum Yum was more interested in catching spiders, but Koko's nose was virtually glued to the raw wood as he explored all its shapely turnings. His ears were swept backward, and occasionally he sneezed.

It was mid-afternoon when the blue pickup truck snaked up the driveway. Tom was alone in the cab.

"Where's the log-splitter?" Qwilleran asked cheerily.

"In the back of the truck," Tom said with his mild expression of pleasure. "I like to split logs with a maul, but this is a big tree. A very big tree." He gazed out at the lake. "It's a very nice day. The fog went away. I don't like fog."

The log-splitter proved to be a gasoline-powered contraption with a murderous wedge that rammed the foot-thick logs to produce firewood. Qwilleran watched for a while, but the noise made him jittery and he retreated to the cabin to brush the cats' fur. Their grooming had been neglected for a week.

At the cry of "Brush!" Koko strolled from the lake porch where he had been watching the wildlife, and Yum Yum squirmed out from under the sofa where she had been driven by the racket in the yard. Then followed a seductive pas de deux as the two cats twisted, stretched, writhed, and slithered ecstatically under the brush.

When Tom had finished splitting the wood, Qwilleran went out to help stack it. "So you don't like heavy fog," he said as an opener.

"No, it's hard to see in the fog," Tom said. "It's dangerous to drive a car or a truck. Yes, very dangerous. I don't drive very much in the fog. I don't want to have an accident. A man in Pickax was killed in an accident. He was driving in the fog." Tom's speech was slow and pleasant, with a musical lilt that was soothing. Today there was something different about his face—a three-day growth on his upper lip.

Qwilleran recognized the first symptom of a moustache and smiled. Searching for something to say, he remarked about the quality of sand surrounding the cabin—so fine, so clean.

"There's gold in the sand," Tom said.

"Yes, it sparkles like gold, doesn't it?"

"There's real gold," Tom insisted. "I heard a man say it. He said there's a gold mine buried under this cabin. I wish this was my cabin. I'd dig up the gold."

Qwilleran started to explain the real-estate metaphor but thought better of it. Instead he said: "I often see people picking up pebbles on the beach. I wonder what they're looking for."

"There isn't any gold on the beach," Tom said. "Only agates. The agates are pretty. I found some agates."

"What do they look like?"

"They look like little stones, but they're pretty. I sold them to a man in a restaurant. He gave me five dollars."

They worked in silence for a while. The tall tree had produced a huge amount of firewood, and Qwilleran was puffing with the exertion of stacking it. The handyman worked fast and efficiently and put him to shame.

After a few minutes Tom said: "I wish I had a lot of money."

"What would you do with it?"

"I'd go to Las Vegas. It's very pretty. It's not like here."

"Very true," Qwilleran said. "Have you ever been there?"

"No. I saw it on TV. They have lights and music and lots of people. So many people! I like nightclubs."

"Would you want to work in a nightclub if you went to Las Vegas?"

"No," Tom said thoughtfully. "I'd like to *buy* a nightclub. I'd like to be the boss."

After Tom had raked up the wood chips, Qwilleran invited him in for a beer. "Or would you rather have a shot? I've got some whiskey."

"I like beer," Tom said.

They sat on the back porch with their cold drinks. Koko was entranced by the man's soothing voice, and even Yum Yum made one of her rare appearances.

"I like cats," the handyman said. "They're pretty." Suddenly he looked embarrassed.

"What's the matter, Tom?"

"*She* told me to come up here and look at the telephone. That's why I came. You told me not to come. I didn't know what to do."

"That's perfectly all right," Qwilleran said. "You did the right thing."

"I always do what she tells me."

"You're a loyal employee, Tom, and a good worker. You can be proud of your work."

"I came up here to look at the telephone, and the big cat came out and talked to me."

"That's Koko. I hope he was polite."

"Yes, he was very polite." Tom stood up and looked at the sky. "It's time to go home."

"Here," Qwilleran said, offering him a folded bill. "Buy yourself some supper on the way home."

"I have my supper money. *She* gave me my supper money."

"That's all right. Buy two suppers. You like pasties, don't you?"

"Yes, I like pasties. I like pasties very much. They're good."

Qwilleran felt saddened and uneasy after the handyman's visit. He heated a can of Scotch broth and consumed it without tasting it. He was in no condition to start writing his novel, and he was relieved when another visitor arrived—this time from the beach.

Buck Dunfield, wearing a skipper's cap, climbed up the dune in the awkward way dictated by loose sand on a steep slope. "You promised me a drink," he called out, "and I'm collecting now while I'm still a bachelor. My wife gets home tomorrow. How's it going?"

"Fine. Come in on the porch."

"I brought you something. Just found it." He handed Qwilleran a pebble. "It was on your beach, so it's yours. An agate!"

"Thanks. I've heard about these. Are they valuable?"

"Well, some people use them to make jewelry. Everybody collects them around here. I brought you something else." Buck drew a foil package from his jacket pocket. "Meat loaf—from Mildred. Her husband never showed up last night." In a lower voice he added: "Just between you and me, she's better off without him."

They settled down in canvas chairs on the porch, with a broadside view of the placid lake. Buck said: "Let me give you a tip. If you use this porch much, remember that voices carry across the lake when the atmosphere is still. You'll see a fishing boat out there about half a mile, and you'll hear a guy say 'Hand me another beer' just as clear as on the telephone. But don't forget: He can hear you, too."

There were several boats within sight on the silvery lake, which blended into a colorless sky. The boats seemed suspended in air.

"Do you do much fishing, Buck?"

"A little fishing, a little golf. . . . Say, I see you've got one of my candlesticks."

"Picked it up this morning at Sharon's candle shop."

"I'll tell Mildred. She'll be tickled. Nice little shop, isn't it? Nice girl, Sharon. Roger's a good kid, too." He took out his pipe and began the business of lighting it. Pointing the stem at the beach he said: "You've got some dead fish down there."

"You don't need to tell me. They smell pretty ripe when the breeze is off the lake."

"You should bury them. That's what I do. The stink doesn't bother me; I've got chronic sinus trouble, but my wife objects to it, so I bury the fish under the trees. Good fertilizer!"

"If you don't have a good nose," Qwilleran said, "how can you enjoy that pipe? The aroma used to be the big attraction for me."

"Just a nervous habit." Buck watched two long-legged girls strolling down the beach with heads bowed, studying the sand underfoot. "See? What did I tell you? Everybody collects agates. In the middle of summer it's like a parade along this beach." He had another look at the girls. "They're a little twiggy for me. How about you?"

Qwilleran was thinking, smugly: Wait till he sees Rosemary! He said: "Do you know the woman who owns this cabin?"

Buck rolled his eyes expressively. "Lord, do I ever! She hates my guts. I got her license revoked after she rammed a hole in the Pickax police station. She didn't know forward from reverse. I hope she's not your grandmother or something."

"No. No relation."

"Just because she's got all the money in the world, she thinks she can do anything she pleases. A woman of her age shouldn't be allowed to carry a firearm. She's crazy enough to shoot up a city council meeting some day." He puffed on his pipe aggressively. "Her name's Fanny, but she calls herself

Francesca, and anybody who names their kid after her gets written in her will. There are more Francescas in Pickax than in Rome, Italy."

When the second drink was poured Buck leaned over and said confidentially: "All foolin' aside, how do you size up this place?"

"What do you mean?"

"Mooseville. Do you think everything is out in the open?"

From the man's conspiratorial manner it was clear that he was not talking about the landscape. Qwilleran stroked his moustache. "Well . . . they have a tendency, I would say, to gloss over certain situations and explain them away very fast."

"Exactly! It's their way of life. The *Picayune* didn't even report it when some tourists were mauled by bears at the village dump. Of course, the stupid jerks climbed the fence and teased the bears, and after that the town put up a double fence. But nothing was ever printed in the paper."

"I'm wondering if this vacation paradise is as free of crime as they want us to believe."

"Now you're talking my language." Buck glanced around quickly. "I suspect irregularities that should be investigated and prosecuted. You've worked on the crime beat; you know what I mean. I'm friendly with a few detectives Down Below, and they speak highly of you."

"Do you know Lieutenant Hames?"

"Sure do." Buck chuckled. "He told me about

your smart cat. That's really far-out! I don't believe a word of it, but he swears it's true."

"Koko's smarter than I am, and he's sitting under your chair right now, so be careful what you say."

"Cats are all right," Buck said, "but I prefer dogs."

"Getting back to the subject," Qwilleran went on, "I think the authorities up here want to operate in their own way without any suggestions or embarrassing questions from outsiders."

"Exactly! The locals don't want any hotshot city-types coming up here and telling them what's wrong."

"What do you think is wrong?"

Buck lowered his voice again and looked over his shoulder twice. "I say there are crimes that are being conveniently overlooked. But I'm working on it— privately. Once a cop, always a cop. Did you ever eat at the FOO? The customers are a mixed bag, and the battleax that runs the joint has larceny in her heart, but it's hooked up to the best grapevine in the country. . . . Now, mind you, I'm not going to stick my neck out. I'm at the age when I value every day of my life. I've got good digestion, a good woman, and something useful to do. Know what I mean? Only . . . it would give me a lot of satisfaction to see a certain criminal activity cleaned up. I'm not saying the police are corrupt, but they're hogtied. Nobody wants to talk."

Qwilleran sat in silence, grooming his moustache

with his knuckles as the panorama of his adventure on the *Minnie K* unreeled before his mind's eye.

"I had an interesting experience the other day," he began. "It might support your theory, although I have no actual evidence. How about you?"

"I've been doing some snooping, and I'm getting there. Something may break very soon."

"Okay. Let me tell you what happened to me. Did you ever hear of a boat called the *Minnie K?*" The newsman went on to recount the entire fog-bound tale, not missing a single detail.

Buck listened attentively, forgetting to relight his pipe. "Too bad we don't know the name of the boat where the guys were having the fight."

"It probably docks in the same godforsaken area where we boarded the *Minnie K*. It was a sleazy part of the shoreline. I haven't been back there since the fog lifted, so I don't know how much activity there is in the vicinity."

"I know that area. It's the slum of the waterfront. Mooseville would like to see it cleaned up, but it's beyond the village limits. Want to drive out there with me—some day soon?"

"Be glad to. I'm having company from Down Below for about a week, but I can work it in."

"Gotta be going," Buck said. "Thanks for the booze. I've gotta get rid of a sinkful of dirty dishes before the old gals get home and give me hell. I've got a wife *and* a sister on my tail all the time. You don't know how lucky you are." He looked at the sky. "Storm tonight."

He left the same way he had come, slipping and sliding down the dune to the beach. The leggy girls were returning from their walk, and Buck fell into step behind them, throwing an OK finger-signal to Qwilleran up on the porch.

Koko was still sitting under the chair, very quiet, folded into a compact bundle. There was something about the visitor that fascinated him. Qwilleran also appreciated this new acquaintance who spoke his language and enjoyed the challenge of detection. They would have a few investigative adventures together.

The day was unusually calm. Voices could be heard from the fishing boats: "Anybody wanna beer? . . . Nah, it's time to go in." There was something portentous about the closeness of the atmosphere. One by one the boats slipped away toward Mooseville. There was a distant rumble on the horizon, Koko started throwing himself at the legs of tables and chairs, while Yum Yum emitted an occasional shriek. By nightfall the storm was overhead. The rain pelted the roof and windows, claps of thunder shook the cabin, and jagged bolts of lightning slashed the night sky and illuminated the lake.

EIGHT

When the sirens went screaming down the highway, Qwilleran was having his morning coffee and one of Aunt Fanny's cinnamon buns from the freezer, thawed and heated to pudding consistency in the microwave. Several acres of woods separated the cabin from the main road, but he could identify the sound of two police cars and an ambulance speeding eastward. Another accident! Traffic was getting heavier as the vacation season approached. Vans, recreation vehicles, and boat trailers were turning a country road into a dangerous thoroughfare.

That morning Qwilleran had lost another round in his feud with the fireplace. Why, he asked himself, can a single cigarette butt start a forest fire when I can't set fire to a newspaper with eleven matches? When he finally managed to ignite the sports section, smoke billowed from the fireplace and flakes of charred newsprint floated about the room before settling on the white linen sofas, the oiled wood floors, and the Indian rugs.

After breakfast he began to clean house. He started by dusting the bookshelves and was still there two hours later, having discovered books on Indians, raccoons, mining history, and common weeds. The dissertation on poison ivy included a sketch of the sinister vine. At once Qwilleran left the cabin with book in hand to scout the woods beyond the septic tank—that particular area that monopolized the cats' attention.

All of nature was reacting ebulliently to the violence of the recent storm. Everything was cleaner, greener, taller, and more alive. Two little brown rabbits were gnawing pine cones. Small creatures rustled through the ground cover of pine needles and last year's oak leaves. There was no poison ivy, however. Back to the dusting, Qwilleran thought.

Then another opportunity for procrastination presented itself. He had never entered the toolshed except to select a canoe paddle. It was a cedar hut with a door, no window and no electric light. Immediately inside the entrance were the paddles, long-handled garden tools, and a ladder. The far end of the shed was in darkness, and Qwilleran went back to the cabin for a flashlight. As he expected, his activities were being monitored by two Siamese in the east window.

In the inner gloom of the shed the flashlight beam picked out paint cans, coils of rope, a garden hose, axes, and—against the far wall—a dingy cot with a limp pillow. On the wall above hung faded magazine pages with a two-year-old dateline and the unmistakable razzle-dazzle of Las Vegas. Mosquitoes were bounding off Qwilleran's neck and ears, and a loud buzzing suggested something worse. Qwilleran made a quick exit.

He had resumed his desultory housecleaning when he heard a rumbling in Koko's throat. The cat rushed to the windows overlooking the lake. Moments later a lone walker on the beach started to climb the dune. Mildred Hanstable's head was bowed, and she was dabbing her eyes with a tissue.

Qwilleran went out to meet her. "Mildred! What's wrong?"

"Oh, God!" she wailed. "It's Buck Dunfield."

"What's happened?"

"He's dead!"

"Mildred, I can't believe it! He was here yesterday and healthy as an ox." She all but collapsed in his arms, and he took her indoors and seated her on a sofa. "Can I get you something? Tea? A shot of whiskey?"

She shook her head and controlled herself with effort. Koko watched, his eyes wide with alarm.

"Sarah and Betty got home—from Canada—a little while ago and—and found him in the basement—workshop." She put her hands over her face. "Blood all over. He'd been killed—beaten—with one of the—one of the big—candlesticks." Her words drowned in her tears, and Qwilleran held her hand and let her cry it out, while he coped with his own shock and outrage.

When she was calm she said, between fits of sniffling: "Sarah passed out—and Betty came screaming over to my house—and we called the police. I told them I hadn't heard anything—not even the machinery. The storm drowned everything out."

"Do you know if the motive was burglary?"

"Betty says nothing was touched. I'm shattered. I don't know what I'm doing. I'd better go home. Sharon and Roger are coming over as soon as they can."

"Let me walk you home."

"No, I want to walk alone—and straighten myself out. Thanks, though."

Qwilleran tried to straighten out his own thinking. First he had to deal with the bitter realization that violence like this could take place in Mooseville. Could it be someone from Down Below? The area was being inundated by outsiders. . . . Then there was genuine grief. He liked Buck Dunfield and had looked forward to a summer of good talk and shared adventures. . . . And there was anger at the senseless killing. Buck had been so glad to be alive and to be doing something useful. . . . After that came uneasiness. No matter what the local custom, locks on doors were now an imperative. He hurried to the phone and called Pickax.

"*Aunt Fanny!* This is Jim calling from Mooseville. I want you to listen carefully. This is important. I need to find a locksmith immediately. I *must have locks* on these doors, or keys for the existing locks. Someone entered my neighbor's house and killed him. Someone has also been using this cabin for some shady purpose. I know this is Sunday, but I want to be able to call a locksmith early tomorrow. The whole idea of leaving doors open to strangers is unsafe, absurd, and medieval!"

There was a long pause before the scratchy baritone response: "Bless my soul! My dear boy, I didn't realize a journalist could get so upset. You are always so *contained*. Never mind! Hang up, and I'll make some arrangements. How is the weather on the shore? Did you have thunder and lightning last night?"

Qwilleran replaced the receiver and groaned. "What do you bet," he asked Koko, "that she'll send Tom, the resident genius?" To Yum Yum, who came struggling out from under the sofa, he said: "Sorry, sweetheart, I didn't know I was shouting." To himself he said: Fanny didn't even ask who had been murdered.

Barely ten minutes elapsed before a car could be heard winding its careful way among the trees and over the rolling dunes. Koko rushed to his checkpoint on the porch. The visitor was a young man with curly black hair, dressed in Mooseville's idea of Sunday Best: a *string tie* with his plaid shirt and jeans, and *no cap*.

With deference in his tone and courteous manner he said: "Good afternoon, Mr. Qwilleran. I hear you have a problem."

"Are you the locksmith?"

"No, sir. Mooseville doesn't have a locksmith, but I know something about locks. I'm an engineer. My wife and I were having our usual Sunday dinner at the hotel, and Miss Klingenschoen tracked us down. She's a very persuasive woman. I came as soon as I finished my prime rib. Very good prime rib at the hotel. Have you tried it?"

"Not yet," Qwilleran said, trying to conceal his impatience. "We've been here just a few days."

"That's what my wife told me. She's postmistress in Mooseville."

"Lori? I've met her. Charming young lady." Qwilleran relaxed a little. "And your name?"

"Dominic. Nick for short. What seems to be the trouble?" After the situation was explained he said: "No problem at all. I'll bring some equipment tomorrow and take care of it."

"Sorry to bother you on a Sunday, but a man at Top o' the Dunes was murdered. It's been a great shock."

"Yes, it's too bad. Everyone is wondering what effect it will have on the community."

"You mean people know about it already? They didn't find the body until a couple of hours ago."

"My wife heard the news in the choir loft," Nick said. "She sings at the Old Log Church. I heard it from one of the ushers during the offering."

"Murder is not what I'd expect in Mooseville. Who would do such a thing? Some camper from Down Below?"

"Well-l-l," replied the engineer. "I could make a guess."

Qwilleran's moustache bristled. He sensed a source of information. "May I offer you a drink, Nick?"

"No, thank you. I'll get back to my wife and my dessert. We like the deep-dish apple pie at the hotel."

Qwilleran walked with him to the car. "So you're an engineer. What kind of work do you do?"

"I'm employed at the prison," Nick said. "See you tomorrow."

Qwilleran went back to his housecleaning—in the desultory manner that was his specialty. He was shaking the Indian rugs in the parking lot when he heard a sound that made his heart leap: a car with a faulty muffler. Rosemary had never found time to have it replaced. He caught a glimpse of her little car between the trees and gasped. She had a passenger! If she had brought Max Sorrel—that pushy opportunist, that viper with a shaved head and facile smile—there might be another murder in Mooseville. The car disappeared in a gully, then rumbled back into view. Seated next to the driver, mouth agape and eyes staring, was the polar bear rug from the apartment at Maus Haus.

Rosemary tumbled out of the car, laughing at Qwilleran's spluttering amazement. "How—what—how—?"

"The former tenant offered to sell it for fifty dollars, and I thought you could afford that much," she said. "I had fun driving up here with the bear in the front seat, but the state troopers stopped me and said it was a motoring hazard. I pushed the head down under the dashboard, but it kept popping up. . . . What's the matter, dearest? You're rather subdued."

"There's been a shocking incident here," Qwilleran told her, "and if you want to turn around and go home, I won't blame you."

"What on earth—?"

"A murder, half a mile down the beach."

"Someone you know?"

He nodded sadly.

Rosemary raised her chin in the determined way she had. "Of course I'm not going home. I'm going to stay here and cheer you up. You've been too solitary, and you've probably been eating all the wrong food, and you've been spending too much time at the typewriter instead of getting exercise."

That was his Rosemary—not as young as some of the women he had been seeing; in fact, she was a grandmother. But she was an attractive brunette with a youthful figure, and she was comfortable to have around. Once, when he had made some foolish attempt at rigorous exercise, she had given him a remarkably skillful massage.

"Please bring in my luggage, dearest, and show me where I'm going to sleep. I'd love to have a shower and a change of clothes. Where are the beautiful cats? I've brought them some catnip."

Koko and Yum Yum remembered her from Maus Haus and reacted to her presence without feline wariness but also without overt friendliness. Occasionally, when she had visited Qwilleran's apartment, they had been locked in the bathroom.

Rosemary's vitality and dewy complexion and bright eyes were the result, she claimed, of eating the Right Food, some of which she had brought along in a cooler. With the Right Food warming in the oven and the bear-skin rug grinning on the hearth, the cabin felt homey and comfortable. Koko walked across the cassette player, and they had music.

"*Aimez-vous* Brahms?" Qwilleran asked.

"What?" Rosemary often missed the point of his quips.

He inquired about the situation at Maus Haus.

"It's terrible. The cook has left. Hixie never says anything funny. Charlotte cries all the time. And one night the immaculate Max had a spot on his tie. You're so lucky to have this cabin for the summer, Qwill. It's so lovely. There are violets and trilliums all along the driveway, and I've never seen so many goldfinches, and the chipmunks are so cute."

Rosemary noted and commented on everything:

the white linen slipcovers on the sofas, the mauve and turquoise tints of the lake as the sun sank, the tall oak candlestick on the porch, the moose head and crosscut saw over the mantel.

"The pickax! Where's the pickax?" Qwilleran exclaimed, jumping to his feet. "There was an antique pickax up there a week ago. I don't know, Rosemary. People walk in and out of this cabin like it's a bus terminal. It's considered unfriendly to lock doors. My good watch has disappeared and—worst of all—the gold pen you gave me. And now the pickax is missing."

"Oh, dear," she said sympathetically.

"Everything around here is strange. The police set up roadblocks just for fun. Nobody has a last name. There are footsteps on the roof in the middle of the night. The cats spend all their time staring at the septic tank."

"Oh, Qwill, you must be exaggerating. You're punchy from eating the wrong food."

"You think so? Well, this is a fact: Koko found a cassette hidden behind the moose head, with a threatening message recorded right in the middle of the music. And when I went fishing, I hooked the body of a man."

Rosemary gasped. "Who was it?"

"I don't know. It went back to the bottom of the lake, and everybody tries to tell me it was an old rubber tire."

"Qwill, dearest, are you sure you're getting enough fresh fruit and vegetables?"

"You're like all the others," he complained, "but there was one person who believed me, and now he's dead, with his skull bashed in."

"Oh, Qwill! Don't meddle with these things. You might be in danger yourself."

"We'll see about that," he said. "Let's eat. But first I want to feed the cats. A nice woman down the beach sent over some meat loaf, and I've conned them into thinking it's pâté de foie gras."

"Have you met many nice women down the beach?" Rosemary inquired sweetly. "I thought you were up here to write a book."

They talked far into the night. Qwilleran couldn't stop. He told her about the Nasty Pasty and the FOO, cherry blossoms and mosquitoes, agates and gravediggers, the Goodwinters and the Whatleys, shipwrecks and poachers, Little Henry and Big George, Night's Candles and Bob's Chop Shop.

Rosemary could no longer control her yawns, which she tried to disguise as laughs, coughs, and hiccups. "Dearest, I've been driving all day," she said. "Isn't it about time . . . ?"

After a prolonged good-night she escaped to the guest room and dislodged the Siamese from their favorite bunk. Qwilleran went to his own bed and thought about Rosemary for ten minutes, worried about the unlocked door for seven, and pondered the mystery of Buck Dunfield's murder for four and a half before falling into a deep sleep.

He was waked by horrendous screaming. He

leaped out of bed. It was just outside his window. "Rosemary!" he shouted.

"What's that?" she cried.

Lights were turned on. Koko dashed about with his ears laid back. Yum Yum hid. Rosemary came running from the guest room in her red nightgown.

The sound of wordless struggle in the underbrush ceased, and the screams gradually diminished in volume, fading away into the night stillness.

Qwilleran grabbed a flashlight and a poker from the fireplace.

"Don't go out there, Qwill!" Rosemary cried. "Call the police!"

"It won't do any good. I reported one incident this week, and they made me feel like a fool."

"Please call them, Qwill. It could be murder, or rape, or abduction. Some woman walking on the beach. It was a woman screaming."

"It sounded like a banshee to me."

Succumbing to Rosemary's pleas he phoned the sheriff's office. He gave his name and location and described the episode as calmly and objectively as possible.

In answer to a question he said: "No, there's not another house for quarter of a mile, but people walk on the beach in the middle of the night. . . . Yes, it's heavily wooded. . . . There were sounds of struggling in the woods. No other voice—just the screams. . . . Very loud at first—utter panic. Then they got weaker and just died away. . . . A what? . . . Hmmm. Very interesting. Do you think that's what it was? . . . It certainly did. . . . Well, thank you, officer. Sorry to bother you."

Qwilleran turned to Rosemary. "It was an owl, swooping down on a rabbit and carrying it away."

"Is that what he said? Well, I don't care; it scared me out of my skin. I'm still shaking. I'd feel a lot safer in your room. Do you mind?"

"No, I don't mind," Qwilleran said, grooming his moustache.

"The cats would like it better, too," said Rosemary. "They seem to think I've taken their bed."

NINE

Qwilleran was feeling particularly happy and agreeable on Monday morning. Although he was not given to using affectionate appellations, he started calling Rosemary "honey." As the day progressed, however, his elation gradually deflated. The first setback occurred when Nick arrived to work on the locks before Qwilleran had had his coffee.

"I see you have a Siamese," Nick said after Koko had inspected him at the checkpoint. "We have three cats, just ordinary ones. My wife would love to see yours."

Recalling the engineer's cryptic remark about

Buck Dunfield's murderer, Qwilleran said: "Why don't you bring your wife over some evening—to meet Koko and Yum Yum? I must apologize again for disturbing your meal yesterday."

"Think nothing of it. Glad to oblige. Besides, nobody ever says no to Miss Klingenschoen." Nick raised his eyebrows in a good-humored grimace.

When he left he was carrying one of Rosemary's catnip toys. "While you're here," he told her, "be sure to visit the flower gardens at the prison. The tulips are out now. Everything is later here than Down Below, you know."

After he had gone Rosemary said: "What a nice young man! I can visit the gardens this afternoon while you're working on your book. I'd also like to get my hair done if I can get an appointment."

The Siamese were delighted with their new plaything, catnip tied in the toe of a sock. Koko was especially dexterous, batting it with a paw, chasing it, tumbling with it, then losing it in some remote nook or crevice.

Qwilleran, on the other hand, was less than delighted with his late breakfast. It consisted of a fresh fruit compote sprinkled with an unidentified powder resembling cement, followed by a cereal containing several mysterious ingredients—some chewy, some gummy, some sandy. He knew it was all the Right Food, and he consumed everything without comment but refused to give up his morning caffeine in favor of brewed herbs.

Rosemary said: "I found some dreadful commercial rolls in your freezer, made with white flour and covered with sugary icing. You don't want to eat that junk, Qwill dearest. I threw them out."

He huffed into his moustache and said nothing.

After her noisy car had chugged down the drive and headed for Bob's Chop Shop, Qwilleran planned his own day. He set up his typewriter on the dining table, together with writing tools and scattered papers, in a realistic tableau of creative industry. Then he telephoned Mildred: "How are you doing?"

"I'm not as hysterical as I was yesterday," she said, "but I feel terrible. Do you realize what it's like to have your next-door neighbor murdered?"

"We've all got to start locking our door, Mildred—the way they do Down Below."

"Buck and Sarah and Betty were such good friends of mine. We played bridge all the time. He'll be buried in his hometown, and the girls have taken off already, so it's quiet and gloomy. I miss hearing the woodworking machines. Would you like to drop in? I'll make a strawberry pie."

"I have a houseguest," Qwilleran said, "and I was going to suggest that you and your husband come for drinks and then be my guests at the hotel dining room."

"You're very sweet," she said, "but he's awfully busy on the farm right now. Why don't you bring your guest down here? I'll read the tarot cards for you."

Next on Qwilleran's agenda was a trip into

Mooseville. Before leaving the cabin he checked the whereabouts of the Siamese, closed the windows, and enjoyed the familiar ritual of locking the door. Leaving the cabin without locking up was an unnatural act that had made him uneasy ever since coming to Mooseville.

For the last three days he had nursed a desire to take another look at the *Minnie K,* simply to convince himself that the boat really existed. He headed west, retracing the route taken with the unforgettable Whatleys. Beyond the Cannery Mall and beyond the FOO the landscape was dotted with ramshackle cottages, each with a junk car in the yard, a TV antenna on the roof, and gray laundry on the clothesline. Finally he turned down the lane alongside the trash-filled canal.

There at the end of the rotting wharf was the boat with the torn, gray, spotted canvas chairs on the deck. But it was no longer the *Minnie K;* it was the *Seagull,* according to the freshly painted stern board. There was no sign of a crew. Farther down the shore other boats of equal dilapidation were moored in Monday morning lassitude.

From one of those moldy decks, Qwilleran was sure, someone had been thrown into the icy lake.

On the return trip to Mooseville he stopped at the FOO for coffee and the Monday edition of the *Pickax Picayune.* The news item he sought was buried at the bottom of page five under the Euchre Club scores. It was headlined: *Incident on East Shore.* Qwilleran read it twice.

Buford Dunfield, 59, retired police officer and longtime summer resident of Mooseville, was found dead in the basement workshop of his posh East Shore cottage Sunday morning, the apparent victim of an unknown assailant, who attacked him with a blunt instrument just a few hours before his wife, Sarah Dunfield, 56, and his sister, Betty Dunfield, 47, returned home from their annual summer visit to Canada, where they attended three Shakespearean plays. Police are investigating.

The restaurant was buzzing with conversation about fishing. Qwilleran suspected the customers switched to that subject automatically whenever an outsider walked in.

His next stop was the tourist bureau. Roger was seated at his desk, bantering with a visitor—a fresh-faced youth who lounged in a chair expertly balanced on two legs, with his feet propped on Roger's desk.

"Qwill! You're just in time to meet the managing editor of the *Pickax Picayune*," Roger exclaimed. "This is Junior Goodwinter, one of your admirers. We were just talking about you."

The young man jumped to his feet. "Wow! The great man in person!"

"And yet another of the famous Goodwinters," Qwilleran said. "I knew you were a journalist by the way you balanced that chair. Congratulations on your coverage of the Dunfield murder. That was the most succinct seventy-one-word sentence I've ever read."

"Wow! You counted!"

"You omitted only one pertinent fact: the titles of the plays that the ladies attended in Canada."

"Now you're putting me on," said Junior.

"At last I realize why you don't have any crime up here. You have 'incidents' instead. Brilliant solution to the crime problem."

"Aw, take the nails out, will you? I know we do things in a different way up here—different from what I learned in J school anyhow. We're country, and you're city. Would you mind if I interviewed you some day?"

"My pleasure. Maybe I'd learn something."

"Well, so long. I've got to get out and sell some ads," Junior said.

Qwilleran was shocked. "Don't tell me you sell advertising as well as edit the paper!"

"Sure, we all sell ads. My father owns the paper, and he sells ads and sets the type."

The managing editor loped out of the office in his jogging shoes, and Qwilleran's face registered amazement and amusement. "Isn't he young for a managing editor?" he said to Roger.

"He's been working at the paper since he was twelve. Worked his way up. Graduated from State last year. Ambitious kid."

"I've always wanted to own a small newspaper."

"You could buy the *Picayune* cheap, but it would take a lot of dough to drag it into the twentieth century. It was founded in 1859 and hasn't changed since. . . . Anything I can do for you today?"

"Yes. You have all the answers. Tell me who killed Buck Dunfield."

Roger flushed. "That's a tough one. I haven't heard any scuttlebutt. Sharon and I went over to see Mildred yesterday, and she was really shook up."

"Was it a random killing? Did Dunfield have enemies? Or was he involved in something we don't know about?"

Roger shrugged. "I don't know much about the summer people."

"He lived next door to your mother-in-law and made candlesticks to sell in your wife's store. You never met him?"

"I guess I met him on the beach a couple of times and had a few words."

"You're lying, Roger. Are you practicing to be a politician?"

Roger raised both hands. "Don't shoot!" Then he gave Qwilleran a mocking grin. "Been doing any fishing from the *Minnie K* lately?"

"Tell you something interesting," Qwilleran said. "I went back to have another look at the old scow this morning, and the name's been changed to *Seagull* with the *S* painted backward."

Roger nodded. "I can tell you why, if you want to know. The skipper was probably afraid you'd go around blabbing about a body in the lake, and you'd involve the *Minnie K*. Then he'd be fined for operating an illegal charter service. Boats have to be registered before they can take trolling parties. From what you say about the *Minnie K*, she'd never pass the inspection."

Qwilleran had one more mission to pursue that afternoon. His curiosity about the buried pail kept luring him back to the cemetery, and now that he could identify poison ivy he was ready for another expedition. Weekend activity in the lovers' lane had increased the amount of picnic litter, and the sunny days and rainy nights had done wonders for the weeds in the graveyard itself. He found the vicious vines with three pointed leaves around the small headstones, and he remembered how he had torn at them to read the inscriptions. Then he followed the faint foot-trail behind the Campbell monument.

The pail was still camouflaged by scattered weeds, and it was still empty. But it had been used for some purpose. There were bits of straw in the bottom of the pail, and the top-handle on the lid, which Qwilleran had left at right angle to the headstone, was now askew.

Qwilleran didn't linger. He hurried back to the cabin in order to arrive before Rosemary. The whiffs of rotting fish, increasing in pungency, aggravated his cheerless mood. Rosemary, on the other hand, breezed into the cabin bubbling with enthusiasm and carrying an armload of yellow, white, pink, red, and purplish-black tulips.

"The prison gardens are lovely," she said. "You must go to see them, Qwill dearest. A charming man gave me these to bring home. How many pages did you write today?"

"I never count," Qwilleran said.

"It's a lovely new prison. A very friendly woman outside the gate invited me to join PALS. That's the Prisoner Aid Ladies' Society, or something like that. They write letters to the inmates and send them little presents."

"Did you hear any gossip about the murder?"

"Not a word! Do you have any vases for these tulips? I have some groceries in the car for our dinner. I picked up some fresh fish and *lovely* parsnips and brussels sprouts—and some carrots for the kitty cats. You should grate a little carrot and mix it with their food every day."

Brussels sprouts! Parsnips! Qwilleran had been thinking about a sixteen-ounce steak and French fries with ketchup and Parker-House rolls and a Roquefort salad and deep-dish apple pie with cheddar cheese and three cups of coffee.

"Will the fish keep?" he asked. "I'd like to take you to the Northern Lights Hotel for dinner. My day hasn't been productive, and I need a change of scene."

"Why, of course! That sounds lovely," Rosemary said. "Do I have time to walk on the beach for an hour?"

"You won't like it. The beach is covered with dead fish."

"That won't bother me," she said. "It's part of nature."

Leaving tulips in a lemonade pitcher on the mantel, in a flour canister on the dining table, and in an ice bucket on the bar, Rosemary tripped jubilantly down the slope to the beach.

Qwilleran sprawled on one of the sofas. "Koko, I feel like an idiot," he told the cat, who was studying him intently from the back of the sofa. "I don't have a single clue. What are we working with? A dead body in the lake, the murder of a retired cop, and a message on a cassette. Someone has been using this cabin for some kind of illicit or illegal purpose. Never mind *who*. We don't even know *what*."

"YOW!" said Koko, blinking his large blue eyes.

Qwilleran brought the cassette from his dresser drawer and once more played *Little White Lies*. The voice cut in: ". . . bring up more stuff . . . gotta make some changes . . . things are gettin' hot . . . at the boat dock after supper." It was a high-pitched nasal voice with a monotonous inflection.

"I've heard that voice before," Qwilleran said to Koko, but the cat was playing with his catnip toy. "Things were getting hot because Buck was closing in on his investigation. Some changes had to be made because the cabin was no longer available as a depot."

That voice! That voice! He had heard it at the post office, or at the FOO, or at the General Store, or in the hotel dining room.

No! Qwilleran snapped to attention. The voice on the cassette was the voice he had heard in the fog, when two men were brawling on another boat. One voice had a deep rumble and a British accent. The other man spoke with a piercing twang and a flat inflection. As he recalled, something had happened to the engine, and they were arguing, apparently, about the best way to get it started.

CLUNK!

Qwilleran recognized the clunk of a book being pushed from a bookshelf and landing on the floor. Koko had done it before. He was never clumsy; if he knocked something down it was for a good reason.

Koko was on the second shelf, digging behind a row of books to extricate his sockful of catnip. The book he had dislodged was a treatise on historic shipwrecks. It was lying open on the floor—open to a page marked by a folded slip of paper.

There on page 102 was an account of the sinking of the *Waterhouse B. Duncan,* a freighter carrying a rich cargo of copper ingots. It went down in treacherous water north of Mooseville during a severe storm in November 1913. All lives were lost: three passengers and a crew of twenty-three, including a woman cook.

The folded slip that marked page 102 was a penciled agreement to rent a boat for thirteen summer weekends, terms to be decided. It was dated the previous year and was signed S. Hanstable.

There was something about this information that jogged Qwilleran's memory. Somewhere in one of her letters Aunt Fanny had mentioned . . . what? The recollection was a vague one. He delved into his correspondence file and groaned; not only were her letters cross-written, but her handwriting was extremely individual, and the multitude of dashes made each page a dazzling plaid.

He put on his reading glasses and squinted through half a dozen pages before he found the reference that was nagging his memory. On April third she had first offered him the use of the cabin. Written in her telegraphic style, the letter read:

> Charming little place—built entirely of logs—quite comfortable—I'm getting older—don't enjoy it so much—last summer decided to rent—two handsome young men—interested in marine history—came up on weekends—their girlfriends stayed all week—horrid creatures—played games with spaghetti—threw it at the ceiling—unspeakable mess—two weeks to clean the place—never again!

Qwilleran's moustache bristled, the way it did when he thought he had found a clue. The bookmark raised other questions: Did Roger's wife own a boat? Did she print like a kindergarten teacher? Did she spell "decided" with an *s*?

TEN

Before taking Rosemary out to dinner Qwilleran fed the cats, both of whom fastidiously avoided every shred of carrot that contaminated their corned beef.

He had made a reservation at the Northern Lights Hotel in order to get one of the high-backed booths constructed from the salvaged cabins of retired fishing boats. Diners in these booths had to be careful to avoid splinters, and in humid weather the booths exuded haunting reminders of their origin, but they were ideal for confidential conversation.

Rosemary was wearing a Mooseville T-shirt and a braided leather necklace from the prison gift shop, and she looked so youthful, so vibrant, so healthy that Qwilleran found it hard to believe she had a grandson old enough to be in medical school. She hung her shoulder-strap bag on a hook at the entrance to the booth. "Isn't it wonderful," she said, "not to worry about theft! At home, when I go to a restaurant, I put this bag on the floor, keep my foot on it, and wind the strap around my ankle."

The menu cover reproduced an engraving of a terrifying storm on the lake, and the paper placemats listed the dates of major shipwrecks plus the number of lives lost. *Bon appetit*, Qwilleran thought.

He said to Rosemary: "You can order the poached scrod with cauliflower if you wish, but I'm going to have a large steak with fries. . . . Don't look so shocked. I know the Right Food has done wonders for you; you don't seem a day over thirty-nine. But it's too late for me. The only time I ever looked thirty-nine was when I was twenty-five."

"Truce! Truce!" she said, waving a paper napkin. "I didn't mean to be a nag, Qwill. You order whatever you want, and don't apologize. You're under creative pressure with your book, and you've earned a treat. How many chapters have you written? Would you read me a few pages tonight?"

"And another thing, Rosemary: Please don't keep asking about my progress. I don't have a daily quota or a deadline, and when I'm not sitting at my typewriter I want to forget about it entirely."

"Why, certainly, Qwill. I've never known an author personally. You'll have to tell me how to behave."

He kept glancing across the room toward a party of four seated beneath a large painting of a drowning sailor in shark-infested water. "Don't look now," he said, "but the two men over there are wreck-divers, I've been told. They loot sunken ships."

The men were tall, lean, and stony-faced. "They look like cigarette ads," Rosemary said, "and the girls with them look like models. How did they get those gorgeous tans so early in the season? And why don't they look happy? Their diet is probably inadequate."

"I've seen the girls walking on the beach," Qwilleran said. "I think they're staying at a cottage near ours. They may be the four who rented Fanny's cabin last year." He told how Koko had attracted his attention to the shipwreck book and how he had waded through the cross-written correspondence. "If you're looking for a quick way to get a headache," he added, "I'll lend you a few of Fanny's letters."

"When am I going to meet her?"

"Tomorrow or Wednesday. I'd like to ask her about these so-called marine historians and about her relationship with Buck Dunfield. There's one obstacle; it's hard to get her attention."

"Some types of deafness are caused by a diet deficiency," Rosemary said.

"She's not deaf, I'm sure. She simply chooses not

to listen. Maybe you'll be able to get through to her, Rosemary. She seems to favor women. . . . Excuse me a moment. I want to catch those people before they leave."

He crossed the room to the wreck-divers and addressed the more formidable of the two. "Pardon me, sir. Aren't you a correspondent for one of the wire services?"

The man shook his head. "Sorry, you're on the wrong track," he said in a deep and less-than-cordial voice.

"But you're a journalist, aren't you? Didn't you do graduate work at Columbia? You covered the last presidential election."

"Sorry, none of the above."

Qwilleran made a good show of bewilderment and turned to the second man. "I was sure you were a press photographer, and you two worked together on big assignments."

More genially the other man said: "Nothin' like that, suh. We're jest a coupla bums up heah awn vacation."

Qwilleran apologized, wished them a pleasant holiday, and returned to the booth.

"What was that all about?" Rosemary asked.

"Tell you later."

On the way home he explained: "I think there's a syndicate operating around here. They've been using Fanny's cabin for an underground headquarters. It's secluded; the doors have always been unlocked; and there are three avenues of access or escape: from the beach, from the highway, and from the woods. The boss has been giving tape-recorded orders to his henchmen, hiding the cassette behind the moose head."

Rosemary laughed. "Qwill, dear, I know you're kidding me."

"I'm serious."

"Do you think it's drug-related?"

"I think it's shipwreck-looting. The lake is full of valuable wrecks, and there's a book at the cabin that pinpoints their location and describes their cargoes. Some of the boats went down more than a hundred years ago."

"But wouldn't the cargo be ruined by this time?"

"Rosemary, they weren't shipping automobiles and TV sets in 1850. They were shipping copper ingots and gold bullion. The shipping manifests tell exactly what was aboard each vessel when it sank— how many barrels of whiskey, how many dollars in banknotes and gold. At one time this part of the country was booming."

"Why did you talk to the men at the hotel?"

"I thought one of them might be the ringleader, but there's no similarity between their voices and the one on the cassette. None at all. But the ringleader is around here somewhere."

"Oh, Qwill! You have a fantastic imagination."

When they arrived at the cabin Qwilleran unlocked the door and Rosemary entered. He heard her yelp: "Oh! Oh! There are tulips all over the floor!"

"Those cats!" Qwilleran bellowed—loud enough to send both of them flying to the guest room.

"They pulled out all the *black* tulips, Qwill."

"I don't blame them. Tulips were never intended to be black."

"But you told me once that cats can't distinguish colors."

He picked up the flowers, and Rosemary rearranged the bouquets in the impromptu vases on mantel, bar, and dining table. Then they went to the lake porch to await the sunset, stretching out in varnished steamer chairs old enough to have sailed on the *Titanic*.

Seagulls soared and swooped and squabbled over the dead fish on the beach. Rosemary identified them as herring gulls. The flycatchers, she said, who were performing a nonstop aerial ballet were purple martins. Something brown and yellow that kept whizzing past the porch was a cedar waxwing.

"I hear an owl," Qwilleran said, to prove he was not totally ignorant about wildlife.

"That's a mourning dove," she corrected him. "And I hear a cardinal . . . and a phoebe . . . and I think a pine siskin. Close your eyes and listen, Qwill. It's like a symphony."

He touched his moustache guiltily. Perhaps he had been listening to the wrong voices. Here he was in the country, on vacation, surrounded by the delights of nature, and he was trying to identify miscreants instead of cedar waxwings. He should be reading the bird book instead of cross-written letters.

Rosemary interrupted his thought. "Tell me some more about Aunt Fanny."

"Ah—well—yes," he said, shifting his attention back to the moment. "For starters . . . she wears flashy clothes and bright lipstick, and she has a voice like a drill sergeant. She's spunky and bossy and full of energy and ideas."

"She must have a wonderful diet."

"She has a houseman who drives her around, runs errands, takes care of the garden, cleans the house, and knows how to repair everything under the sun."

Rosemary giggled. "He'd make a wonderful husband. How old is he?"

"But I have a suspicion he's also a petty thief."

"I knew there was a catch," Rosemary said. "How does Koko react to him?"

"Very favorably. Tom has the kind of gentle voice that appeals to cats."

Koko heard his name and wandered nonchalantly onto the porch.

"Have you been walking Koko on his leash?"

"No, but I've contemplated a reconnaissance maneuver. He spends a lot of time staring out the guest room window, and I'd like to know what he finds so interesting."

"Rabbits and chipmunks," Rosemary suggested.

"There's something more." Qwilleran stroked his moustache. "I have a hunch . . ."

"Let's take him out."

"Now?"

"Yes. Let's!"

On several occasions Koko had been strapped into his blue harness and taken for a walk. A twelve-foot nylon cord donated by a *Fluxion* photographer served as a leash and gave him a wide range. Frequently Koko's inquisitive nose and catly perception led to discoveries that escaped human observation.

The appearance of the harness produced a noisy demonstration, and when the buckles were tightened Koko uttered a gamut of Siamese sounds denoting excitement. Yum Yum thought he was being tortured and protested loudly.

For the first time since his arrival Koko left the cabin. Outside the porch he found the rope hanging from the brass bell, stretched until he could catch it with a claw, and gave the bell a peal or two. Without hesitation he then turned eastward—past the porch, beyond the cabin itself, around the sandy rectangle that covered the septic tank, and toward the woods. When he reached the carpet of pine needles, acorns, and dried oak leaves, every step was a rustling, crackling experience unknown to a city cat. Squirrels, rabbits, and chipmunks retired to safety. A frantic robin tried to distract him from her nest. Koko merely walked resolutely toward the woods on top of the dune. Behind a clump of wild cherry trees was the toolshed.

"How do you like that?" Qwilleran whispered to Rosemary. "He made a beeline for the toolshed."

He opened the door, and Koko hopped across the threshold. He gave a single sniff to a canoe paddle and two sniffs to the trash can. "Quick, Rosemary, run and get the flashlight. It's hanging inside the back door."

In the inner gloom of the shed Koko glanced at the collection of paint cans and went directly to Tom's cot. Jumping on the threadbare blanket he started pawing industriously, all the while making guttural noises and flicking his tail in wide arcs. He pawed the sorry excuse for a pillow, pawed the wall with the faded Las Vegas pictures, and returned to pawing the blanket.

"What are you looking for, Koko?" Qwilleran pulled aside the blanket, and Koko dug into the thin mattress.

Rosemary was beaming the flashlight on the drab scene. "He's very determined."

"There might be a nest of mice in the mattress."

"Let's pull the whole dirty thing off onto the floor."

The mattress slid off the flat springs of the cot, and with it came a large manila envelope. Rosemary held the light closer. The envelope was addressed to Francesca Klingenschoen and postmarked two years before. The return address was that of a Florida real estate firm.

"Look inside, Qwill."

"Money! Mostly fifties."

"Here, let me count it. I'm used to counting money." She snapped the bills with professional speed. The total sum was almost twelve hundred dollars. "What shall we do with it?"

"It belongs to Fanny's houseman," Qwilleran

said. "We'll put it back, and tidy the bed, and get out of here before the mosquitoes bring up their reserves."

Late that night he lay awake wondering about Tom's cache in the toolshed. Was the poor fellow saving up for a downpayment on a Las Vegas nightclub? Where was he getting the money? Not from Aunt Fanny. It appeared that she doled out a few dollars at a time.

Qwilleran heard heavy footsteps on the roof. He hoped Roger was right. He hoped it was a raccoon.

ELEVEN

Tuesday morning Qwilleran drove to town before breakfast to buy eggs. Rosemary insisted there was nothing better than a soft-boiled egg for easy digestibility. Qwilleran couldn't remember eating a soft-boiled egg since the time he stayed home from second grade with a case of mumps. Nevertheless, he bought a dozen eggs, and when he returned Rosemary met him at the door. Her face was stern.

"Koko has been naughty," she said.

"Naughty!" No one had ever accused Koko of being naughty. Perverse, perhaps, or arrogant, or

147

despotic. But naughtiness was beneath his dignity. "What has he done?"

"Pulled out all the black tulips again. I saw him do it. I scolded him severely and locked him in the bathroom. Yum Yum has been sitting outside the door whimpering, but Koko is very quiet inside. I'm sure he knows he did wrong."

Qwilleran opened the door slowly. The scene was like the aftermath of a blizzard. A roll of paper towels was reduced to confetti. The wastebasket was overturned and its contents scattered. A fresh box of two hundred facial tissues was empty, and the toilet tissue was unrolled and festooned about the room. Bath salts and scouring powder were sprinkled liberally over all.

Koko sat proudly on the toilet tank as if he had completed a work of conceptual art and was ready for a press conference.

Qwilleran drew his hand across his face to erase a wicked smile, but Rosemary burst into tears.

"Don't be upset," he said. "Go and boil the eggs, and I'll clean up this mess. I think he's trying to tell us something about black tulips."

Conversation was strained at the breakfast table. Rosemary asked meekly: "When are we going to see Aunt Fanny?"

"I'll phone her after breakfast. Today we should take your car to Mooseville to get the muffler fixed. While we're there we can visit the museum and have lunch at the Nasty Pasty. . . . I'd also like to suggest that we eliminate the black tulips."

The telephone call to Pickax required the usual patience.

"Of course, I would *adore* to see you and your lady friend tomorrow," said Aunt Fanny in her chesty voice. "You must come for lunch. We'll have pork chops or nice little veal collops. Do you like spinach soufflé? Or would you rather have cauliflower with cheese sauce? I have a splendid recipe for the soufflé. How's the weather on the shore? Is there anything Tom can do for you? I could make an orange chiffon pie for dessert if you . . ."

"Aunt Fanny!"

"Yes, dear?"

"Don't plan a big lunch. Rosemary has a small appetite. I could use Tom's services, though, if it isn't inconvenient. We have some dead fish on the beach that should be buried."

"Of course. Tom enjoys working on the beach. Are you making good progress with your book? I'm so eager to read it!"

Rosemary was unusually subdued all morning, and Koko—being a master of one-upmanship—devised a subtle way to press his advantage. He followed her around the cabin and repeatedly maneuvered his tail under her foot. His blood-curdling screeches after each incident reduced her to nervous confusion.

Qwilleran, though amused at Koko's ingenuity, began to feel sorry for Rosemary. "Let's get out of here," he said. "In a battle with a Siamese you never win."

They dropped off her car at the garage, and Qwilleran paid close attention to the mechanic's manner of speech. Compared with the voice on the cassette, he had the right pitch but the wrong timbre and wrong inflection.

The museum occupied an opera house dating from the nineteenth century, when loggers, sailors, miners, and millhands paid their dimes and quarters to see music hall acts. Now it was filled with memorabilia of the old lumbering and shipping industries. Rosemary pored over the cases containing scrimshaw and other seamen's crafts. Qwillerman was attracted to the scale models of historic ships that had gone to the bottom. So were two other men, whom he recognized. They studied the ship models and mumbled to each other.

A third man—young and enthusiastic—came hurrying over. "Mr. Qwilleran, I'm glad you've honored us with a visit. I'm the museum curator. Roger told me you were in town. If you have any questions, I'll try to answer them." Qwilleran noted that the pitch, timbre, and inflection were all wrong.

He said to Rosemary: "I've got to do an errand. I'll be back in half an hour, and we'll go to lunch."

He hurried to the visitors' center and waited impatiently while five tourists inquired about the bears at the dump. Then he threw a slip of paper on Roger's desk. "What can you tell me about this?"

Roger read the boat rental agreement. "That's my father-in-law's signature."

"Does he have a boat?"

"Everybody up here has a boat, Qwill. He likes to go fishing whenever he can get away from those stupid turkeys."

"Did he rent it to wreck-divers last summer?"

"I don't know for sure, but I think he'd do anything for a buck." Roger wriggled uncomfortably. "The truth is: He and I don't get along very well. Sharon was her daddy's girl, and I came along and stole her. Get the picture?"

"Too bad. I got into that situation myself. . . . Another question, Roger. What do you know about the people who run the FOO?"

"They're a weird couple. She's a hundred pounds overweight, and when she's at the cash register, you'd better count your change. He was in some kind of industrial accident Down Below. When he collected compensation, they came up here and bought the FOO. That was before the *D* dropped off."

"Is that her husband who does the cooking? Little man with thinning hair."

"No, Merle is a big guy. Spends all his time on his boat."

"Where does he keep it?"

"In the dock behind the restaurant. . . . Say, did you see the UFO last night?"

"No, I didn't see the UFO last night," Qwilleran said, starting for the door.

"We get a lot of them up here," Roger called after him. But Qwilleran was gone.

Here was the opportunity to check the voice of a

likely suspect. The FOO had raised his suspicions from the beginning—for several reasons. Something that didn't look like coffee was frequently served in coffee cups. There were rooms for rent upstairs. Customers slipped money to Mrs. FOO surreptitiously and received a slip of paper. As for the little man with thinning hair, he shuffled about in a furtive manner and made ghastly pasties.

Now Qwilleran wanted to meet Merle. Still leaving Rosemary at the museum he drove to the FOO, parked in the lot, and ambled down to the dock. A good-sized boat in shipshape condition was bobbing alongside the pier, but no one was in sight. He called to Merle several times, but there was no response.

As he returned to his car, the cook sidled out of the back door, smoking a cigarette. "Lookin' for sumpin'?" he inquired.

"I want to see Merle. Know where he is?"

"He went somewheres."

"When will he be back?"

"Anytime."

Qwilleran returned to town and took Rosemary to the Nasty Pasty. She had recovered from her tiff with Koko and was brimming with conversation. The museum was so interesting; the curator was so friendly; the restaurant was so cleverly decorated.

Qwilleran, on the other hand, was disappointed at missing Merle, and he jingled three pebbles in his sweater pocket.

"What's the matter, Qwill? You seem nervous."

"I'm just revving up my good luck tokens." He threw the pebbles on the table. "The green one is polished jade that a collector gave me. The ceramic bug is a scarab that Koko found. The agate is one that Buck Dunfield picked up on our beach—last agate he ever found, poor guy."

"And here's another one for your collection," Rosemary said, producing a dime-size disc of yellowed ivory with the face of a cat etched in the surface. "It's scrimshaw, and quite old."

"Great! Where did you find it?"

"In the antique shop behind the museum. The curator told me about it. Have you been there?"

"No. Let's go after lunch."

"An old sea captain runs it, and I'm warning you: It's a terrible place."

The Captain's Mess was an apt name for the jumble of antiquities and fakes that filled the shop behind the museum. A little storefront, it was older than the opera house itself, and the next nor-easter would be sure to blow it down. The building was so loose and out-of-joint that only the solid oak door held it upright. When the door was open, the building slouched to one side, and it was necessary to push the door jamb back into position before the door could be closed. Qwilleran sniffed critically. He detected mildew and whiskey and tobacco.

There were marine lanterns, bits of rigging, unpolished brass objects, ships in dusty bottles, water-stained charts, and—sitting in the midst of the clutter—an old man with a stubby beard and well-worn captain's cap. He was smoking a carved pipe from some far-off place, but his tobacco was the cheapest to be found in the corner drug store. Qwilleran knew them all.

"Ye back again?" shrilled the captain when he spied Rosemary. "I told ye—all sales final. No money back."

Qwilleran asked: "Do you still go to sea, captain?"

"No, them days is over."

"I suppose you've sailed around the globe more times than you can remember."

"Yep, I been about a bit."

"How long have you had your shop?"

"Quite a piece."

The pitch of the man's voice was right; the timbre was right; the inflection was almost right, but the delivery lacked the force of the voice on the cassette. The captain was too old. Qwilleran was looking for someone younger, but not too young. He rummaged among the junk and bought a brass inkwell guaranteed not to slide off a ship captain's desk in a rolling sea.

They returned to the cabin, and Rosemary suggested a walk on the beach. While she changed clothes Qwilleran ambled around the property. He knew Tom had been there; the brass bell had a fresh sheen, and the putrid little carcasses on the beach had been buried.

Rosemary appeared in a turquoise sundress. "I

wanted to wear my new apricot jumpsuit, but I can't find my coral lipstick."

"You look beautiful," Qwilleran said. "I like you in that color."

Koko glared at them silently when they went down the slope to the beach.

Rosemary said: "I think he wants me to go home."

"Nonsense," Qwilleran said, and yet the same idea had crossed his mind. Koko had never approved of the women in his life.

Heading eastward they trudged through deep sand in silence, the better to enjoy the peacefulness of the lonely beach. Then came the row of summer houses on top of the dune. One resembled the prow of a ship. Another, sided with cedar shakes, looked like a bird with ruffled feathers. Some of the cottagers were burying their dead fish. Two girls were sunning on the deck of a rustic A-frame.

"They're the models we saw at the hotel," Rosemary said, "and they're not wearing tops or bottoms."

Qwilleran pointed out the redwood house where Buck had been murdered. "Now it's even more of a mystery," he said. "At first I thought there was some connection between Buck's private investigation and the message on the cassette, but he was on the track of a *crime,* and the wreck-divers are not criminals. They're shrewd opportunists operating for private gain and not in the public interest, but they're not breaking the law."

Next they passed Mildred's yellow house and traversed another half mile of desolate beach until a creek, bubbling across a bed of stones on its way to the lake, sliced through the sand and barred their way. As they retraced their steps, Mildred waved to them from her porch, beckoning them up the dune and offering them coffee and homemade apple pie. "It's in the freezer," she said. "It won't take a minute to thaw."

The interior of the bungalow was muffled in handmade quilts, hanging on the walls and covering the furniture.

"Did you make all these? They're lovely," Rosemary exclaimed. "You've got a lot of time invested here."

"I've had a lot of spare time to invest," Mildred said with a small sigh. "Did you see the UFO last night?"

"No, but I heard about it," Qwilleran said. "What do you think it was?"

Mildred looked surprised. "Why, everyone *knows* what it was."

It was Qwilleran's turn to look surprised. "Do you actually believe it was an extraterrestrial visitor?"

"Of course. They come here all the time—usually at two or three in the morning. I see them because of my insomnia. I had standing orders to phone the Dunfields at any hour, so they could get up and watch."

Making a mental note to follow up this local idiosyncrasy, Qwilleran said: "Have you heard from Buck's wife and sister?"

"They phoned once—to ask if I'd adopt their geraniums and throw the perishables out of the refrigerator. They don't know when they'll be back."

"Any developments in the case?"

"The men from the police lab have been working at the house. Betty told me that Buck must have been working in his shop when the murderer sneaked in and took him by surprise. There was a candlestick on the lathe and a lot of sawdust. Those power tools make so much noise, Buck wouldn't hear anyone come in, I suppose."

"Can we assume that the killer turned the machine off afterward? That was thoughtful of him."

"No one mentioned it, and I never thought of it."

"He must have tracked sawdust out of the house."

"I don't know. I suppose so."

"Did Buck ever talk about the shipwreck-diving that goes on up here? Or did he hint at any criminal activity?"

Mildred shook her head and lowered her eyes and lapsed into a reverie.

To snap her out of it Qwilleran said: "Okay, Mildred, how about reading the tarot cards? I have a couple of questions."

She drew a deep breath. "Come over to the card table. I'll read for you one at a time. Who wants to go first?"

"Are you serious about this?" Qwilleran asked. "Or is it a gimmick for the hospital fund?"

"I'm serious. Quite serious," she said, "and I have to be in the right state of mind, or it doesn't work. So . . . no fooling around, please."

"Would the cards reveal anything about the murder?"

Her face turned pale. "I wouldn't want to ask them. I wouldn't want to get into that."

Rosemary said: "The cards are spooky—such strange pictures! Here's a man hanging upside-down."

"The symbols are ancient, but the symbols only unlock thoughts and insights. Do you have a question, Rosemary?"

Rosemary wanted to know about her business prospects. She sat across the table from Mildred and shuffled the cards. Then Mildred arranged a dozen of the cards in a pattern and meditated at length.

"The cards are in sync with your question," she murmured, "and with some of the questions you didn't ask. Everything points to change. Business, home, romance—all subject to change in the near future. You have had partnerships in the past, and you have lost them, in one way or another. Your present business partner is a woman, I think. That will change. You have always welcomed change, but now you are reluctant to face something new. A broken contract has disappointed you. Don't let it affect your energy and enthusiasm. You will make an inspiring contact soon. And expect good news from a young male of great ambition. I see another figure in the cards—a mature male of great intelligence. You may take a long journey with him. Be alert for two dangers: Avoid conflict between business and personal life, and beware of treachery. All will end happily if you use your natural gifts and maintain an even course." She stopped and drew a deep breath.

"Wonderful!" Rosemary said. "And all so true!"

"Will you excuse me for a moment?" Mildred said weakly. "I want to step outdoors and do some deep breathing before the next reading."

She drifted from the room, and Qwilleran and Rosemary looked at each other. "What do you think about that, Qwill?" she said. "The broken contract is my lease at Maus Haus. My partner at Helthy-Welthy is a woman. The ambitious young man is my grandson, I know. He's trying for a very desirable internship in Montreal."

"How about the other guy? Mature and intelligent. That rules out Max Sorrel."

"Now you're mocking. You're supposed to be serious."

By the time Mildred returned, Qwilleran had composed his face in an expression of sincerity. He shuffled the cards and asked his questions: "Will I accomplish my goal this summer? Why am I balked in everything I try to do in this north country?"

"The cards show a pattern of confusion, which could result in frustration," Mildred said quietly. "This causes you to scatter your forces and waste your energy in trivial detail. You have skills but you are not using them. Change your tactics. Your stubbornness is the obstacle. Be receptive to outside help. I see a male and a female in the cards. The woman is good-hearted and fair in coloring, and she has taken a liking to you. The man is young, dark-complexioned, and intelligent. Let him help you. The cards also see a new emotional entanglement. There may be some bad news, involving you in legal matters, but you will make the best of it. Your summer will be successful, although not as you planned it."

Qwilleran squirmed in his chair. "I'm impressed, Mildred. You're very good!"

She nodded absently and drifted from the room again, after placing a fishbowl on the table. It was labeled *Hospital Donations* and contained a ten-dollar bill. Qwilleran said: "My treat, Rosemary," and added two twenties, a generous sum that would have amazed his friends at the *Fluxion*.

Rosemary said: "I don't like the idea of your new entanglement. It's probably that blonde she mentioned."

"Did you notice that card? The blonde had a black cat. It sounds like the postmistress. The dark male sounds like her husband."

"Or Koko," Rosemary said.

The return walk along the beach was in silence, as each pondered the advice of the cards. One could hear the squeaking of the sand underfoot. Qwilleran made one observation: "Mildred has lost her nervous laugh since the tragedy next door."

At the porch entrance they clanged the brass bell for the sheer pleasure of hearing its pure tone, and when Qwilleran unlocked the door and threw it open for Rosemary, Koko was on the threshold, with Yum Yum not far behind. Koko was carrying a single red tulip in his mouth.

"It's a peace offering," Qwilleran told Rosemary, but he knew very well that Koko never apologized for anything. The cat was trying to convey information, and it was not in the field of horticulture. . . . Tulips . . . Tulips . . . Qwilleran's moustache was sending him signals. The tulips came from the prison gardens. Nick was employed at the prison. . . . He glanced at his watch and grabbed the phone.

Lori answered. "You caught me just in time, Mr. Qwilleran. I was about to lock up and go home."

"You mean you actually *lock* the post office in Mooseville?"

"Seems silly, doesn't it?" she said. "But it's federal regulations."

He made the requisite remarks about the weather and then said: "Would you and Nick like to come over tomorrow evening to have a drink and meet the cats and watch the sunset? I have a charming guest from Down Below, and I don't know how much longer she can stay."

Lori's acceptance was almost too effusive, and Qwilleran said to Rosemary later: "You'd think it was an invitation to the White House or Buckingham Palace."

She raised her eyebrows. "Did I hear you say that your charming guest might not stay much longer?"

"Merely an innocent social prevarication intended to lend convincing authenticity to an alarmingly abrupt invitation."

"You must be feeling good," Rosemary said. "You always get wordy when you're feeling good."

TWELVE

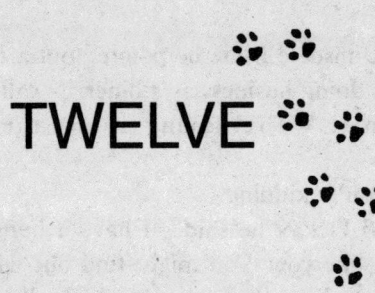

"What shall I wear to visit Aunt Fanny?" Rosemary asked on Wednesday morning. "I'm all excited."

"You look nice in your white suit," Qwilleran said. "She'll be dressed like Pocahontas or the Empress of China. I'm going to wear my orange cap." He knew Rosemary was not enthusiastic about his new headgear.

On the road to Pickax he pointed out the turkey farm. "Mildred brought us some turkey from the farm one day, and it was the best I've ever tasted."

"That's because it was raised naturally," Rosemary explained. "And it was fresh. No preservatives."

Near the old Dimsdale Mine he pointed out a dilapidated boxcar doing business as a diner. "I call it the Dismal Diner. We're having dinner there tonight."

"Oh, Qwill! You're kidding."

As they neared Pickax he said: "I have a hunch Aunt Fanny will like you. You might find out why she rented to those divers last summer. And tell her the pickax disappeared from the cabin."

"Why me?"

"I'm going to take a walk and let you girls get acquainted. You could mention the murder of Buck Dunfield and see how she reacts. I'm also curious to know why an eighty-nine-year-old woman with a live-in bodyguard carries a handgun in a county that has no crime."

"Why don't you ask the questions and I'll take a walk," Rosemary suggested. "I'm no good at snooping."

"With me she's evasive. With another woman she might open up. She likes women lawyers and women doctors, I happen to know."

They drove past crumbling buildings that had been shaft houses for the mines, past old slag heaps that made unnatural bumps in the landscape, past rows of stone rectangles that had been the foundations of miners' cottages. Then the road reached the crest of a hill, and Pickax City lay in the valley below, with the circular park in dead center.

"Fanny lives on the circle," Qwilleran said. "Best location in town. Her ancestors made a pile of money in mining."

When they pulled into the driveway of the great fieldstone house, Tom was working on the perfectly groomed lawn and his blue pickup was parked in front of the carriage house. Qwilleran waved to him and noticed that the growth on the young man's lip was beginning to resemble a moustache.

Aunt Fanny greeted them in a flowing purple robe of Middle Eastern design with borders embroidered in silver. A purple scarf was knotted about her head, and her long dangling earrings were set with amethysts. Rosemary was spellbound, and Aunt Fanny was volubly cordial.

Qwilleran brought up an insignificant rear as the hostess swept them into the large pretentious dining room for lunch. He tried hard to pretend he was enjoying his cup of tomato soup, half a tuna sandwich, and weak coffee. He listened in amazement as Rosemary gushed and twittered and Aunt Fanny proved she could answer questions in a normal way.

"When was this lovely old house built?" Rosemary asked.

"Over a hundred years ago," Aunt Fanny said. "In horse-and-buggy days it was considered the grandest house in town. Would you like me to show you around after lunch? Grandfather brought over Welsh stonemasons to build the house, and there's an English pub in the basement that was imported from London, piece by piece. The third floor was supposed to be a ballroom, but it was never finished."

"While you ladies are taking the grand tour," Qwilleran said, "I'd like to walk downtown, if you'll excuse me. I want to see the *Picayune* offices."

"Oh, you journalists!" Aunt Fanny said with a coy smirk. "Even when you're on vacation you can't forget your profession. I admire you for it!"

Leaving the house, Qwilleran looked for Tom, but the handyman and the blue truck had gone.

The commercial section of Main Street extended for three blocks. Stores, restaurants, a lodge hall, the post office, the home of the *Picayune,* a medical clinic, and several law offices were all built of stone with more exuberance than common sense. Cotswold cottages nestled between Scottish castles and Spanish forts. Qwilleran gave the *Picayune* office a wide berth and turned into the office of Goodwinter and Goodwinter.

"I don't have an appointment," he told the gray-haired secretary, "but I wonder if Mr. Goodwinter is available. My name is Qwilleran."

The secretary was undoubtedly a relative; she had the narrow Goodwinter face. "You've just missed him, Mr. Qwilleran," she said pleasantly. "He's on his way to the airport and won't be back until Saturday. Would you like to speak to his partner?"

The junior partner bounded out of her office in a cloud of expensive perfume, extending a well-manicured hand, and smiling happily. "Mr. Qwilleran!

I'm Penelope. Alex has told me about you. He's attending a conference in Washington. Won't you come in?"

She too had the long intelligent face that Qwilleran had learned to recognize, but it was softened by a smile that activated tantalizing dimples.

Qwilleran said: "I just dropped in to report on something your brother discussed with me."

"About the mysterious liquor purchases?"

"Yes. I don't find any evidence that our elderly friend is tippling."

"I agree with you," said the attorney. "That's my brother's private theory. He thinks she's developing a whiskey voice. I say it's hormones."

"How do you account for the houseman's liquor purchases?"

"He must buy it to treat friends. He has an apartment in the carriage house, and he must have some social life of a sort, or it would be a very lonely life."

"He's a strange young man."

"But gentle and rather sweet," Penelope said. "He's a good worker and carries out orders perfectly, and some of our affluent families would *kill* to get him."

"Know anything about his background?"

"Only that a friend of Fanny's in New Jersey arranged for Tom to come out here and help her. Isn't she a remarkable woman? She amassed her fortune in the days before women were supposed to have brains."

"I thought she inherited her money."

"Oh, no! Her father lost everything in the twenties. Fanny saved the family property and went on to make her own millions. She'll be ninety next month, and we're giving a party. I hope you'll join us. How are you enjoying Mooseville?"

"It's never dull. I suppose you know about the murder."

She nodded without any emotion, as if he had said: "Do you know it's Wednesday?"

"It was a shocking thing to happen in a place like Mooseville," he said. "Do you have any theories?"

She shook her head.

She knows something, Qwilleran thought, but the Legal Curtain has descended. "Wasn't Dunfield the police chief who was feuding with Fanny a few years ago? What was the trouble?"

The attorney looked up at the ceiling before answering coolly. "Simply small-town politics. It goes on all the time."

Qwilleran liked her style. He enjoyed his half hour in the company of an intelligent young woman with dimples and chic. Rosemary was attractive and comfortable to be with, but he had to admit he was captivated by career women in their thirties. Fondly he remembered Zoë the artist, Cokey the interior designer, and Mary the antiques dealer.

On his way back to the stone house he spotted another Goodwinter face. "Dr. Melinda, what are you doing here?" he said. "You're supposed to be repairing tourists at the Mooseville Limp-in Clinic."

"My day off. Buy you a cup of coffee?" She guided him around the corner to a luncheonette. "Second worst coffee in the county," she warned him, "but everybody comes here."

He tested the coffee. "Who's in first place? They'd have to try hard to beat this."

"The Dimsdale Diner takes top honors," Melinda said with a flourish. "They have the *worst* coffee in the county and the worst *hamburgers* in northeast central United States. You should try it. It's an old boxcar on the main highway, corner of Ittibitti-wassee Road."

"You're not going to make me believe *Ittibitti-wassee*."

"No joke. It's the road to the Ittibittiwassee River. The Indians had a village there at one time. Now it's time-sharing condos."

"Tell me something, Melinda. I've seen the remains of the Dimsdale Mine and the Goodwinter Mine. Where's the Klingenschoen Mine?"

Melinda studied his eyes to see if he could possibly be serious. Finally she said: "There is no Klingenschoen Mine. There *never* was a Klingenschoen Mine."

"How did Fanny's grandfather make his money? In lumbering?"

She looked amused. "No. He was a saloon-keeper."

Qwilleran paused to digest the information. "He must have been highly successful."

"Yes, but not highly respected. The K Saloon was

notorious for half a century before World War I. Fanny's grandfather built the most luxurious house in town, but the Klingenschoens were never accepted socially. In fact, they were ridiculed. The miners had a marching song that went like this: *We mine the mines and the K mines us, but who mines Minnie when the something something something.* I don't know the punch line, and I'm not sure I want to know."

"Then Minnie K was . . ."

"Fanny's grandmother, a very friendly lady, according to the stories. You can read about it in the local history section of the public library. Fanny's father inherited the saloon but went bankrupt during Prohibition. Fortunately Fanny had her grandfather's talent for making money, and when she came back here at the age of sixty-five, she could buy and sell anyone in the county."

As Qwilleran returned to the stone house he walked with a springier step. There was nothing like a juicy morsel of news to buoy his spirit, even when he was not on assignment.

Rosemary was equally exhilarated when he picked her up for the ride home. She had had a *lovely* visit. The house was *lovely*—full of antiques. Francesca had given her a Staffordshire pitcher from her collection, and Rosemary thought it was *lovely*. Qwilleran thought it was ugly.

He said: "I've been hungry ever since lunch, and we ought to have an early dinner because Nick and

Lori are coming at seven. Let's try the Old Stone Mill."

The restaurant was an authentic old mill with a water wheel, and the atmosphere was picturesque, but the menu was ordinary—from the chicken noodle soup to the rice pudding.

"All I want is a salad," Rosemary said.

"I'm going to order the mediocre pork chops, a soggy baked potato, and overcooked green beans," Qwilleran said. "That's the Moose County specialty. Why don't you have the chicken julienne salad? It's probably tired lettuce and imitation tomatoes with concrete croutons and slivers of invisible chicken. No doubt they serve it with bottled dressing from Kansas City and a dusting of grated Parmesan that tastes like sawdust. This used to be a sawmill, you know."

"Oh, Qwill! You're terrible," Rosemary admonished.

"What did you two emancipated females talk about while I was taking my walk?"

"You. Aunt Fanny thinks you are so talented, so sincere, so kind, so sensitive. She even likes your orange cap. She says it makes you look dashing."

"Did you tell her about the missing pickax?"

"Yes. She said the Historical Society wanted it for their museum, so she had Tom pick it up."

"She might have let me know. And what about the divers?"

"They wrote to a real estate firm in Mooseville, asking for a summer house to rent. They turned out to be very undesirable tenants. Especially the girls who spent the summer with them. She called them a name that I wouldn't repeat."

"Aw, c'mon. Tell me."

"No."

"Spell it."

"No, I won't. You're just teasing me."

Qwilleran chuckled. He liked to tease Rosemary. She was the epitome of the Perfect Lady circa 1902.

She said: "I have a lot more to tell you, but I don't want to talk here."

When they resumed their drive north he said: "Okay, let's have it. You and Fanny seemed to hit it off pretty well."

"She thinks you and I are engaged, and I didn't dispute it because I wanted her to talk. It was really flattering, the way she took me into her confidence."

"Good girl! What did she confide?"

"Her method of getting what she wants. She manipulates people with big promises and little threats. She says everybody *wants* something or is *hiding* something. The trick is to find their weakness. I think she makes it a kind of *hobby.*"

"The little old rascal! That's the carrot-and-stick technique."

"Of course, it works better if you have a lot of money."

"Of course. What doesn't?"

"She showed me a little gold pistol that she carries. That's to intimidate people. It's just a joke."

"She has a quaint sense of humor. What did she say about Dunfield's murder?"

"Oh my! She really hated that man. She got so mad I thought she was going to have a stroke."

"Buck was the only one she couldn't manipulate."

Rosemary giggled. "He accused her of growing marijuana in her backyard. Can you imagine that?"

"Yes, I can."

"About his murder, she said that people who play with fire can expect to get burned, and then she used some *very bad language*. I was shocked."

Qwilleran smiled into his moustache. He reminded himself that Rosemary shocked easily.

"Such a nice little old lady," Rosemary went on. "Where did she pick up such a vocabulary?"

"In New Jersey, probably."

There was more to relate: about the library with four thousand leather-bound books, unread; the four closets filled with Aunt Fanny's spectacular wardrobe; the Staffordshire collection in the breakfast room, the envy of three major museums; the Georgian silver in the dining room . . .

"Stop!" Rosemary cried as they approached the turkey farm. "I'll run in and see if they have a dressed turkey. Then I can cook it for you before I leave."

Qwilleran pulled into the farmyard alongside the inevitable blue pickup. "Make it snappy. It's getting close to seven o'clock."

Alongside the row of poultry coops there was a

metal shed with a sign on the door: *Retail and Wholesale*. Someone was moving about inside.

Rosemary ran into the building and in two minutes flat she was out again, carrying a bulbous object in a plastic sack. She looked green. She tossed the bundle into the back seat. "Get me out of here before I throw up! The odor was incredible!"

"No one said a turkey farm is supposed to smell like a rose garden," Qwilleran said.

"You don't need to tell me about barnyards," she said indignantly. "I grew up on a farm. This was something different."

She was unusually quiet until they reached the parking lot of the cabin. "I want to change clothes before they come," she said. "I feel like wearing something red."

Qwilleran handed her the key. "You go in and start changing. I'll bring the bird. I hope it'll fit in the refrigerator."

She hurried toward the cabin and stepped onto the porch. A moment later she screamed.

"Rosemary! What is it?" Qwilleran shouted, running after her.

"Look!" she cried, staring toward the locked door.

Dangling there was a small animal, hanging by the neck, the rope looped over one of the porch beams.

"Oh my God!" Qwilleran groaned. He felt sick. Then he said in astonishment: "It's a wild rabbit!"

"At first I thought it was Yum Yum."

"So did I."

It was one of the little brown rabbits that gnawed pine cones near the toolshed. It had been shot and then trussed up in a hangman's noose.

Qwilleran said: "You go down to the beach and calm down, Rosemary. I'll take care of this." He wondered: Is this a threat? Or a warning? Or just a prank? Someone had come out of the woods on the crest of the dune—the thicket that the cats were always watching. Anyone approaching the cabin by stealth would come from that direction.

He left the sad bit of fur hanging there and went to the other side of the cabin to let himself in. Koko and Yum Yum came running in a high state of nervous excitement, dashing about without direction or purpose, Koko growling and Yum Yum shrieking. They had seen the prowler from their favorite window. They had heard the shot. They had smelled the presence of the dead animal.

"If only you could talk," Qwilleran said to Koko.

A vehicle was chugging over the roller-coaster terrain of the driveway, and he went out to meet the visitors. His face was so solemn that Nick's happy smile faded instantly.

"Is anything wrong, Mr. Qwilleran?"

"Let me show you something unpleasant."

"Oh, no! That's a dirty trick!" Nick exclaimed. "Lori, come and look at this!"

She gasped. "A poor little cottontail! For a moment I thought it was one of your cats, Mr. Qwilleran."

Nick advised calling the sheriff. "Where's your phone? I'll call him myself. Don't touch the evidence."

While Nick was phoning, Lori was on her hands and knees, crooning to the disturbed Siamese. Gradually they responded to her soothing voice and even played games with her golden hair, which she was wearing in two long braids tied with blue ribbons. Rosemary served raw vegetables and a yogurt dip, and Qwilleran took orders for drinks. Lori thought she would like a Scotch.

"Watch it, kid," her husband warned her, with one hand covering the mouthpiece of the phone. "You know what the doctor told you."

"I'm trying to get pregnant," she explained to Rosemary, "but so far we haven't had anything but kittens."

Nick replaced the phone in the kitchen cupboard. "Okay. The sheriff's coming. And I'll have a bourbon, Mr. Qwilleran."

"Call me Qwill."

They sat on the porch and enjoyed the tranquilizing effect of the placid blue lake. Koko, who was not inclined to be a lap cat, jumped onto Lori's lap and went to sleep.

"I'm not sure I want to stay around Mooseville," Qwilleran suddenly announced. "If I leave the cabin, and the cats are sitting on the windowsill, what's to prevent that maniac from taking a shot through the glass? This incident might be a warning. He might come again."

"Or she," said Lori quietly.

Three questioning faces were turned in her direction, and Qwilleran asked: "Do you have a reason for switching genders?"

"I'm only trying to be broadminded."

"I suppose you know everyone at the Top o' the Dunes Club," he said to her.

"My wife knows everyone in the whole postal district," Nick said proudly, "including how many stamps they buy and who gets stuff in plain brown wrappers."

Qwilleran said: "I know the Hanstables and the Dunfields. Who are the others?"

Lori counted on her fingers. "There are three retired couples. And an attorney from Down Below. And a dentist from Pickax. Don't go to him; he's a butcher. Then there are two cottages for sale; they're empty. Another is in probate, and it's being rented to two *very good-looking men*." She threw a sly glance at her husband. "I think they're professors from somewhere, doing research on shipwrecks. The school superintendent from Pickax lives in the shingled house, and an antiques dealer lives in the one that looks like a boat."

"That fraud!" Nick interjected. "And how about the people who own the FOO?"

"Their place is up for sale. They lost it. The bank owns it now. . . . By the way," she said to Qwilleran, "the homeowners on the dune are worried about the future of this property. Miss Klingenschoen said she might leave it to the county for a park. That would be good for business in Mooseville, but it would hurt property values on the dune. Do you know what your aunt intends to do?"

"She's not my aunt," Qwilleran said, "and I don't know anything about her will, but if the subject ever comes up, I'll know what the local sentiments are." He was pouring the third round of drinks. "It doesn't look as if the sheriff's coming. He probably thinks I'm a nut. I called him about an owl the other night, and last week I reported a dead body in the lake, which everybody seemed to think was a rubber tire."

Nick turned to him abruptly. "Where did you see this body?"

"I was trolling and brought it up on my fish-hook." Qwilleran related the story of the *Minnie K* with relish, appreciating the rapt attention of his listeners.

Nick asked: "What was the date? Do you remember?"

"Last Thursday."

"How about the voices on the other boat? Could you hear them distinctly?"

"Not every word, but well enough to know what was going on. The engine had conked out, and they were arguing about how to fix it, I think. One guy had a high-pitched unmusical voice. The other guy's name was Jack, and he had what I would call a British working-class accent."

Nick glanced at Lori. She nodded. Then he said: "Englishmen are always called Jack up here. It's a custom that started way back in mining days. Last week one of the inmates went over the wall. He was a fellow with a Cockney accent."

Qwilleran looked at him in amazement mixed with triumph. "He was trying to escape to Canada! Someone was ferrying him across—in the fog!"

"They all try it," Nick said. "It's suicide, but they try it. . . . This is off-the-record, Qwill. Everybody knows about the ferry racket, but we don't want it getting in the papers. You know the media. They blow everything up."

"Do many inmates escape?"

"The usual percentage. They never head south. A poor bastard gives a local skipper good money to ferry him to Canada, and when they're a few miles out . . . *splash*! Just like you said. The water's so cold that a body goes down once and never comes up."

"Incredible!" Qwilleran said. "That's assembly-line murder. Do you think there are many guys working in the racket?"

"Everything points to one skipper, who happens to have a good contact inside. But so far they've never been able to apprehend him."

"Or her," Lori said softly.

"I see," Qwilleran said, smoothing his moustache. "No bodies—no evidence—no trace."

"Frankly," Lori said, "I don't think the authorities are trying very hard to catch anybody."

Nick snapped at her: "Lori, don't shoot off."

"How about the drug problem inside?" Qwilleran asked.

"No more than what they expect. It's impossible to stop the smuggling entirely."

His wife piped up again. "They don't want to stop it. Pot and pills make the inmates easier to control. It's the liquor that causes trouble."

A car door slammed. "That's one of the sheriff's men," Nick said, jumping to his feet. Qwilleran followed.

Lori said to Rosemary: "Don't you just love the hats the deputies wear—with the two little tassels in front? I'd love to have one."

THIRTEEN

When the telephone rang, Koko and Yum Yum were sitting on the polar bear rug, washing up after their morning can of crabmeat. Rosemary was in the kitchen, preparing the turkey for the oven. Qwilleran was having his third cup of coffee on the porch when the phone bleated its muffled summons from the kitchen cupboard.

He was trying to organize his wits. The dead rabbit was one more mismatched piece in the Mooseville Puzzle. Nick's revelation about escaped convicts reassured him, however, that he could still tell a human body from an automobile tire. Now it was clear that the ferry racket—and not wreck-looting—was the focus of Buck's do-it-yourself investigation; if one could identify the cold-blooded skipper, it would undoubtedly solve the mystery of Buck's murder. He (or she, as Lori would say) was someone who was used to killing.

Qwilleran had no way of knowing what clues the police had found in the sawdust or what progress they were making in the investigation. At the *Daily Fluxion* he could count on the police reporter to tip him off, but in Mooseville he was an outsider who registered alarm over a marauding owl or a dead rabbit or a body snagged by a fishhook. One thing was certain: The voice in the fog matched the voice on the cassette. If he could find that voice in Mooseville, he would have useful information for the investigators. Yet, the *message* on the cassette seemed to have nothing to do with the premeditated drownings.

Rosemary appeared on the porch. "Telephone for you, Qwill. It's Miss Goodwinter."

He thought at once of perfume and dimples, but the pleasurable tremor subsided when he heard the attorney's grave voice.

"Yes, Miss Goodwinter. . . . No, I haven't had the radio turned on. . . . No! How bad? . . . Terrible! I can't believe it! . . . What is being done? . . . Is there anything I can do? . . . Yes, I certainly will. Right away. Where shall we meet? . . . In about an hour."

"What's happened?" Rosemary demanded.

"Bad news about Aunt Fanny. Sometime last night she fell down a flight of stairs."

"Oh, Qwill! How terrible! Is she . . . She can't have survived."

He shook his head. "Tom found her at the bottom of the stairs this morning. Poor Aunt Fanny! She was so spirited—had such a youthful outlook. She enjoyed life so much. She never complained about being old."

"And she was so generous. Imagine giving me a Staffordshire pitcher! I'm sure it's valuable."

"Penelope wants me to meet her at the house as soon as possible. There are things to discuss. You don't have to go with me, but I'd appreciate it if you would."

"Of course I'll go with you. I'll put the turkey back in the fridge."

Before leaving for Pickax, Qwilleran latched all the windows and closed the interior shutters so that the cats could not be seen by a prowler. He locked front and back doors to keep them from the screened porches. "I'm sorry to do this to you guys," he said, "but it's the only safe way."

To Rosemary he said: "Who would think such security measures would be necessary in a place like this? I'm going to move back to the city next week. Now that Aunt Fanny's gone, the cabin might not be available to me anyway. That's probably what the attorney wants to discuss."

"It was too good to be true, wasn't it?"

"It would have been ideal—without the complications. But the simple country life is not all that simple. They'll razz me when I show up at the Press Club next week. I'll never live it down."

When they arrived at the stone house in Pickax, Tom was working in the yard, but his head was bowed and he didn't wave his usual eager greeting.

Penelope answered the doorbell, and Qwilleran introduced his houseguest. "This is Rosemary Whiting. We were both stunned by the news."

Rosemary said: "We lunched with her yesterday, and she was so *chipper*!"

"One would never guess she would be ninety next month," the attorney said.

"Is this where it happened?" Qwilleran pointed to the staircase.

Penelope nodded. "It was a terrible tumble, and she was such a fragile little person. She had been having fainting spells, and Alex and I urged her to move into a smaller place, all on one floor, but we couldn't convince her." She shrugged in defeat. "Would you like a cup of tea? I found some teabags in the kitchen."

Rosemary said: "Let me fix the tea while you two talk."

"Very good of you, Miss Whiting. We'll be in the conservatory."

They went into the room with the French doors and the rubber plants and Aunt Fanny's enormous wicker rocking chair. Qwilleran said: "Fanny called this the sun parlor."

Penelope smiled. "When she moved back here

after years on the East Coast, she took great pains to conceal her sophistication. She tried to talk like a little old granny, although we knew she was nothing of the sort. . . . I phoned Alex in Washington this morning, and he told me to contact you, as next of kin. He can't possibly return until Saturday."

"Fanny and I were not related. She was a close friend of my mother's, that's all."

"But she referred to you as her nephew, and she had great affection and admiration for you, Mr. Qwilleran. She has no other relatives, you know." The attorney opened her briefcase. "Our office handled all of Fanny's affairs—even her mail, to protect her from hate mail and begging letters. She deposited a sealed envelope in our file, detailing her last wishes. Here it is. No funeral, no visitation, no public display, just cremation. The *Picayune* is running a full-page obituary tomorrow, and we plan a memorial service on Saturday."

"Did she have a church affiliation?"

"No, but she made annual contributions to all five churches, and the service will probably be held at the largest. It will be very well attended, I'm sure—people coming from all over Moose County."

During the conversation the telephone rang frequently. "I'm not answering," Penelope said. "They're just curiosity-seekers. Legitimate inquiries will go to the office."

Qwilleran asked: "What about the open-door policy that seems to prevail in these parts? Won't people walk into the house?"

"Tom has instructions to turn them away."

Then Rosemary served the tea, and conversation drifted into polite reminiscences. Penelope pointed out Fanny's favorite rocker. Qwilleran commented on her flair for exotic clothes.

Finally he said: "Well, everything seems to be under control here. Are you sure there's nothing we can do to help?"

"There is one little matter that Alex said I should discuss with you." She paused dramatically. "We don't have Fanny's will."

"What! With all that money and all that real estate—she died intestate? I can't believe it!"

"We are positive that a holographic will exists. She insisted in writing it herself to protect her privacy."

"Is that a legal document?"

"In this state, yes . . . if it's written in her own hand and signed and dated. Witnesses are not required. That was the way she wanted it, and one didn't argue with Fanny! Naturally we advised her on the terminology to avoid ambiguity and loopholes. Its location should have been noted in her letter of instructions, but unfortunately . . ."

"And now what?"

Penelope looked hopefully at Qwilleran. "All we have to do is find it."

"Find it!" he said. "Is that what you want me to do?"

"Would you object strenuously?"

Qwilleran looked at Rosemary, and she nodded

enthusiastically. She said: "Fanny gave me a tour of the house yesterday, and I don't think it would be difficult."

"Call me at the office if you have any problems," Penelope said, "and don't answer the phone; it will only prove a nuisance."

Then she left them alone, and Qwilleran confronted Rosemary. "All right! If you think it's so easy, where do we begin?"

"There's a big desk in the library and a small one in Fanny's sitting room upstairs. Also an antique trunk in her bedroom."

"You're amazing! You notice everything, Rosemary. But has it occurred to you that they might be locked?"

She ran to the kitchen and returned with a handful of small keys. "These were in the Chinese teapot I used for the tea. Why don't you start in the library? I'd like to tackle the trunk."

That was a mistake, considering Qwilleran's obsession with the printed word. He was awed by the rows of leather-bound volumes from floor to ceiling. He guessed that Grandfather Klingenschoen tucked away a few pornographic classics on the top shelf. On one shelf he found a collection of racy novels from the twenties, with Aunt Fanny's personal bookplate, and he was absorbed in *Five Frivolous Femmes* by Gladys Gaudi when Rosemary rushed into the room.

"Qwill, I've made a terrific discovery!"

"The will?"

"Not the will. Not yet. But the trunk is filled with Fanny's scrapbooks as far back as her college days. Do you realize that dear Aunt Fanny was once an exotic dancer in New Jersey?"

"A stripper? In burlesque houses?"

Rosemary looked gleeful. "She saved all the ads and some 'art photographs' and a few red hot fan letters. No wonder she wanted you to write a book! Come on upstairs. The scrapbooks are all dated. I've just started."

They spent several hours exploring the trunk, and Qwilleran said: "I feel like a voyeur. When she told me she was in clubwork, I visualized garden clubs and hospital auxiliaries and afternoon study clubs."

Actually her career had been pursued in Atlantic City nightclubs, first as an entertainer, then as a manager, and finally as an owner, with her greatest activity during the years of Prohibition. There were excerpts from gossip columns, pictures of *Francesca's Club,* and photos of Francesca herself posing with politicians, movie stars, baseball heroes, and gangsters. There was no mention of a marriage, but there was evidence of a son. His portraits from babyhood to manhood appeared in one scrapbook until—according to newspaper clippings—he was killed in a mysterious accident on the New York waterfront.

But there was no will.

Qwilleran telephoned Penelope to say they would continue the search the next day. He made the chore sound tedious and depressing. In fact, the excitement of Fanny's past life erased the sadness of the occasion, and both he and Rosemary were strangely elated.

She said: "Let's do something reckless. Let's eat at the Dismal Diner on the way home."

The boxcar stood on a desolate stretch of the highway with not another building in sight—only the rotting timbers of the Dimsdale shaft house. There were no vehicles in the pasture that served as a parking lot, but a sign in the door said OPEN, contradicting another sign in one window that said CLOSED.

The side of the boxcar was punctuated with windows of various sorts, depending on the size and shape available at some local dump. The interior was papered with yellowing posters and faded menus dating back to the days of nickel coffee and ten-cent sandwiches. Qwilleran raised his sensitive nose and sniffed. "Boiled cabbage, fried onions, and marijuana," he reported. "I don't see a maître d'. Where would you like to sit, Rosemary?"

Along the back wall stretched a worn counter with a row of stools, several of them stumps without seats. Tables and chairs were Depression-era, probably from miners' kitchens. There was only one sign of life, and that was uncertain. A tall, cadaverous man, who may not have eaten for a week, came forward like a sleepwalker from the dingy shadows at the end of the diner.

"Nice little place you've got here," Qwilleran said brightly. "Do you have a specialty?"

"Goulash," the man said in a tinny voice.

"We were hoping you'd have veal cordon bleu. Do you have any artichokes? . . . No? . . . No artichokes, Rosemary. Do you want to go somewhere else?"

"I'd like to try the goulash," she said. "Do you suppose it's real Hungarian goulash?"

"The lady would like to know if it's real Hungarian goulash," Qwilleran repeated to the waiter.

"I dunno."

"I think we'll both have the goulash. It sounds superb. And do you have any Bibb lettuce?"

"Cole slaw is all."

"Excellent! I'm sure it's delicious."

Rosemary was eyeing Qwilleran with that dubious, disapproving look she reserved for his playful moments. When the waiter, who was also the cook, shambled out of his shadowy hole with generous portions of something slopped on chipped plates, she transferred the same expression to a study of the food. She whispered to Qwilleran: "I thought goulash was beef cubes cooked with onions in red wine, with sweet paprika. This is macaroni and canned tomatoes and hamburger."

"This is Mooseville," he explained. "Try it. It tastes all right if you don't think about it too much."

When the cook brought the dented tin coffeepot, Qwilleran asked genially: "Do you own this delightful little place?"

"Me and my buddy."

"Would you consider selling? My friend here would like to open a tearoom and boutique." He spoke without daring to look at Rosemary.

"I dunno. An old lady in Pickax wants to buy it. She'll pay good money."

"Miss Klingenschoen, no doubt."

"She likes it a lot. She comes in here with that quiet young fellah."

When Qwilleran and Rosemary continued their drive north, she said: "There's an example for you. Fanny made irresponsible promises to the poor man, and you're just as bad—with your jokes about tearooms and artichokes."

"I wanted to check his voice against the cassette," Qwilleran said. "It doesn't fit the pattern I'm looking for. When you stop to think about it, he doesn't fit the role of master criminal either . . . although he could be arrested for that goulash. My chief suspect now is the guy who owns the FOO."

When they turned into the private drive to the cabin, Rosemary said: "Look! There's a Baltimore oriole." She inhaled deeply. "I love this lake air. And I love the way the driveway winds between the trees and then suddenly bursts into sight of the lake."

Qwilleran stopped the car with a jolt in the center of the clearing. "The cats are on the porch! How did they get out? I locked them in the cabin!"

Two dark brown masks with blue eyes were peering through the screens and howling in two-part harmony.

Qwilleran jumped out of the car and shouted over his shoulder: "The cabin door's wide open!" He rushed indoors, followed by a hesitant Rosemary. "Someone's been in here! There's a bar stool knocked over . . . and blood on the white rug! Koko, what happened? Who was in here?"

Koko rolled over on his haunches and licked his paws, spreading his toes and extending his claws.

From the guest room Rosemary called: "This window's open! There's glass on the floor, and the shutter's hanging from one hinge. The screen's been cut!"

It was the window overlooking the septic tank and the wooded crest of the dune.

"Someone broke in to get the cassette," Qwilleran said. "See? He set up a bar stool to reach the moose head. He fell off—or jumped off in panic—and gave the stool a back-kick. I'll bet Koko leaped on the guy's head from one of the beams. His eighteen claws can stab like eighteen stilettoes, and Koko isn't fussy about where he grabs. There's a lot of blood; he could have sunk his fangs into an ear."

"Oh, dear!" Rosemary said with a shudder.

"Then the guy ran out the door—maybe with the cat riding on his head and screeching. Koko's been licking his claws ever since we got home."

"Did the man get the cassette?"

"It wasn't up there. I have it hidden. Don't touch anything. I'm going to call the sheriff—again."

"If my car had been parked in the lot, this wouldn't

have happened, Qwill. He'd think someone was home."

"We'll pick up your car tomorrow."

"I'll have to drive home on Sunday. I wish you were coming with me, Qwill. There's a dangerous man around here, and he knows you've found his cassette. What are you going to tell the sheriff?"

"I'm going to ask him if he likes music, and I'll play *Little White Lies*."

Later that evening Rosemary and Qwilleran sat on the porch to watch the setting sun turn the lake from turquoise to purple. "Did you ever see such a sky?" Rosemary asked. "It shades from apricot to mauve to aquamarine, and the clouds are deep violet."

Koko was pacing restlessly from the porch to the kitchen to the guest room and back to the porch.

"He's disturbed," Qwilleran explained, "by his instinctive savagery in attacking the burglar. Koko is a civilized cat, and yet he's haunted by an ancestral memory of days gone by and places far away, where his breed lurked on the walls of palaces and temples and sprang down on intruders to tear them to ribbons."

"Oh, Qwill," Rosemary laughed. "He smells the turkey in the oven, that's all."

FOURTEEN

Rosemary picked up her car at the Mooseville garage, and Qwilleran picked up his mail at the post office.

"I heard the bad news on the radio," Lori said. "What a terrible way to go!"

"And yet it was in character," Qwilleran said. "You've got to admit it was dramatic—the kind of media event that Fanny would like."

"Nick and I want to go to the memorial service tomorrow."

He said: "We're on our way to Pickax now, and we're taking the cats. There was a break-in at the cabin yesterday, and we think Koko attacked the burglar and drove him away."

"Really?" Lori's blue eyes were wide with astonishment.

"There was blood on the rug, and Koko was licking his claws with unusual relish. If one of your postal patrons turns up with a bloody face, tip me off. Anyway, I'm not leaving Koko and Yum Yum at the cabin alone until this thing is cleared up. They're out in the car right now, disturbing the peace on Main Street."

Rosemary drove her car back to the cabin and parked it in the clearing. Then the four of them headed for Pickax at a conservative speed that would not alarm Yum Yum.

Rosemary mentioned that the garage mechanic was going to the memorial service.

"Fanny had a real fan club in Moose County," Qwilleran said. "For a name that used to be despised, *Klingenschoen* has made a spectacular comeback."

He swerved to avoid hitting a dead skunk, and the Siamese raised noses to sniff-alert, with ears back and whiskers forward.

Rosemary said: "I've been thinking about that odor at the turkey farm. It wasn't a barnyard smell; it was a bad case of human B.O. I think the farmer has a drastic diet deficiency. I wish I could suggest it to his wife without offending her."

Next the car hit a pothole, and Yum Yum

launched a tirade of Siamese profanity that continued all the way to Pickax.

Qwilleran parked in the driveway of the imposing stone house with its three floors of grandeur. "Here we are, back at Manderley," he quipped.

"Oh, is that the name of the place?" Rosemary asked innocently.

The two animals were shut up in the kitchen with their blue cushion, their commode, and a bowl of water, while Qwilleran and Rosemary continued their search for the will.

The library desk was a massive English antique, its drawers containing tax records, birth and death documents, insurance policies, real estate papers, investment information, paid bills, house inventories, and hundred-year-old promissory notes . . . but no will. The desk in Aunt Fanny's sitting room was a graceful French escritoire devoted to correspondence: love letters from the twenties; silly chit-chat about "beaux" written by Qwilleran's mother when she and Fanny were in college; brief notes from Fanny's son at boarding school; and recent letters typed on *Daily Fluxion* letterheads. But still no will.

"Here's something interesting, Qwill," Rosemary said. "From someone in Atlantic City. It's about Tom, asking Fanny to hire him as a man-of-all-work." She scanned the lines hastily. "Why, Qwill! He's an ex-convict! It says in this letter he's about to be paroled . . . but he needs a place to go . . . and the promise of a job. He's not real sharp, it says . . . but he's a hard worker . . . obeys orders and never makes any trouble. . . . Listen to this, Qwill. He took a rap and got ten years . . . but he's being released for good behavior. . . . Oh, Qwill! What kind of people did Fanny know in New Jersey?"

"I can guess," Qwilleran said. "Let's go to lunch."

He checked the Siamese; they were perched on their blue cushion on top of the refrigerator and were as contented as could be expected under the circumstances. He found the handyman working in the yard.

"Hello, Tom," he said sadly. "This is an awful thing that has happened."

Tom had lost his bland, boyish expression and looked twenty years older. He nodded and stared at the grass.

"Are you going to the memorial service tomorrow?"

"I never went to one. I don't know what to do."

"You just go in and sit down and listen to the music and the speeches. It's a way of saying goodbye to Miss Klingenschoen. She'd like to know that you were there."

Tom leaned on his rake and bowed his head. His eyes brimmed.

Qwilleran said: "She was good to you, Tom, but you were also a great help to her. Remember that. You made the last years of her life easier and happier."

The handyman smeared his wet face with his

sleeve. His grief was so poignant that Qwilleran felt—for the first time since hearing the news—a constriction in his throat. He coughed and started talking about the broken window at the cabin. "I've got a piece of cardboard in the window now, but if it rains hard and the wind blows from the east . . ."

"I'll fix it," Tom said quietly.

The luncheonette that served the second worst coffee in Moose County was crowded at the lunch hour and buzzing with chatter about the Klingenschoen tragedy. No church was large enough for the expected crowd, so the memorial service would be held in the high school gymnasium. Pastors of all five churches would give eulogies. The Senior Citizens' Glee Club would sing. A county commissioner would play taps on a World War I bugle. Fanny Klingenschoen's favorite wicker rocker would be on the platform, and kindergarten children would file past, each dropping a single rosebud in the empty chair.

There was, of course, much speculation about the will. The great stone house had been promised to the Historical Society for a museum, and the carriage house had been promised to the Art Society for a gallery and studio. It was rumored that a lump sum would go to the Board of Education for an Olympic-size swimming pool. Altogether there was an atmosphere of mingled sorrow and excitement and gratitude among the customers at the luncheonette, especially the younger ones, several of whom were named Francesca.

Qwilleran said to Rosemary: "I hope she remembered Tom in her will. I hope she left him the blue truck. He takes care of it like a baby."

"What if we don't find the will?"

"The government and the lawyers will get everything."

After lunch the search continued in the drawing room, where a Chinese lacquer desk was stuffed with photographs: tintypes, snapshots, studio portraits, and glossy prints from newspapers. Qwilleran wanted to guess which whiskered chap was Grandfather Klingenschoen, and which bright-eyed girl with ringlets was Minnie K, but Rosemary dragged him away.

Upstairs there were marble-topped dressers, tall chests, and wardrobes. Rosemary organized the search, taking Fanny's suite herself and directing Qwilleran to the other rooms. Then they compared notes, sitting on the top stair of the long flight that had been the scene of the accident.

Rosemary said: "All I found was clothing. Real silk stockings and silk lingerie, imagine! White linen handkerchiefs by the gross . . . lots of white kid gloves turning yellow . . . everything smelling of lavender. What did you find?"

Qwilleran's list was equally disappointing. "Sheets by the ton. Blankets an inch thick, smelling of cedar. Enough white towels for a Turkish bath. And tablecloths big enough to cover a squash court."

"Where do we go from here?"

"There might be a safe," he said. "It could be built into a piece of furniture or set in a paneled wall or hidden behind a picture. If Fanny was so concerned about concealing the nature of her will, she'd keep it in a safe."

"It could take weeks to find it. You'd have to pull the whole house apart."

A distant howl echoed through the quiet rooms. "That's Koko," Qwilleran said. "He objects to being shut up for so long. You know, Rosemary, that little devil has a sixth sense about things like this. We could let him walk through the house and see what turns him on."

As soon as Koko was released from the kitchen, he stalked through the butler's pantry into the dining room with the dignity of a visiting monarch, head held regally, ears worn like a coronet, tail pointing aloft. He sniffed ardently at the carved rabbits and pheasants on the doors of the mammoth sideboard, but it stored only soup tureens and silver serving pieces. In the foyer he was entranced by a spot on the rug at the foot of the stairs, until Qwilleran scolded him for bad taste. In the drawing room he examined the keys of the old square piano and rubbed against the bulbous legs. There was nothing to interest him in the library or conservatory, but he found the basement stairs and led the way to the English pub.

It was a dark paneled room with a stone floor and several tavern tables and crude wooden chairs. The bar was ponderous, and there was a backbar elaborately carved and set with leaded glass. Koko nosed about behind the bar, then struck a rigid pose. In slow motion he approached a cabinet under the bar. He waited, staring at the bottom of the cabinet door. Qwilleran put his finger to his lips. Neither he nor Rosemary dared to move or even breathe. Then Koko sprang. There were tiny squeaks of terror, and Koko pranced back and forth in frustration.

"A mouse," Qwilleran mouthed in Rosemary's direction. He tiptoed behind the bar and opened the cabinet door. A tiny gray thing flew out, and Koko took off in pursuit.

"Let him go," Qwilleran said. "This is it!" Inside the cabinet was an old black-and-gold safe with a combination lock. "Only one problem. How do we open it?"

"Call Nick."

"Nick and Lori are coming into town for the service tomorrow. The safe can wait until then. Let's go home and eat that turkey."

They bought a copy of the *Pickax Picayune* and found that Fanny's obituary filled the front page. Even the classified ads that usually occupied column one of page one were omitted. The text of the obituary was set in large type in a black-bordered box in the center of the page, surrounded by white space and then another wide black border. In fine print at the bottom on the page it was mentioned that the obituary was suitable for framing.

Rosemary read it aloud on the way back to Mooseville, and Qwilleran called it a masterpiece of evasion and flowery excess. "They wrote obituaries like that in the nineteenth century. Wait till I see the editor! It's not easy to write a full-page story without saying anything."

"But there are no pictures."

"The *Picayune* has never acknowledged the invention of the camera. Read it to me again, Rosemary. I can't believe it."

The headline was simple: *Great Lady Called Home.*

Rosemary read:

Elevated to the rewards of a well-spent life, without enduring the pangs of decay or the sorrow of parting or pain of sickness, and happy in her consciousness of having completed to the best of her ability her work for mankind, Fanny Klingenschoen, at the advanced age of eighty-nine, slipped suddenly into the sleep from which there is no waking, during the midnight hours of Wednesday at her palatial residence in downtown Pickax. In the few brief moments when The Reaper called her home, she passed from the scene of her joy and happiness, closed her eyes to the world, and smiled as the flickering candle of life went out, casting a gloom over the county such as rarely, if ever, has been felt on a similar occasion.

No pen can describe the irreparable loss to the community when the cold slender fingers of death gripped the heart strings that inspired so many of her fellow creatures—inspired them for so many years—inspired them with an amplitude of leadership, poise, refined taste, cultivated mind, forthrightness, strength of character and generous nature.

Born to Septimus and Ada Klingenschoen almost nine decades ago, she was the granddaughter of Gustave and Minnie Klingenschoen, who braved the trackless wilderness to bring social betterment to the rugged lives of the early pioneers.

Although her spirit has taken flight, her forceful presence will be felt Saturday morning at eleven o'clock when a large number of county residents representing every station of life will assemble at Pickax High School to do honor to a woman of sterling qualities and unassuming dignity. Business in Pickax will be suspended for two hours.

Rosemary said: "I don't know what you object to, Qwill. I think it's beautifully written—very sincere—and rather touching."

"I think it's nonsense," Qwilleran said. "It would make Fanny throw up."

"YOW!" said Koko from the back seat.

"See? He agrees with me, Rosemary."

She sniffed. "How do you know if that's a yes or a no?"

They arrived at the cabin in time to hear the telephone struggling for attention inside a kitchen cupboard.

"Hello, there," said a voice that Qwilleran despised. "Have you got my girl up there? This is your old pal, Max Sorrel."

Qwilleran bristled. "I have several girls here. Which one is yours?"

After Rosemary had talked with Max she was moody and aloof. Finally she said: "I've got to start driving home tomorrow right after the memorial service."

"YOW!" Koko said with more energy than usual, and it sounded so much like a cheer that both Qwilleran and Rosemary looked at him in dismay. The cat was sitting on the mantel, perilously close to the Staffordshire pitcher. One flick of the tail would . . .

"Let's move your pitcher to a safe place," Qwilleran suggested. Then: "Did Max say something to upset you, Rosemary?"

"He's decided to buy me out and go through with the restaurant deal, and I'm nervous."

"You don't like him much, do you?"

"Not as much as he thinks I do. That's what makes me nervous. I'd like to go for a walk on the beach and do some thinking."

With some concern Qwilleran watched her go. Reluctantly he admitted he was not entirely sorry to see her move to Toronto. He had been a bachelor for too long. At his age he could not adjust to a supervised diet and Staffordshire knickknacks. He had

given up his pipe at Rosemary's urging, and he often
longed for some Groat and Boddle, despite his attempts to rationalize. Although she was attractive—
and companionable when he was tired or lonely—he
had other moods when he found younger women
more stimulating. In their company he felt more
alive and *wittier*. Rosemary was not tuned in to his
sense of humor, and she was certainly not tuned in
to Koko. She treated him like an ordinary cat.

The cooling of the relationship was only one development in a vacation that had hardly been a success. It had been two weeks of discomfort,
mystification, and frustration—not to mention guilt;
he had not written a word of his projected novel. He
had not enjoyed evenings of music or walked for
miles on the beach or lolled on the sand with a good
spy story or paid enough attention to the sunsets.
And now it was coming to an end. Even if the executors of the estate did not evict him, he was going
to leave. Someone had been desperate enough to
break into the cabin. Someone had been barbarous
enough to club a man to death. A rabbit-hunter
could come out of the woods with a rifle at any moment.

The cabin was quiet, and Qwilleran heard the
scurrying of little feet. Koko was playing with his
catnip toy, dredged up from some remote corner. He
batted it and sent it skidding across the floor,
pounced on it, clutched it in his front paws and
kicked it with his powerful hind legs, then tossed it
into the air and scampered after it.

Qwilleran watched the game. "Koko bats to right-field . . . he's under it . . . he's got it . . . throws wild to second . . . makes a flying catch . . . he's down, but he's got the ball . . . here comes a fast hook over the plate . . . foul to left."

The catnip ball had disappeared beneath the sofa. Koko looked questioningly at the precise spot where it had skidded under the pleated skirt of the slip-cover. The sofa was built low; only Yum Yum was small enough to struggle under it.

"Game's over," Qwilleran said. "You've lost by default."

Koko flattened himself on the floor and extended one long brown leg to grope under the sofa. He twisted, squirmed, stretched. It was useless. He jumped to the back of the sofa and scolded.

"Tell your sidekick to fish it out for you," the man said. "I'm tired."

Koko glared at him, his blue eyes becoming large black orbs. He glared and said nothing.

Only a few times had Qwilleran seen that look, and it had always meant serious business. He hoisted himself off the comfortable sofa and went to the porch for the crude pitchfork hanging there. With the handle he made a swipe under the piece of furniture and brought forth some dustballs and one of his navy blue socks. He made another swipe and out rolled Rosemary's coral lipstick and a gold ball-point pen.

Both cats were now standing by, enjoying the performance.

"Yum Yum, you little thief!" Qwilleran said. "What else have you stolen?"

Once more he raked under the sofa with the handle of the pitchfork. The catnip ball appeared first— and then his gold watch—and then some folded bills in a gold money clip. "Whose money is this?" he said as he counted the bills. Thirty-five dollars were tucked into what looked like a jumbo paper clip in shiny gold.

At that moment Rosemary climbed up the dune from the beach and wandered wearily into the cabin.

"Rosemary, you'll never believe what I found," Qwilleran said. "The gold pen you gave me! I thought Tom had stolen it. And your lipstick! Yum Yum has been stashing things under the sofa. My watch, one of my socks, and some money in a gold money clip."

"I'm so glad you found the pen," she said quietly.

"Are you okay, Rosemary?"

"I'll be all right after a good sleep. I'd like to go to bed early."

"We haven't even had dinner."

"I'm not hungry. Will you excuse me? I'll have a long drive tomorrow."

Qwilleran sat on the porch alone, hardly noticing the foaming surf and the gliding seagulls. The money clip, he reflected, was the kind that Roger used. Had Roger been in the cabin? If so, for what purpose? The place had been locked for several days. No, he refused to believe that his young friend was involved in any devious operation. Certainly it was not his voice on the cassette.

He sat on the porch until dusk, then made himself a turkey sandwich and a cup of coffee. He chopped a little turkey for the cats also. Yum Yum devoured her share, but—surprisingly—Koko was not in the least interested. There was no way to predict, understand, or explain the moods of a Siamese.

FIFTEEN

There were four documents in Aunt Fanny's safe. Three were envelopes sealed with red wax and labeled *Last Will and Testament* in her unmistakable handwriting. These Qwilleran turned over to Goodwinter and Goodwinter along with some velvet cases of jewelry to put in the attorneys' safe. The fourth item was a small address book bound in green leather, which he slipped into his pocket.

Nick and Lori had arrived at the stone house an hour before the memorial service, giving Nick time to crack the safe and giving Rosemary time to show Lori the handsome rooms with their antique furnishings. Then, leaving Koko and Yum Yum on top of the refrigerator, all four of them joined the crowd at the Pickax High School.

Everyone was there. Qwilleran saw Roger and Sharon and Mildred, the fraudulent sea captain who sold fake antiques, Old Sam, Dr. Melinda Goodwinter in a sea-green suit to match her eyes, the two boys from the *Minnie K,* a.k.a. the *Seagull,* the museum curator, the Mooseville garage mechanic—everyone. The emaciated cook from the Dismal Diner arrived by motorcycle, riding behind a burly man wearing a large diamond ring and a leather jacket with cut-off sleeves. Tom was there, huddled shyly in the back row. Even the proprietors of the FOO were there with their furtive cook.

The managing editor of the *Pickax Picayune* was standing on the front steps, making note of important arrivals.

"Junior, you've surpassed yourself!" Qwilleran said in greeting. "You hit seventy-eight in a single sentence! That must be a record. What genius writes your obituaries?"

The young editor laughed off the question. "I know it's weird, but they've been written that way since 1859, and that's what our readers like. A flowery obit is a status symbol for the families around here. I told you we do things our own way."

"You weren't serious, I hope, when you said Fanny's obit was suitable for framing."

"Oh, sure. A lot of people up here collect obits as a hobby. One old lady has more than five hundred in a scrapbook. There's an Obituary Club with a monthly newsletter."

Qwilleran shook his head. "Answer another question, Junior. How does the Dimsdale Diner stay in business? The food's a crime, and I never see anyone there."

"Didn't you ever see the coffee crowd? At seven in the morning and then at eleven o'clock the parking lot's full of pickups. That's where I go to gather news."

At that moment the FOO delegation arrived, and Qwilleran grasped the chance to speak to the elusive Merle. He was a mountain of a man—tall, obese, forbidding, with one eye half-shut and the other askew.

"Excuse me, sir," Qwilleran said. "Are you the owner of the FOO restaurant?"

His wife, the beefy woman who presided at the cash register, said: "He don't talk no more. He had a accident at the factory." She made a throat-cutting motion with her hand. "And now he don't talk."

Qwilleran made a fast recovery. "Sorry. I just wanted to tell you, Merle, how much I enjoy your restaurant, especially the pasties. My compliments to the cook. Keep up the good work."

Merle nodded and attempted to smile but only succeeded in looking more sinister.

While the preachers and politicians paid glowing tributes to Fanny Klingenschoen, Qwilleran fingered the little green book in his pocket. It was indexed alphabetically and filled with names, but instead of addresses there were notations of small-town malfeasance: shoplifting, bad checks, infidelity, graft, conflict of interest, errant morals, embezzlement. Nothing was documented, but Fanny seemed to know. Perhaps she too was a regular patron of the coffee hour at the Dismal Diner. It was her hobby. As others collected obituaries, Fanny had collected the skeletons in local closets. How she used her information, one could only guess. Perhaps the little green book was the weapon she used in saving the courthouse and getting new sewers installed. Qwilleran decided he would build a fire in the fireplace before the day was over.

After the service Rosemary said: "I've had a lovely time, Qwill. Sorry I can't stay for lunch, but I have a long drive ahead."

"Did you remember to take the Staffordshire pitcher?"

"I wouldn't forget that for anything!"

"It's been good to have you here, Rosemary."

"Write and tell me how the estate is settled."

"Send me your address in Toronto, and don't get too involved with our friend Max."

There was a note of friendly affection in their farewell, but none of the warmth and intimacy there had been a week ago. Too bad, Qwilleran thought. He collected the Siamese and drove back to the cabin. It was clear that Koko had disliked Rosemary. He had always been a man's cat. The night before, Koko had refused to eat the turkey that

Rosemary had so thoughtfully purchased and roasted.

"Okay, Koko," Qwilleran said when they reached the cabin. "She's gone now. We'll try the turkey once more."

A tempting assortment of white meat and dark meat was arranged on the cats' favorite raku plate— a feast that would send any normal Siamese into paroxysms of joy. Yum Yum attacked it ravenously, but Koko viewed the plate with distaste. He arched his back and, stepping stiffly on long slender legs, circled the repast as if it were poison—not once but three times.

Qwilleran stroked his moustache vigorously. In the few years he had known Koko, the Siamese had performed this ritual twice. The first time he pranced around a dead body; his second macabre dance had been the clue to a ghastly crime.

The telephone emitted its stifled ring.

"Hello, Qwill. It's me. I'm calling from Dove Lake."

"Oh-oh. Car trouble?"

"No, everything's fine."

"Forget something?"

"No, but I remembered something. You know that money you found under the sofa. The money clip looked familiar, and now I know why."

"The candle shop carried them. Roger has one, and I tried to buy one myself," Qwilleran said.

"Maybe so, but the one I remember was at the turkey farm. That man with the terrible problem got out his money clip to give me a dollar in change, and it looked like a big gold paper clip."

Qwilleran combed his moustache with his fingertips. Rosemary had bought the turkey on Wednesday. The break-in was Thursday. The money clip could have popped out of a pants pocket when the man jumped or fell from the bar stool and fled from those eighteen claws.

"Did you hear me, Qwill?"

"Yes, Rosemary. I'm putting two and two together. There's something about that turkey you bought—it's turning Koko off. He's getting vibrations. Yum Yum thinks it's great, but Koko still refuses to touch it. I think he's steering me to that turkey farm."

"Be careful, Qwill. Don't take any chances. You know what almost happened to you at Maus Haus when you meddled in a dangerous situation."

"Don't worry, Rosemary. Thanks for the information. Drive carefully, and stop if you get sleepy."

So that was the clue! Turkey! Qwilleran grabbed the money clip with the thirty-five dollars, locked the cats in the cabin, and hurried to his car.

It was only a few miles to the turkey farm. The bronze backs were pitching and heaving as usual. The blue pickup was in the yard. He parked and headed for the door that invited retail and wholesale trade. The wind was from the northwest, so there was very little barnyard odor, but once he stepped inside the building he was staggered by the stench.

There was nothing to account for it. The premises

were spotless: the white-painted walls, the scrubbed wooden counter with its stainless steel scales and shiny knives, the clean saw-dust on the floor in the manner of old butcher shops. There was a bell on the counter: *Ring for service*. Qwilleran banged it three times, urgently.

When the tall, hefty man stepped out of a walk-in cooler, Qwilleran tried to control his facial reaction of revulsion. It was the post office experience all over again, but there was more. The man's face and neck were covered with red, raw scratches. There was an adhesive bandage on his throat. One ear was torn. He was wearing the inevitable feed cap, and its visor had apparently protected his eyes when Koko attacked, but the sight was worse than Qwilleran had imagined, and the odor was nauseating.

He stared at the farmer, and the man returned the stare, impassively, defensively. Someone had to say something, and Qwilleran brought himself to make the natural comment: "Looks like you had a bad accident."

"Damn turkeys!" the man said. "They go crazy and kill each other. I should learn to stay outa the way."

That was all that was necessary for Qwilleran's practiced ear. It was the voice on the cassette.

He threw the money and the gold clip on the counter. "Does this belong to you? I found it in my cabin. I also have a cassette that might be yours." He looked the disfigured farmer squarely in the eye.

The man's expression turned hostile; his eyes

flashed; his jaw clenched. With a yell he leaped over the counter, grabbing a knife.

Qwilleran bolted for the door but tripped over a doorstop and went down on one knee—his bad knee. He sensed an arm raised above him, a knife poised over his head. It was a frozen pose, a freeze-frame from a horror movie. The knife did not descend.

"You drop that," said a gentle voice. "That's a very bad thing to do."

The knife fell to the sawdust-covered floor with a muffled clatter.

"Now you turn around and hold your hands up."

Tom was standing in the doorway, pointing a gun at the farmer, a small pistol with a gold handle. "Now we should call the sheriff," he said to Qwilleran mildly.

"You idiot!" his prisoner screamed. "If you talk, I'll talk!"

There was no doubt about it; that was the voice: high pitch, metallic timbre, flat inflection.

Two deputies took Hanstable away, and Qwilleran agreed to go to the jail later to sign the papers.

"How did you happen to stop here?" he asked Tom.

"I went to fix your window. The door was locked. I couldn't get in. Then I went to Mooseville to buy a pasty. I like pasties."

"And then what?"

"I was going home. I saw your car here. I came in to get the key."

"Come on back to the cabin and have a beer," Qwilleran said. "I don't mind telling you, I've never been so glad to see anyone in my life! That's a nice little gun you've got there." How a pistol from Fanny's handbag happened to be in Tom's pocket was a matter of interest that Qwilleran did not pursue at the moment.

"It's very pretty. It's gold. I like gold."

"How can I repay you, Tom? You saved my life."

"You're a nice man. I didn't want him to hurt you."

Qwilleran drove back to the cabin, the handyman following in his blue truck, shining like new. They sat on the south porch in the shelter of the building because the northwest wind was blowing furiously, lashing trees and shrubs into a green frenzy.

Qwilleran served a beer and made a toast. "Here's to you, Tom. If you hadn't come along, I might have ended up as a turkey hot dog." The quip, such as it was, appealed to the handyman's simple sense of humor. Qwilleran wanted to put him at ease before asking too many questions. After a while he asked casually: "Do you go to the turkey farm often, Tom?"

"No, it smells bad."

"What did the farmer mean when he said he would talk if you talked?"

A sheepish smile flickered across the bland face.

"It was about the whiskey. *He told me* to buy the whiskey."

"What was the whiskey for?"

"The prisoners."

"The inmates at the big prison?"

"I feel sorry for the prisoners. I was in prison once."

Qwilleran said sympathetically: "I can see how you would feel. You don't drink whiskey, do you? I don't either."

"It tastes bad," Tom said.

The newsman had always been a sympathetic interviewer, never pushing his questions too fast, always engaging his subjects in friendly conversation. To slow down the interrogation he got up and killed a spider and knocked down a web, commenting on the size of the spider population and their persistence in decorating the cabin, inside and out, with their handiwork. Then:

"How did you deliver the whiskey to the prisoners?"

"*He* took it in."

"Excuse me, Tom. I hear the phone."

It was Alexander Goodwinter calling. He had just returned from Washington and was at a loss to express his sadness at the death of the gallant little lady. He and Penelope were about to drive to Mooseville and would like to call on him in half an hour to discuss a certain matter.

Qwilleran knew what that certain matter would be. As executors of the estate they would want a thousand a month for the cabin. He returned to the porch. Koko had been conversing with Tom in his absence.

"He has a loud voice," the handyman said. "I stroked him. His fur is nice. It's soft."

Qwilleran made a few remarks about the characteristics of Siamese, mentioned Koko's fondness for turkey, and then sidled into the inquiry again. "I suppose you had to deliver the whiskey to the turkey farm."

"I took it to the cemetery. He told me to leave it in the cemetery. There's a place there."

"I hope he paid you for it."

"He gave me a lot of money. That was nice."

"It's always good to have a little extra money coming in. I'll bet you stashed it away in the bank to buy a boat or something."

"I don't like banks. I hid it somewhere."

"Well, just be sure it's in a safe place. That's the important thing. Are you ready for a beer?"

There was time out for serving and for comments on the velocity of the wind and the possibility of a tornado. The temperature was abnormally high, and the sky had a yellow tone. Then: "Did you buy the liquor in Mooseville? They don't have a very good selection."

"He told me to buy it in different places. Sometimes he told me to buy whiskey. Sometimes he told me to buy gin."

Qwilleran wished he had a pipeful of tobacco. The business of lighting a pipe had often filled in the pauses and softened the edges of an interview when the subject was shy or reluctant. He said to Tom: "It would be interesting to know how the farmer got the liquor into the prison."

"He took it in his truck. He took it in with the turkeys. He told me to buy pint bottles so they would fit inside the turkeys."

"That's a new way to stuff a turkey," Qwilleran said, getting a hilarious reaction from the handyman. "If you didn't go to the farm, how did you know what kind of liquor to buy?"

"He came here and talked into the machine. I listened to it when I came here to work. That was nice. I liked that." Something occurred to Tom and he giggled. "He left it behind the moose."

"I always thought that moose looked kind of sick, and now I know why."

Tom giggled some more. He was having a good time.

"So you played the cassette when you came here."

"It had some nice music, too."

"Why didn't the farmer just leave you a note?" Qwilleran performed an exaggerated pantomime of writing. "*Dear Tom, bring five pints of Scotch and four pints of gin. Hope you are feeling well. Have a nice day. Love from your friend Stanley.*"

The handyman found this nonsense highly entertaining. Then he sobered and answered the question. "I can't read. I wish I could read and write. That would be nice."

Qwilleran had always found it difficult to believe

the statistics on illiteracy in the United States, but here was a living statistic, and he was struggling to accept it when the telephone rang again.

"Hello, Qwill," said a voice he had known all his life. "How's everything up there?"

"Fine, Arch. Did you get my letters?"

"I got two. How's the weather?"

"You didn't call to ask about the weather, Arch. What's on your mind?"

"Great news, Qwill! You'll be getting a letter from Percy, but I thought I'd tip you off. That assignment I told you about—investigative reporting—Percy wants you to come back and start right away. If the *Rampage* gets someone first, Percy will have a heart attack. You know how he is."

"Hmmm," Qwilleran said.

"Double your salary and an unlimited expense account. Also a company car for your own use—a new one. How's that for perks?"

"I wonder what the *Rampage* is offering?"

"Don't be funny. You'll get Percy's letter in a couple of days, but I wanted to be the first . . ."

"Thanks, Arch. I appreciate it. You're a good guy. Too bad you're an editor."

"And something else, Qwill. I know you'll need a new apartment, and Fran Unger is giving up hers and getting married. It's close to the office, and the rent is reasonable."

"And the walls are papered with pink roses and galloping giraffes."

"Keep it in mind anyway. Be seeing you soon. Say hello to that spooky cat."

Qwilleran was dizzy with shock and elation, but Tom was starting to leave and he had to thank him once more. He picked up the antique brass inkwell from the top of the bar.

"Here is something I'd like you to have, Tom. It needs polishing, but I know you like brass. It's an inkwell that traveled around the world on sailing ships a hundred years ago."

"That's very pretty. I never had anything like that. I'll polish it every day."

The handyman measured the broken window and drove into Mooseville to buy glass, while Qwilleran sat down to contemplate the offer from the *Fluxion*. Now that he was leaving this beautiful place he was filled with regret. He should have spent more time enjoying the verdure, the moods of the lake, the dew glistening on a spider web. Now he could look forward to the daily irritations of the office: the pink memos from Percy; electric pencil sharpeners always out-of-order; six elevators going up when a person wanted to go down; VDTs that made the job harder instead of easier. Suddenly he realized how much his knee was paining him.

He propped his leg on a chaise. From the back of a nearby chair, where a hawk had once perched, he was being watched intently by a pair of blue eyes in a brown mask.

"Well, Koko," Qwilleran said, "our vacation didn't turn out the way we expected, did it? But the time hasn't been wasted. We've cracked a one-man crime operation. Too bad we couldn't have stopped him before he got Buck Dunfield. . . . Too bad no one around here will ever know you deserve all the credit. Even if we told them, they wouldn't believe it."

Howling wind and crashing surf drowned out the sound of the Goodwinter car as it pulled into the clearing. Qwilleran hobbled out to greet them—Alexander looking impeccably well-groomed and Penelope looking radiant and a trifle flushed. When they shook hands she added an extra squeeze, and in addition to her perfume there was a hint of mint breath-freshener.

"You're limping," she said.

"I tripped over a toadstool. . . . Come in out of the wind. I think we're going to have a tornado."

Alexander went directly to his previous seat on Yum Yum's sofa. Penelope went to the windows overlooking the turbulent lake and rhapsodized about the view and the cabin's desirable location.

Qwilleran thought: The rent just went up to twelve hundred. Won't they be surprised when I break the news!

"It is regrettable," Alexander was saying, "that I was in Washington when this unfortunate incident occurred. My sister tells me you were of great assistance, making many trips back and forth and spending long hours searching through the Klingenschoen archives. It cannot have been a pleasant task."

"There was a lot of material to sift through,"

Qwilleran said. "Luckily I had a houseguest from Down Below who was willing to help." He refrained from mentioning Koko's contribution; he doubted whether the Goodwinters were ready for the idea of a psychic cat.

"I regret I could not get a return flight in time to attend the memorial service, but it appears that Penelope organized it efficiently and tastefully, and it was well attended."

His sister had wandered over to the table that presented such a convincing picture of authorial industry, and now she dropped onto the other sofa. "Alex, why don't you get to the point? You're keeping Mr. Qwilleran from his writing."

"Ah, yes. The will. A problem has arisen in connection with the will."

"I don't envision any problem," Penelope retorted. "You're inventing one before it arises."

The senior partner threw a remonstrative glance in her direction, cleared his throat, and opened his briefcase. "As you know, Mr. Qwilleran, Fanny left three wills in the safe, written in her own hand. She had written many wills during the years, changing her mind frequently. Only the last three wills were saved (this on our recommendation). They were dated, of course, and only the most recent is valid. Having the three wills gives us an enlightening overview of the lady's feelings in the last few years."

Qwilleran's gaze dropped from the attorney's face to his shoe; the little brown triangle of a face was appearing under the skirt of the sofa. Koko, on the other hand, was perched on the moose head with the authority of a presiding judge.

"The oldest will, which is invalid, bequeathed Fanny's entire estate to a foundation in Atlantic City, for the purpose of rehabilitating a certain section of the city which apparently had nostalgic significance for her, although it would be considered by most of us to be—ah—unsavory."

Yum Yum's paw was reaching out from her hiding place with stealth. Penelope had noticed the maneuver, and her face reflected a heroic effort to control mirth.

Goodwinter went on. "The second will, which is also invalid, I am mentioning merely to acquaint you with the change in Fanny's sympathies. This document bequeathed half her estate to the Atlantic City foundation and the other half to the schools, churches, cultural and charitable organizations, health care facilities, and civic causes in Pickax City. Considering the extent of her holdings there was plenty to distribute equitably, and she had promised sizable sums to all of the aforementioned."

Qwilleran checked Yum Yum's progress and glanced at Penelope, who returned his glance and exploded with laughter.

"Penelope!" her brother said in consternation. "Please allow me to conclude. . . . The most recent will leaves the sum of one dollar to each of the beneficiaries heretofore named—a wise precaution in our estimation, inasmuch as . . ."

"Alex, why don't you come to the point of this

discussion," said Penelope, waving a hand gaily, "and tell Mr. Qwilleran that he gets the whole damned thing."

"YOW!" came a howl from the vicinity of the moose head.

Goodwinter cast a quick disapproving eye at Penelope and then at Koko. "Excepting only the token bequests I have indicated, Mr. Qwilleran, you are indeed the sole heir to the estate of Fanny Klingenschoen."

Qwilleran was stunned.

"That," the attorney said, "sums up the intent and purpose of the most recent will, dated April first of this year, thus revoking all prior documents. The formal reading of the will is scheduled to take place Wednesday afternoon in our office."

Qwilleran shook his head like a wet dog. He could think of nothing to say. He looked at Penelope for help, but she merely grinned in an idiotic way.

Finally he said: "It's an April Fools' joke."

Goodwinter said: "I assure you it is legitimate. The problem, as I see it, might be that the bequest will be challenged by the numerous organizations expecting generous sums."

"They were verbal promises that Fanny made to everyone in town," Penelope reminded her brother. "Mr. Qwilleran's claim is the only legal one."

"Nevertheless, one might foresee a class action suit on behalf of the Pickax charities and civic institutions, questioning Fanny's testamentary capacity, but I assure you . . ."

"Alex, you neglected to mention the proviso."

"Ah, yes. The assets—bank accounts, investments, real estate, etc.—are held in trust for five years with the entire income going to you, Mr. Qwilleran, provided you consent to make Pickax your residence for that period of time and maintain the Klingenschoen mansion as your address—after which time the trust is dissolved and the estate is transferred to you in toto."

There was silence in the room, and stares all around. A window slammed in the guest room.

Goodwinter looked startled. "Is there someone else in the house?"

"Only Tom," Qwilleran said. "He's fixing a broken window."

"Well?" Penelope asked. "Don't keep us in suspense."

"What happens if I decline the terms?"

"In that case," Goodwinter said, "the will specifies that the entire estate goes to Atlantic City."

"And if it goes to Atlantic City," Penelope added, "there will be rioting in the city of Pickax, and you will be lynched, Mr. Qwilleran."

"I still think you're pulling my leg," he said. "There's no reason why Fanny should make this . . . this incredible gesture. Until a couple of weeks ago I hadn't seen her for forty years or more."

Goodwinter reached into his briefcase and drew

out a paper covered with Fanny's idiosyncratic handwriting. "She claims you as her godchild. Your mother was a friend she regarded as a sister."

Penelope giggled. "Come on, Alex, tie your shoelace and let's go. I have a dinner date tonight."

Tom's pickup truck had already gone when the attorneys drove away, following handshakes and congratulations. Penelope had staggered a little, Qwilleran thought. Either she had been celebrating something, or she had been drowning her disappointment.

Thu-rump . . . thu-rump . . . thu-rump. It was the familiar sound of a cat jumping down from the moose head in three easy stages.

"Well, Koko," Qwilleran said, "what do you think about that?"

Koko rolled over on the base of his spine and licked his tail assiduously.

SIXTEEN

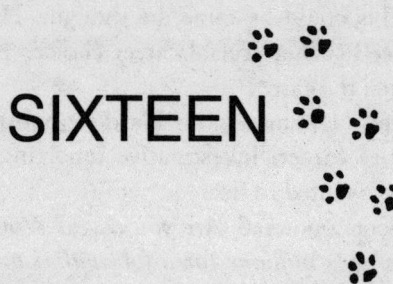

In a daze Qwilleran prepared a dish of turkey for the Siamese. He was so preoccupied with the bombshells dropped by Arch Riker and Alexander Goodwinter that he prepared a cup of instant coffee for himself minus the essential ingredient. Then he carried his coffee mug to the lakeside window and sipped the hot water without noticing that something was lacking.

Foaming white breakers pounded the shore; the beach grasses rippled in the wind; the trees waved their branches frantically; even the little wildflowers bobbed their heads bravely under the tumultuous sky. He had never seen anything so violent and yet so beautiful. This could be mine, he thought. Had anyone ever faced such a crucial career choice? His two selves argued the case:

The Dedicated Newsman said: It's the opportunity of my entire career. Investigative reporting—what I've always wanted to do.

The Canny Scot countered: *Are you crazy? Would you pass up Fanny's millions for a job with a midwestern newspaper? The first time the* Fluxion *gets slapped with a lawsuit, Percy will change his mind. Then where will you be? Back on the restaurant beat—or worse.*

But I'm a newsman. Reporting is my life! It's not a job; it's what I *do*.

So buy your own newspaper with Fanny's money. Buy a chain of newspapers.

I never wanted to be a newspaper tycoon. I like to get out in the field, dig up stories, and bang them out with two fingers on an old black manual typewriter.

If you own the paper, you can do anything you damn please. You can even set the type, like the guy at the Picayune.

And I don't *need* a lot of money or possessions. I've always been satisfied with what I earned.

But you're not getting any younger, and all you've got in the bank is $1,245.14. Forget the Fluxion *pension; it won't keep the cats in sardines.*

I'd have to live in Pickax, and I need the stimulation of a big city. I've never lived in a small town.

You can fly to New York or Paris or Tokyo any time you feel like it. You can even buy your own plane.

"YOW!" cried Koko in his most censorious voice. He was still waiting for his evening meal. Qwilleran had absentmindedly put the plate of turkey in the cupboard with the telephone.

"Sorry, kids," he said. He waited for Koko's reaction to the food. Twice this remarkable cat had rejected turkey from Stanley Hanstable's farm—until he succeeded in getting his message across. Now he devoured it with gusto. "Yow . . . gobble gobble . . . yow," Koko said as he gulped the white meat, leaving the dark meat for Yum Yum.

Qwilleran felt the need to talk to someone with a larger vocabulary and he telephoned Roger MacGillivray. "What time are you through at the office? . . . Why don't you run out here for a drink? . . . No, don't bring Sharon. Not this time. I want to speak to you privately."

Koko had finished his repast and was doing his well-known busybody act—restless meandering accompanied by grunts and chirps and squeals and mutterings. He inspected the fireplace, the stereo, the bathroom faucets. He pressed two keys on the typewriter (*x* and *j*) and sniffed a title on the lowest bookshelf (the bird book). When he ambled into the guest room, Qwilleran followed.

The lower berth of the double-decker was the spot where Koko and Yum Yum liked to sleep. During Rosemary's visit they had been banished to the upper level. Now Koko explored the lower bunk, muttering to himself and pawing the bedcover industriously. The bunk abutted the log wall, and soon he was reaching down between the mattress and the logs, trying first one paw and then the other, stretching to the limit until he dredged up a prize—a pair of sheer pantyhose. Still he was not satisfied. He fished in the narrow crevice until he retrieved a gold chain bracelet.

Qwilleran grabbed it. "That's Mildred's! How did it get down there?"

Mildred had said it might have fallen off her wrist when she delivered the gift of turkey the week before. Mildred had been there on that occasion with someone who smoked Groat and Boddle, although Buck Dunfield claimed he had never visited the cabin.

Qwilleran found Fanny's green leather address book, still in his jacket pocket, and flipped it open to the page indexed *H*.

HUNT, R.D.—Bought three farms while commissioner; sold for airport six months later.

HANSTABLE, S—Low bidder for prison turkey contract. *Too low.*

HANSTABLE, M—Sleeping around.

Qwilleran turned to the page indexed *Q* and found himself described as a former alcoholic. There was nothing under *M* for Roger, but Dunfield was labeled a womanizer, and there were two pages of Goodwinters, who appeared to have committed every sin in the book.

Qwilleran tossed the thing in the fireplace, emptied his wastebasket on top of it, added some twigs from the coal scuttle, and opened the damper. Just as the brass bell clanged at the back door, he struck a match and threw it in the grate. Almost immediately he had second thoughts about losing such a choice compendium of scandal. If he decided to move to Pickax, it might be useful. Too late! The tremendous draft of a windy day had whipped the debris into an instant blaze.

It was a subdued young man who waited at the door. Roger's white skin was whiter, and his black beard seemed blacker.

"Come in and make yourself comfortable," Qwilleran said. "It's too noisy to sit on the porch. The wind must be fifty miles an hour, and the surf is deafening."

Roger slumped on one of the sofas and stared into the fire, saying nothing.

"I saw you and Sharon and Mildred at the memorial service. What did you think of the turnout?"

"About what I expected," the young man said in a monotone. "Everyone there was expecting to inherit something. The Queen of Pickax went around making promises."

"Had she made any promises to you?"

"Oh, sure. A couple of hundred thousand to start an underwater preserve. . . . I suppose I should congratulate you."

"For what?"

"For inheriting half of Pickax and three quarters of Moose County."

"How did you find out? They didn't open the will until a couple of hours ago."

"I have to protect my sources," Roger said testily.

Qwilleran huffed into his moustache. He suspected that the Goodwinters' secretary was Junior's mother or aunt; she had the family resemblance. And Junior had undoubtedly rushed to phone Roger. "Well, Roger my boy, I haven't accepted the terms of the will, as of now. If you're lucky, I'll go back to the *Fluxion,* and half of Pickax and three quarters of Moose County will belong to Atlantic City."

"Sorry," Roger said. "I didn't mean to be snotty, but we're all miffed about your aunt's broken promises."

"She wasn't my aunt, and furthermore I wouldn't live up here for any amount of money. Your newspaper is a farce. The radio station should be put off the air. The restaurants massacre the food. And the whole county is insular and probably inbred. I won't even mention what I think about the mosquitoes."

"Wait a minute! Don't get excited," Roger said. "We'd rather see the money stay here with you than end up in New Jersey, restoring some red-light district."

"All right, let's have a drink and bury the hatchet. Scotch? Beer?"

They talked politely about the amenities of the

cabin. "It's neat," Roger said. "Sharon and I want a place like this some day. Mildred's cottage is okay, but it's like the houses in town. This cabin is perfect for the woods. I wonder who shot that moose." Suddenly he stiffened. "My God! There's a cat up there! I'm leery of cats. I got bitten by a barn cat when I was a kid."

"You were probably pulling its tail and deserved what you got," Qwilleran said. "You're looking at Koko up there. He's harmless if you behave properly. I suppose you know what happened to your father-in-law."

Roger shook his head dolefully. "I know he's in jail. It was inevitable, of course. Stanley has been on the skids for ten years."

"It's a strange thing," Qwilleran admitted. "Just because he's your father-in-law and Mildred's husband, I felt guilty about turning him in. But he came after me with a knife. . . . And still I hated to do it."

Roger agreed without enthusiasm. "That's the way it is up here. Everyone knows what's going on, but no one wants to do anything about it. Everyone is a relative or an old school chum or a war buddy or a member of the lodge."

"The sheriff's deputy apologized to Stanley for arresting him. They'd known each other since kindergarten. If you don't mind my saying so, it makes a perfect climate for corruption." Qwilleran poked the fire and threw two more logs into the grate. "What happened to Stanley ten years ago?"

"I was just beginning to date Sharon when it started. He'd been living high and suddenly got this incredible B.O. It was like a curse. His own family couldn't tolerate it. Mildred couldn't live in the same house. Sharon and I had to elope because the father-of-the-bride couldn't be stomached at a regular wedding. The guy became an outcast, that's all."

"Didn't he consult any doctors?"

"All kinds. They suspected abscessed lungs, infection of the sweat glands, chronic uremic poisoning, and you-name-it. But nothing checked out, and nothing seemed to help. Dr. Melinda—you know her—told me some people just have an idiopathic stink."

"Didn't Mildred consider divorce?"

"She was afraid to divorce him. He said he'd kill her, and she believed it. For a healthy, loving woman that was a helluva way to live, you know, so she was wide open for male companionship."

"Meaning Buck Dunfield?"

"He wasn't the first—only the unluckiest."

"Is that why Stanley killed him?"

"Well, it was no secret that he hated Buck. He knew what was going on."

"The real reason, I suspect—he found out Buck was snooping into his racket. The ferry racket."

"One thing I don't understand," Roger said. "How could Stanley *sneak up* on Buck undetected? That's what happened, they say."

"I know how. Buck had lost his sense of smell.

Even the dead fish on the beach didn't bother him. Did Mildred suspect he was a killer?"

"Everyone knew. The police had a good idea, but they hadn't collected enough evidence. They were waiting for something to break."

"Everyone knows! The motto of Moose County ought to be *Omnes Sciunt*. What was Stanley's connection at the prison?"

"He made the lowest bid to supply turkeys. Pretty good contract. They have five thousand inmates."

"It had to be more than just a low bid, chum. He had a clientele inside for liquor and maybe drugs. He could also smuggle out an inmate in his truck-bed, rolled up in a tarpaulin. Did you know he was transporting escapees halfway to Canada?"

"There was gossip, but no one would blow the whistle. It had to be an outsider like you."

Qwilleran told Roger about the cassette and his efforts to match it with voices around town. He wondered if he should reveal Koko's role in solving the mystery. The cat had found the cassette, directed attention to the prison connection and later to the turkey farmer, attacked the man when he broke into the cabin, and brought the final clue to light: the money clip.

No, Qwilleran thought. Roger wouldn't buy such a fantastic story. Aloud he said: "Let's drop this depressing subject. . . . Have you seen any extraterrestrial aircraft lately?"

Just before leaving, Roger said: "I almost forgot. Some woman from Down Below phoned the visitors' center. She wanted to know how to reach you. I took her number. You're supposed to call her soon as possible."

He handed over a slip of paper with the phone number of the *Morning Rampage* and the name of the woman who was managing editor.

Qwilleran returned her call, then drove into Mooseville—first for the formalities at the jail and then for dinner at the Northern Lights Hotel. He sat alone in a booth and longed for his pipe. If he decided to accept the terms of Fanny's will, his first act would be to order a couple of tins of Groat and Boddle Number Five. And if he accepted the new assignment at the *Fluxion* or *Morning Rampage* he would soon regard these two weeks in Moose County as a visit to another planet. Already his orange cap was beginning to look ridiculous.

After dinner he drove back to the cabin slowly, savoring every picturesque stand of birch, every grotesque jack pine, every sudden view of the raging lake as the highway dipped in and out of the woods. All the beauties of the landscape that he had ignored during the last two weeks now became treasures to stow away in his memory. He might never see this wild and wonderful country again, and he had not even taken the trouble to watch for the Northern Lights. Or a UFO.

A sheriff's car with the siren wailing sped past him, followed by the red truck of the volunteer fire department. Qwilleran's throat choked with dread and he pressed the accelerator. The cabin! The fire in the fireplace! *The cats!*

By the time he reached the Klingenschoen driveway the firefighters were working on a burning truck that had run off the road near the site of the old log schoolhouse. Several cars had stopped.

"Anyone hurt?" he asked the onlookers. No, they said. No sign of a driver, they said. Lucky it didn't start a forest fire, they said, considering the force of the wind.

As Qwilleran started up the long driveway a chilling thought occurred to him. The charred hulk looked like a blue pickup.

As soon as he parked the car he heard Koko howling inside the cabin. As soon as he unlocked the door the cat rushed onto the porch and dashed crazily from one side to the other, stopping only to jump at the rattail latch of the screened door.

Qwilleran found the harness in a hurry and buckled it around the taut belly of the Siamese. Then he played out the long leash and opened the door. Koko immediately bounded toward the toolshed, forcing Qwilleran into a painful run.

The door of the shed was open; that was unusual. The interior of the windowless building was murky, but Qwilleran could see money blowing around on the floor. Stealthily the cat stalked the deep shadows of the shed, unearthly moans coming from the depths of his chest. A gust of wind stirred up another flurry of bills, and Qwilleran kicked an empty whiskey bottle. Then Koko started to

howl—not his usual emphatic statement but a prolonged high-pitched wail. Qwilleran looped up the
slack of the leash and edged warily into the shadows.

There was one bright spot in the gloom. Lying on
the floor was a small handgun with a Florentine
gold handle. The body of the handyman was
sprawled on the shabby cot.

Snatching Koko, Qwilleran hobbled back to the
cabin and phoned the sheriff's dispatcher.

In a matter of minutes a deputy's car pulled into
the clearing. "We were right down there on the
highway," the officer said. "Pickup on fire. Total
loss. Looks like arson."

After the body had been carried away in the ambulance, Koko prowled through the cabin with long
purposeful strides, wandering everywhere, a portrait
of indecision. Yum Yum huddled with her haunches
elevated and watched him with concern.

Qwilleran stood at the front windows, staring at a
hundred miles of water. Who could fathom the
moods and motives of a poor fellow like Tom? He
was so willing to do anything suggested, so easily
exploited, so pleased to be given a job to do, a
pasty, or even a kind word. Fanny had bossed him
and given him a home; Hanstable had given him orders and a regular payoff that encouraged that unre-
alistic dream of buying a nightclub. Without them, it
seemed to Qwilleran, Tom had felt suddenly cut
adrift.

A burst of music interrupted his uncomfortable

reverie. It was the forceful introduction to Brahms' Double Concerto followed by the cello's haunting melody. Abruptly, in the middle of a phrase, the music was replaced by the spoken word—a gentle voice:

"I did it. . . . I pushed her. . . . She was a nice old lady. She was my friend." There was a choked sound. *"He told me* to do it. He said I would get a lot of money to buy a nightclub. He said we would be partners. . . . She promised me the money. She promised to leave me everything. She said I was like her son. . . . Why did she say it? She didn't mean it."

The voice trailed away, and the mike picked up the roar of the wind and waves and the cry of a cat. Then it cut out, and the music resumed with the plaintive theme and the solo violin.

Qwilleran coughed to dispel the lump in his throat. The cat was sitting alongside the stereo, studying the little red light. Qwilleran stroked Koko's head. "Did he say anything to you, Koko? Did he say goodbye?"

Mooseville, Sunday

Dear Arch,

Your news on the telephone has left me in a state of terminal shock. Now I have news for you! The *Rampage* has made a better offer, and they have a prettier managing editor. Do you think Percy is prepared to meet their terms?

There's been a little excitement here. We had
a B-and-E at the cabin, and Koko bloodied the
burglar. I almost got knifed by the same man.
He killed one of our neighbors last weekend.
Aunt Fanny died suddenly on Thursday, and
her houseman shot himself yesterday—in my
toolshed. Otherwise it has been a quiet vacation.

There is one little problem. The new assignment sounds great, but I've just found out that
I'm the sole heir to Aunt Fanny's sizable fortune. Naturally there's a catch. I have to live in
Pickax. What to do? What to do?

You won't believe a word of this, and I don't
blame you.

Qwill

As he ripped the sheet out of the typewriter the
two nagging voices in his head were still debating.
Be true to your profession, said the Dedicated
Newsman. *Take the money and run,* said the Canny
Scot.

Koko was sitting on the table studying the keys
and levers of the machine, while Yum Yum made
playful passes at his tail.

"Tell me what to do, Koko," the man said.
"You're always right. Shall I take the new assignment?"

Yum Yum was licking Koko's ears now, and both

cats were cross-eyed with enjoyment. "Yow," he murmured weakly.

Qwilleran huffed into his moustache. Was that *yes* or *no*?

Penguin Putnam Inc.

Online
Your Internet gateway to a virtual environment with hundreds of entertaining and enlightening books from Penguin Putnam Inc.

While you're there, get the latest buzz on the best authors and books around—

Tom Clancy, Patricia Cornwell, W.E.B. Griffin, Nora Roberts, William Gibson, Robin Cook, Brian Jacques, Catherine Coulter, Stephen King, Ken Follett, Terry McMillan, and many more!

Penguin Putnam Online is located at http://www.penguinputnam.com

PENGUIN PUTNAM NEWS
Every month you'll get an inside look at our upcoming books and new features on our site. This is an ongoing effort to provide you with the most up-to-date information about our books and authors.

Subscribe to Penguin Putnam News at http://www.penguinputnam.com/newsletters

"In every business and operation, and even with the best systems, stuff happens and we have to fix it. This insightful book reaffirms the fact that painful as it may be, we ultimately make things better after problems occur and no problem is bigger than we are . . . a great message for these times!"

> — Frank Vitiello,
> president, founder, and
> CEO, Vitech Systems Group

"Everyone has had that fickle finger of fate deal them a blow now and then. That's what this book handles so intelligently—how to deal with all that bad stuff and still have a happy life."

> — John Badham,
> feature film director, *Saturday Night Fever,*
> *Whose Life is it Anyway, Point of No Return,*
> *War Games, Stakeout, Drop Zone, Nick of Time*

"This book tells it like it is. Without the benefit of this information, some 'get it' some don't. Anyone can read this and 'get it!' The fact is that life throws stuff at all of us and fixing stuff is what growth, development, and survival in life is all about. According to Alston and Thaxton, no challenge is bigger than you."

> — Roger Crawford,
> USPTA tennis professional, speaker, and
> author of *How High Can You Bounce?*
> *The 9 Keys to Personal Resilience*

"In the global, competitive world of modern business, innovation and a timely response to market needs is the key to profits when stuff happens—and stuff will happen! This book is for those who want to achieve, sharpen their edge and meet the demands of the dynamic reality of the twenty-first century."

> — Dr. Glen Toney,
> retired Group Vice President,
> Applied Materials, Inc.

Praise for Stuff Happens (and then you fix it!)

"Every once in a while a book comes along that is both simple in its presentation and profound in its impact. This is such a book."
— From the Foreword by Jack Canfield,
coauthor, *Chicken Soup for the Soul*

"Bad stuff happens to everyone! This easy-to-read, lighthearted book takes the sting out of painful events and puts perspective into life by using principles that everyone can relate to. A must read!"
—Mark Victor Hansen,
co-creator of the #1 New York Times best-selling
series *Chicken Soup for the Soul* and
coauthor, *The One Minute Millionaire*

"We've all had bad stuff happen to us. In a fun reading way, this book, Stuff Happens, is invaluable for showing how to take that bad stuff, deal with it, and be thankful for the life you already have."
— Jerry Lewis

"Throughout life, stuff happens. Some good. Some bad. When the bad hits you, read this book. It can help you bounce back and feel like dancing again."
— Dick Clark

"This book has a lot of soul and if it seems that life has been dumping all kinds of stuff on you lately, sit down and read it. I'll make the bet that you'll soon stand up and sing I FEEL GOOD!"
—James Brown,
The Godfather of Soul

"*Stuff Happens* is a must for anyone who ever hit bottom at one time in their lives."

> — Mace Neufeld,
> feature film producer, *Sum Of All Fears,*
> *The General's Daughter, Clear and Present*
> *Danger, Beverly Hills Cop, Patriot Games,*
> *Hunt for Red October*

"It's about time that we get to read a book that is rooted in reality. *Stuff Happens* (and then you fix it!) is concrete, practical, and appealing and offers a sensible 'slice of life' view that is uplifting. It is a NO WHINE approach to life and its complexities that has a sweet simplicity of solutions."

> —Susan RoAne,
> keynote speaker and author of *How to Work a*
> *Room and The Secrets of Savvy Networking*

STUFF HAPPENS

(and then you fix it!)

STUFF HAPPENS

(and then you fix it!)

**9 Reality Rules to Steer Your
Life Back in the Right Direction**

JOHN ALSTON and LLOYD THAXTON

JOHN WILEY & SONS, INC.

Published by John Wiley & Sons, Inc., Hoboken, New Jersey.
Published simultaneously in Canada.

For general information on our other products and services please contact our Customer Care Department within the U.S. at (800) 762-2974, outside the United States at (317) 572-3993 or fax (317) 572-4002.

Wiley also publishes its books in a variety of electronic formats. Some content that appears in print may not be available in electronic books. For more information about Wiley products, visit our web site at www.wiley.com.

Library of Congress Cataloging-in-Publication Data:

Alston, John W., 1945–
Stuff happens (and then you fix it!) : 9 reality rules to steer your life back in the right direction / John Alston, Lloyd Thaxton.
p. cm.
Includes bibliographical references.
ISBN 0–471–27360–0 (cloth : alk. paper)
1. Life change events—Psychological aspects. I. Thaxton, Lloyd, 1927– II. Title.
BF637.L53 A47 2002
158—dc21   2002014904

Printed in the United States of America.
10 9 8 7 6 5 4 3 2 1

STUFF HAPPENS!

Life and reality are a combination of what
we do and what happens to us.
Stuff motivates us to get on with living!
Some get it. Some don't.
Some will. Some won't.
Those that do, do.
Those that don't, don't.

FIX IT

To make firm, stable, or stationary, or to give a permanence to final form. To set in order. Adjust. To get ready. Prepare, repair, mend, restore, cure. *(Merriam-Webster)*

To recover by improving, repairing, straightening out, getting unstuck, uprighted, and balanced after having been thrown off a bit when stuff happens. *(Alston-Thaxton)*

Acknowledgments

Thanks from John and Lloyd

To Senior Editor Matt Holt at John Wiley & Sons, whose enthusiasm and knowledge of how to write a good book pushed us along like a jet engine. He made it fun. He made it happen. He affirmed what we already knew: There's something worth reading here!

To our wonderful agents, the witty Michael Larsen and the lovely Elizabeth Pomada. They had the wisdom to yell, "It's a slam dunk!" when they first read our book and shared their excitement with us. And they also know the best restaurants in San Francisco!

To friend and colleague Jack Canfield, who wrote the wonderful Foreword. It certainly was chicken soup for our souls.

To Jerry Lewis, Dick Clark, Mark Victor Hansen, John Badham, Mace Neufeld, Roger Crawford, James Brown, Frank Vitiello, Dr. Glen Toney, and Susan RoAne. These talented and famous people took time out from their busy schedules to consider our little book and bless it with their endorsements.

To Linda Indig, Senior Associate Managing Editor at John Wiley & Sons, and Claire Huismann, Senior Project Coordinator at Impressions Book and Journal Services, Inc., and their teams, who gave us the wonderful look of this book and made sure we knew the difference between *its* and *it's*, *then* and *than*, and *who's* and *whose*.

From Lloyd

A big thank you and a kiss to my wonderful, talented, and very funny wife, Barbara. She always is able to make me laugh even when bad stuff happens. Her penetrating feedback and meticulous sense of continuity was essential to the writing of every single word in this book.

It's been about two years getting this material from the inside of our minds to the pages of this book. The catalyst for all this was and still is John Alston. My hope is that every reader of *Stuff Happens* will someday get the chance to hear John speak. He is the greatest. What I learned just from listening to him talk could (and will) fill the pages of many books to come. Thanks, John. You certainly fixed my stuff. I am so proud to be a part of your life.

From John

Many thanks to my daughter, Lindsay, for her love and support. And to my lovely wife and partner, Karen Mills-Alston thanks for being there when I wasn't always organized and on track. No one achieves anything alone, and the partnership we have and the teamwork we engage in has made all of this possible.

To my speaking colleagues of Gold Coast Speakers, who encouraged my forward momentum as a cheering squad while I struggled between professional and personal obligations.

To Lloyd Thaxton, my partner in the most wonderful writing collaboration I have ever had. This book is balanced in effort between the two of us in every sense one can imagine. Energy, insight, and all the spirit makes for the tempering of the 9 steely reality principles.

There is nothing more satisfying when you are hungry than to have a good dining experience and not just a mouth-stuffing, stomach-filling, fast-food special, wolfed down while rushing to the next appointment. I mean a dining experience with wonderful ambiance, relaxation, good drink, sumptuous food, and stimulating conversation with an exchange of ideas, sentiments, and humor.

Good stuff happens when you get the right mix going. You have to have a good recipe, the right ingredients, the right company, collaboration, and time to put it all together. You taste the dishes as you progress to ensure that what you are preparing is on course for creating a satisfying experience. Such was the way this book came about. Lloyd Thaxton and I, with a range of diverse experiences, verified the 9 principles herein, which resulted in a true collaboration.

This could not have happened without us working together. So to Lloyd, my friend, colleague, and cowriter, I say thank you for being in the kitchen, where we endured the heat and created food for thought. Thanks for being there, thanks for being you and for contributing to what we've forged together to create a dining experience for hungry minds.

Contents

Foreword

Jack Canfield
Coauthor, *Chicken Soup for the Soul*®

Every once in a while a book comes along that is both simple in its presentation and profound in its impact. This is such a book. It contains 9 rules about reality that can significantly and positively change your life—deeply and permanently. All you have to do is read this book and apply these powerful principles to your life.

This book is written by two award-winning authors: John Alston—award-winning speaker, educator, and author—and Lloyd Thaxton, five-time Emmy award—winning television personality, writer, producer, and director. I first met John Alston in 1982 when I presented him with the Foundation for Self-Esteem's Golden Apple

Award for his unique contributions in the field of education. Since that time John has gone on to write four wonderful books and to win the highest award presented by the National Speakers Association — induction into the CPAE Speaker Hall of Fame.

In addition to their 50 years of combined experience in studying the human condition, John and Lloyd bring their own life experiences, including lots of ups and downs in the challenging and competitive fields of entertainment and professional speaking, to the writing of this book. These are two successful guys who have seen a lot of stuff happen and who have earned the right to talk about how to "fix it."

That's what *Stuff Happens (and then you fix it!)* is all about — the realization that life, as good as it is, is going to shovel some dirt on you now and then. Stuff happens! The point of this book is that it's not what happens to you that's important. It's how you respond to what happens. And how you respond depends on how you think, feel, believe, and live your life — how you deal with reality. To realize that nothing makes you change, improve yourself, or make a positive move in your life until you deal with the stuff that happens. In other words, nothing happens until stuff happens.

Stuff Happens (and then you fix it!) offers 9 reality rules to help you prepare for and deal with all that stuff — to fix it and get your life back on track. It is filled with stories of people bouncing back from all kinds of big and little problems by applying one or more of the 9 reality rules.

Some of this stuff is pretty demanding. But as the authors point out, "Never confuse that which is hard with that which is impossible." Just because something is difficult to do doesn't mean it can't be done!

John and Lloyd say, "Some get it. Some don't. Some will. Some won't. Those that do, do. Those that don't, don't." If you read this book, you're sure to get it. And then you will be one of those who does instead of one of those who doesn't. And you will be better off for it—much better off!

Stuff Happens (and then you fix it!) is an uplifting can-do book with a happy ending. The happy ending is your life—the life you have always wanted but have not yet created. What could be more refreshing than that?

Introduction

Thanks for picking up our book, *Stuff Happens (and then you fix it!): 9 Reality Rules to Steer Your Life Back in the Right Direction*. If you've read this far, you're already off to a good start.

You most likely were intrigued by the title. After all, stuff happens to everyone—in fact, without stuff happening, nothing would happen at all. Stuff is the catalyst for change in our lives. Good, bad, indifferent, there is stuff happening to us all of the time. It just so happens that when people say, "Stuff happens!" they are most often referring to bad events that make them miserable. Things such as job loss, divorce, a sense of failure or unworthiness, unhappiness concerning one's career choice, a loss of material possessions, a relationship gone bad, and so on. All trying events, but without stuff happening we wouldn't change. This isn't to say that we want bad things to happen to us, but face it, it's inevitable. Bad things will continue to happen to us all. Pain is nature's doorbell. It gets our attention. The trick is how we deal with this bad "stuff." It isn't what happens to you that's important—it's how you respond to what happens.

The goal of our book is to offer approaches and advice to the millions of people who suffer from bad stuff that happens to them. We give you, the reader, 9 reality rules to help fix these problems and get your life back on track as fast as possible. We are driven by our beliefs, a philosophy that drives us to affirm that life is a gift—don't trash it.

We certainly don't suggest that every problem has an easy fix. Sometimes there are very difficult decisions to make, pains to endure, and complex stuff to deal with. Life can be hard. But we encourage you to come to the awareness that hard does not mean impossible.

Life is good. Yes, bad stuff will continue to happen. Jobs will be lost, marriages will end, and relationships will go sour. Accidents will occur, and we will always need wisdom and help to get through all those big and little obstacles to living a good and meaningful life. In the process, new relationships will form, opportunities will be created, and joy will be rekindled. We hope that some of the answers to your problems are in this book and that by reading it, you will find a way over, under, around, and through all the stuff that happens.

Pain may be a wake-up call, but loss is many times there to remind us of what not to take for granted. It is all balanced out as we put forth our effort and direct our energies supporting, encouraging, inspiring, and energizing each other to be the best and most decent human beings we can be.

Throughout this book we use stories to illustrate how people deal with stuff that happens and how they've fixed it. Most of the stories are either composites of people we know or based on situations that actually happened to one of us. In stories like The Donkey Story and Sam and Tom, the authors are unknown and were passed to us from friends, relatives, or acquaintances. The stories of Laura Hillenbrand, Itzhak Perlman, Roger Crawford, Charles Plumb, and John Naber are based on real-life stories. They all inspire by offering proof that when bad stuff happens, it can be fixed.

If you, the reader, have a "stuff happens" story you would like to share with us for our next book, e-mail it to stuff@stuffhappens.net, or mail it to Stuff Happens, 419 N. Larchmont Blvd. #9, Los Angeles, California 90004.

Prologue

The most common use of the phrase "Stuff happens!" is when bad stuff happens. Bad stuff has the ability to get in our way, slow us down, or stop us from achieving what we want to achieve. But in reality, stuff is the fertilizer of life. Stuff gets our attention, and stuff makes things grow.

Reality does not stop because stuff happens to you. Remember when you were a kid? There were public parks filled with recreational equipment that you loved to play on. There were jungle gyms, swing sets, and tetherballs. One of the most fun pieces of equipment was the push-around merry-go-round. It was like a large flat plate and had handles that stood up extending from the center and sectioning off portions of the plate like pieces of pie. It had to be pushed by all the kids to get spinning; then you would all jump on and ride it until it slowed down. Once it stopped, you would push it again and jump on. It was fun. But if you fell off while it was rotating, that was it. You couldn't get back on again until it stopped. What was more, no one stopped it in order for any victims of a fall to dust themselves off and get back on. If you fell off, you just had to wait for another opportunity. Stuff happens!

In the wake of such setbacks some kids would yell, "Hey, wait for me!" Sometimes that worked. There were some who would wait and lend a hand. But more often than not, they didn't wait.

Well, that's life, isn't it? Like the push-around-merry-go-round, life doesn't stop for you just because stuff happens. Life goes on. If you get sick, lose money, go through a divorce, drop out of school, or have a child before you are ready, the world and life continue to spin on and on.

There is a poster of a man climbing a very sheer and rocky cliff. The caption reads, "If it is to be, it is up to me!" This suggests that when it comes to achievement, initiative, and individual effort, it is a choice that each of us is responsible for, and it is up to each one of us to make it happen.

One of the great things about life is that it's never too late to start living; it is only too late if you never begin. Here's the good part: you can begin right now. If you want to learn how to get off the ground when stuff happens to you, read on.

Finding a way over, under, around and through. . .

Reality Rule #1

Wise Up,
Stuff Happens!

Control your impulses or they will control you. It's not what happens to you that's important, it's how you respond.

The Dot.Commer Who Dot.Bombed

•

Harry was very successful. He lived well, drove a Porsche, and had all of the latest high-tech accoutrements, games, and software. He had the cell phones, pagers, laptop computer, online services, and credit cards. He had just made the down payment on a million-dollar home, a piece of cake for Harry. After all, his personal stock portfolio was climbing at a fantastic rate, and he was on his way to becoming a rich man.

He had it all figured out. How was all of this possible at 27 years old? Easy. Harry was the top computer whiz at

Some get it, some don't. Some will, some won't.

Sureshothotshot.com in Cupertino, California, in the heart of Silicon Valley. The future was bright, and the sky was the limit. His company's stock had doubled, then split. They were on a roll. Harry was a happy man. And why not? He had done all of the right things.

He worked long hours, including weekends. He fulfilled every expectation and followed all the rules. He saved his money, saw his dentist twice a year, rotated his tires, ate five servings of vegetables a day, jogged every morning, never left the house with torn or dirty underwear, drank bottled water, got eight hours of sleep a night, avoided too much fat, salt, sugar, and alcohol, deleted old e-mail daily, kept up with the latest tech news, never sat on public toilet seats, called his mother once a week, obeyed the law, had a yearly physical, went to church, gave to charity, and remembered everyone's birthday. Harry had the perfect life—he had the perfect future.

Harry never saw it coming. Despite all the positive hoopla and all the promises, stuff happened. That light at the end of the tunnel turned out to be a speeding train. Without warning, he was given notice. The business had tanked, and the doors to Sureshothotshot.com were locked for good.

After 2 years, 6 months, 3 days, 2 hours, 17 minutes, and 47 seconds of thriving and surviving, they were out of business.

It got worse as 10 other companies also went from dot.com to "dot.bomb." Besides his being on the street, Harry's personal stock plummeted from $95 to 50 cents a share. This sudden turn of events shook Harry to the core, especially when he realized he had nowhere to go. As it

Those that do, do. Those that don't, don't.

turned out, all the other companies he had a relationship with were also dot.bombers. Harry was no longer needed.

"What is happening? Why me? What did I do wrong?" was Harry's lament. His savings wouldn't last forever. Especially now since the close of escrow had made him the owner of a healthy mortgage payment.

"Besides this," Harry asked, "If stuff happens once, what will prevent it from happening again and again and again?" The truth? Nothing. "I did everything right! Why should life be such a worry and struggle?" Harry became worried and frustrated.

•

What to Do, What to Do

Face it. It doesn't matter if you're the whiz at a high-profile dot.com business like Harry, a blue-collar worker in the same job for 20 years, or someone just trying to make it through life. Stuff happens!

Harry's story as told here represents the composite of every person who at one time in their lives has had their dream shattered. Harry had that dream. As a result of his efforts, good stuff happened, and he achieved a lot at an early age. Then the rug was pulled out from under him, and bad stuff happened! Once the bad stuff happened, Harry had to close the door on that former aspect of his life, where comfort, accommodation, and enormous profit made his life a joy. He had to look for another door to open.

There are many stories of people who suffered losses, tragedies, betrayals, setbacks, abuse, and failures. Some are big and some are small. Some are quite simple, like the plumber not showing up and the pipes are still leaking. Some are due to the person's own ignorance or flaws, some are due to the stupidity or the boneheaded plays of others, and some are due to the luck of the draw, fate, karma—whatever you want to call it.

So what do you do? Either you learn how to "fix it" or you adapt to it and move ahead by uttering the only verbal cure we know of to get you back on track—"Next"—and you move on. There is no sense in assuming the position and waiting for a solution to knock at your door.

> "There are two great tragedies in life. One is to lose your life's dream, the other is to get it too early so you have nothing to validate yourself or your life."
> James Michener

Control Your Impulses or They Will Control You

Impulse control is one of the virtues we ascribe to mature individuals. Some people believe that blowing off steam is a good thing to do. They may go off the rails a bit or fly off the handle. Harry could have ranted, raved, and gone ballistic. However, nothing is fixed when you are dealing with the normal stuff of life and fail to control your impulses. So often when stuff happens, our initial response is one of hurt, fear, anger, and frustration, sometimes accompanied by emotional thoughts, ideas, and even rage that can blind us. Then there is the moment when a wise person thinks again. Wise people rarely shoot from the hip; they slow themselves down enough to think a second time.

Fixing It!

Practice getting used to handling stuff by changing your life and building an inner switch you can turn on or off at will. Remember rule #1: "It's not what happens to you that's important—it's how you respond." Realize that you can't change others, but you can and do influence them by how you respond. What is the switch? Simple. The word *Next!* Saying "Next!" is like asking, "Okay, what do I do now, in this instant, to handle this and move on?" You might even consider coupling the phrase "Thank you" with "Next" Why? When painful stuff happens, it's reality's way of getting your attention. Suppose there were no pain? You would not be alerted to something that needs your attention. "Thank you" and then "Next" can be very powerful.

You have to think of the experience as fertilizer, and use it to make yourself grow. To start, throw out the bitter stuff and concentrate on the sweet. What sweet? Well, first thing, you are alive, you are present, you have resources, and you have ability. There is a void for you to fill. The important thing in life is that it isn't what happens to you that's important. It's how you respond to it. Use it or lose it.

•

A farmer's donkey falls into a well. The animal cries piteously for hours as the farmer tries to figure out what to do. Finally, he decides that the animal is very old, and the well needs to be covered up anyway. So he grabs a shovel and begins to shovel dirt into the well.

At first, the donkey cries horribly. Then, to the farmer's amazement, he quiets down. A few shovel loads later, the farmer looks down the well and is astonished at what he sees. With every shovel of dirt that hit his back, the donkey is doing something amazing. He shakes it off and takes a step up. As the farmer continues to shovel dirt on top of the animal, the donkey shakes it off and takes another step up. Pretty soon, the donkey steps up over the edge of the well and trots off.

•

Moral of the story: Life, as good as it gets from time to time, is sometimes going to shovel some dirt on you…all kinds of dirt (stuff happens!). The trick is to shake it off and take that first step up. Each of our troubles is a stepping-stone, and each of us has what is required to get up, over, and out of the deepest wells by not giving up and by seeing the truth and handling what comes. We can get out of the deepest wells by not giving up! We can "get over it!"

The Cellular Olympics

But we're getting ahead of ourselves. Let's start at the beginning. THE REAL BEGINNING. Consider this: You started out life as nothing but a puny little member of the Cellular Olympics. There you were, working out in the cell's gymnasium with millions of other ab-obsessed cells, doing curls, jumping jacks, and swimming laps. Then all of a sudden they ordered, "Everybody to the platform," and there you were on the starting block with the number 2,345,367 printed on the back of your shirt. Then, boom!

The starting gun fires, and everybody takes off. You most likely don't remember any of this, but it was a tough race. All those millions of contestants heading for the same goal.

And guess what. You not only made it—you won. You were number one. You, and only you, were awarded the egg. And if you remember your basic biology, as soon as just one cell gets in that egg, all the rest are shut out.

BEYOND BELIEF

Being number 1 out of over 200 million cells means that you won the lottery. It's like becoming president of the United States. Think about it: 1 in over 200 million.

Congratulations. You have just learned and fulfilled the first requirement of life, the prerequisite for success: SHOW UP! You showed up, and you're already ahead of the game. Life in essence has said yes to you. You are worthy to participate in the next phase of this thing called life!

Okay, so you won your first race. You showed up. What now? Well, for nine months, more or less, you sat in that little tiny room. Life was good, you were hooked up, and it was nice and relaxed. You could just lay back and take it easy. Mom ate a little food, and you thought, "Hey that's pretty good. A little chili, a little spicy, but I can handle that. A little Thai food, you know. Oh, that Italian. Yes, I like that." That was the life.

Then just as you were really settled in—bam! They kicked you out. You were born (talk about stuff happening). And you came into the world without the benefit of instructions. You asked yourself, "What do I do now? How do I work?"

You see, the most important thing we need to know in life is learning how to operate ourselves without that set of written instructions. We don't even rate an owner's manual. Did you see any instruction tag on your toe? No way. This was the first time in your life when you realized you had no idea what to do when stuff happens.

Even without instructions, though, it didn't take you long to learn that you could get just about anything you wanted by crying. After all, it was the only way you had to communicate. You cried, and someone responded. Cool! When you were too hot, you cried; when you were too cold, you cried; when you were tired, you cried. When you were uncomfortable, needed to be changed, restricted from doing what you wanted, lost something, or had a toy taken away, you cried. After all, stuff was happening all around you, and what else was a baby to do? "Look at me! I am the center of the universe."

You cried for somebody, anybody, to "fix it"—make it better. "Gimme, gimme, gimme. Mine, that's mine. I want it now. I am entitled to have what I want!" Then, too soon, there came the day you were told, "If you want something, you are going to have to get it yourself. No one is going to feed you, bathe you, support, and take care of you the rest of your life." Hey, this life thing was starting to get complicated. Why were they changing the game on you? Stuff happens!

This is when you must first start putting together the stories of your life. The stories you accumulate over time. The stories based on your experiences that you hold as the center of your life.

READ ON

Whatever you thought might be in this book, our guarantee is that you will find the encouragement, support, information, and knowledge you need to become more effective. Knowledge that will increase your ability to handle all that stuff out there.

REALITY RULE RECAP
Reality Rule #1

Wise Up, Stuff Happens!

Control your impulses. It's not what happens to you that's important—it's how you respond.

- Stuff happens. In a universe of unlimited opportunities, where things can change in an instant, stuff happens. Even though, like Harry, you think you are doing everything right, what happened should prompt you to start preparing for stuff.
- With preknowledge and controlled intelligent responses, you can handle any stuff that that comes your way. Preparation won't prevent stuff from happening, but it will enable you to handle things better.
- You can't control everything, but you can always control how you respond to things. It may not be your fault, but it is your responsibility.
- Impose discipline on your impulses by making it a practice to "catch" your first impulse. Think before you act. Here are some things to try. They might just stop you from doing something you could later regret:
  — Breathe.
  — Suck in your stomach and tense your muscles.
  — Be still for this instant. Know that you are in control right here and right now.

— Realize that you are ahead of the game because you won the race and SHOWED UP! For this moment in time, be thankful you woke up this morning.

— Imagine that what is going on now is a movie. Now choose to act your role. Write the story, and direct your own performance and desired outcome.

— Keep saying: "It's not what happens to me that's important — it's how I respond to what happens."

— Like the donkey in our story, be prepared to shake stuff off and take those necessary steps up and out.

What do you do now? Now that you are calmed down? Read on.

Wise up,
Stuff Happens!

Reality Rule #2
Take Action

To Win, You Have to Begin

Take that first step.

Get Real

Let's talk a little bit about reality. Reality only respects action!

•

Three ministers were asked at a forum, "What would you like people to say when they look at you in your coffin?" The first minister said, "I want them to say that I was a good man who was faithful to his God and to his congregation." The second minister said, "I want them to say that I was true to my calling and helped many people have better lives." Then

Some get it, some don't. Some will, some won't.

it was the third minister's turn. His reply was, "I want them to say, 'LOOK. HE'S MOVING!'"

•

Taking Those First Scary Steps

Here's one thing you can be sure about: Gravity works! Gravity will never let you down. But to manage gravity, you have to learn how to use one sense that is rarely mentioned with the five senses—taste, touch, sight, smell, and hearing. It is the sense of balance. We can count on gravity, and we must count on our sense of balance to manage to remain upright.

> "The only ones who get anything done by just standing around are mannequins."
> Dean Koontz

Let's get back to Harry, the dot.com expert who lost his dot.com job. Like all of us, he first came into the world totally uninformed. It took a while, but he knew that sooner or later, he would have to figure things out. And when he was born, one of the first things Harry discovered was gravity. BAM! He couldn't walk without falling down. But wait a minute. He saw other people moving around, he heard different things going on, he wanted to learn how to move, and he wanted to do what everybody else was doing: stand up and walk around. So Harry started to move, and BAM! Down he went again. Stuff was happening big time.

It didn't take Harry too long to figure out that in order to get from A to B, he had to first learn how to balance on

Those that do, do. Those that don't, don't.

one leg. However, he found out that when he stood on one leg, this was when he was most unstable. This was when he was most vulnerable to being knocked over, to falling down. So in order to get from A to B, he would just have to make his first move. Pretty scary.

Harry never was that brave. He didn't do it all at once. He started out first in a crawl, but gradually, he did learn how to take that first step. Harry was smart. He didn't become a dot.com expert when he grew up by being dumb. He quickly determined that the longer he stood balanced on one leg, the more unprotected he became. But he knew he had to make his move and make it sooner, not later.

A DIZZYING THOUGHT

Gravity may knock you down, but if you respect it, gravity will never bring you down. People who do stupid things are trying to defy gravity.

Harry is now back at work. Not as a dot.com expert but as a consultant in a computer software company. It's not exactly what he wanted, but he knows the way back. He also knows that stuff could possibly happen again. No problem! He's prepared for it if it does. He knows the right steps.

And that's how life works. If you're going to make a change in your life, you have to stop all that indecision and teetering and take that first step. Yes, you will be nervous; yes, you will be frightened and you will be anxious. Every time you try to challenge gravity, you're going to experience a certain anxiety, discomfort, and sometimes even fear or shame. But you have to do it.

> WARNING
>
> If after you read this book, you go back to doing the same thing that you did before, you will have wasted your time. And your time is the most valuable thing you possess.

Somebody once said, "You are born and you die and everything in between is negotiable. The only thing you have between birth and death is time. How you use your time will define your life." So if you're not interested in improving your life, stop reading now. Don't waste your time.

•

Noted motivational speaker **Roger Crawford** *was born with one leg and no hands. Bummer. Just a finger on one arm and only two fingers on the other. You know what else Roger does for a living? He teaches tennis. Some of you may be saying, "No way!" Yes, there is a way. He wears an artificial leg, and on the arm with the one finger, doctors implanted a thumb from a toe. He takes the one finger, puts it in the bottom of the racket, and places the two fingers from his other arm at the top. He then tosses the ball up and wham! Another "ace." Roger played on a four-year tennis scholarship at Loyola Marymount University. He had to beat 47 guys to make the team, and he did. How did he do it? Because a friend said, "Roger, you can!" and he believed it. Roger did not stand still. He took that first step.*

•

Change Your Story

In the previous chapter, you were told that you start writing the story of the rest of your life the minute you are born. This is important because there is enormous power in stories. If you don't believe stories are powerful, go back to when you were younger. Think of the many childhood stories you no longer believe in, stories that had a tremendous power over your life. The tooth fairy for instance. You would take your baby teeth and put them under the pillow, and the tooth fairy would leave you money. For a kid, the tooth fairy was a powerful story. It was all a lie, of course. But this shows you: A lie can be as powerful as the truth if you can get someone to believe it.

> **KID LOGIC**
>
> One time I went over to my grandmother's house, and her teeth were in a glass. I said, "Grandma, why don't you put them under the pillow? You've got a fortune here."

How many remember believing in the bogeyman? You probably still come home late at night and, if the house is dark, reach around the wall to turn on the lights. Why do you do this? Because, admit it, you still believe in the bogeyman. It's a powerful, powerful story.

As we get older, we drop one set of stories to take on another. Some of us keep some stories that inhibit us. "I was never good in math" is one story we hear a lot. "I don't know, I've always been that way. I can't change" is another. "I can't do it. I just get so embarrassed." And on and on and on and on.

Remember this: Not feeling like doing the right thing is no excuse for not doing the right thing! Sometimes you just have to get over that embarrassment in order to take that next step. Stop trying to tell the same old story. Sometimes for you to get from A to B, you have to change the story. To change your story, change your mind. Go back and look at the story and change it.

It's interesting how people live their lives. Remember, you are born and you die, and everything in between is negotiable. As we move through life, we keep collecting the stories about ourselves, about the world, and about the nature of things. The power of believing in those stories enables us to focus and make things happen. Whatever you believe to be, you act out. It's as if we all have our own drama, our own soap opera that we star in.

> **LIFE'S SONGS**
>
> It's amazing when you listen to the stories told in country and western music. "If you want to keep your beer cold, put it next to my girlfriend's heart." Or, "I'm so lonesome since you're gone it's almost as if you're here." Or, "When your phone don't ring you'll know it's me." As amusing as those lyrics are, they still sum up a lot of people's lives.

We each have our own stories, and we live out the drama. They're based on our past experience and what people tell us. There are a lot of things that keep us from looking ahead, but by and large, it's the story you believe that either helps or hinders you. Change your life? Start changing your story.

THE ULTIMATE MOVERS

Every morning in Africa, a lion gets up and knows that she must run faster than the slowest gazelle or she will starve to death. When the gazelle gets up, he knows that he will have to run faster than the fastest lion or he will be killed and eaten. So whether you're a lion or a gazelle, when you get up in the morning, you've got to get going.

A Call for Action

Wow, you say. All this is not going to be easy. The methods for dealing with life when stuff happens are never going to be a piece of cake or a walk in the park. We're talking about some big changes here. And before anything changes—before you can change—you have to get up off that couch and move it. "Action speaks louder than words" is not an empty quote.

SOLUTIONS

Easy? No! Impossible? No! Doable? Yes! But "doable" means "doing it." Just reading this book and not doing it is like reading the directions on a soup can and not making the soup.

The fact that you've even read this far is proof that you are in the game and ready to play. But are you actually ready to get moving?

REALITY RULE RECAP
Reality Rule #2

To Win, You Have to Begin

Take action! Take that first step.

When you were born, here are some of the things you discovered:

- Gravity.
- You couldn't walk without falling down.
- The longer you stood balanced on one leg, the more unprotected you became.
- You had to make your move sooner, not later.
- To get from A to B, you had to take that first step.

And that's how life continues to work. If you're going to make a change in your life, you have to stop all that indecision and teetering and take that first step. Every time you try to challenge gravity, you're going to experience a certain anxiety, discomfort, and sometimes even shame. The first time you tried to walk, you stumbled and fell down. But to succeed, you had to do it. And you did. It worked then. It still works.

Up to now, you've operated on the stories you believe in, your own personal little dramas, your own soap operas that you act out every day. If you want to change your life for the better, you have to change your story.

If you don't believe all this, think of the many childhood stories you no longer believe in, stories that once had a tremendous power over your life:

- The tooth fairy.
- Santa Claus.
- The bogeyman.
- The Easter bunny.
- The monster under the bed.

They were all lies, of course. But, hey, you believed. *And a lie can be as powerful as the truth if you can get someone to believe it.*

As we get older, we drop one set of stories to take on others we believe. But too many of these stories are downright lies. Falsehoods you keep believing that hold you back. Take a moment and list some of the stories (lies) you still believe. We'll start you off with some familiar ones. You fill in the rest.

1. I'm stupid.
2. I've always been shy. I can't change that.
3. I don't have enough education to succeed.
4. I can't do it.
5. Life stinks!
6. Stuff happens to me because I deserve it.
7. (Start adding your own here.)
8.
9.
10.

Come on, you can think of more than four. Throughout this book, you'll find tools for changing your story. But they just won't work unless you fess up.

> Some get it. Some don't. Some will. Some won't.
> Those that do, do. Those that don't, don't.

We'll talk about this next.

Reality Rule #3
Get Knowledge

Knowledge Is Power

Some get it. Some don't. Some will. Some won't. Those that do, do. Those that don't, don't.

Some Just Don't Get It

> Question: If there is an "it" in life to get, what is it?
> Answer: The "it" is knowledge.

Francis Bacon said, "Knowledge is power!" What he didn't say, and what is equally valid, is that ignorance also has power. What you don't know can hurt you. Ignorance has the power to stop, delay, and prevent prosperity and growth.

There are basics to know and respect about reality. Water quenches thirst, and water can drown you. Fire can

Some get it, some don't. Some will, some won't.

warm you, and fire can destroy. Gravity works, keeping you on the ground, and just one misguided move slams you down. We also must respect the fact that even with the best-laid plans, stuff happens. When stuff happens, it can thwart our best intentions for enduring, thriving, and surviving. Fixing what we can has to be our goal. To do this there is much to know. What often hurts most people is that they just don't know how to live their lives.

It has been said that pain is inevitable but that suffering is optional! In life we suffer more by choice than by happenstance. And too many times we make bad choices based on lack of knowledge.

Facts

In our view knowledge consists of three things. First, knowledge requires facts. You have to know the facts of life, the situation you are in, and then you have to apply them.

Take, for example, Heather and Mickey, who are planning a three-week safari through Africa, which includes going to Kenya and the Congo. They would both be in a lot of trouble if they were to merely rely on imagining what they needed. Although it is important to imagine and visualize taking a trip, dreaming is not enough. *To make dreams come true, you have to wake up!*

Heather and Mickey have to have real knowledge of what the journey will be like and what is required to complete the journey successfully. Their survival and pleasure they derive from the trip will depend on finding out what reality demands.

Those that do, do. Those that don't, don't.

How does this apply to you? Whether you are going to Africa or just going to work, you still have certain realities to face. What you experience on life's journey depends on where you want to go, where you start from, and the resources needed to make that journey a successful one.

For our travelers, this means that to guarantee a successful trip, they must read the latest books and the most current articles and brochures, take instructions and directions, listen to and consult with experienced experts who have made the trips, and rely on the advice of well-informed and well-meaning local residents as well. They may require the assistance of guides, agents, and local-resident experts accustomed to assisting others on such adventurous trips. To do anything less than plan ahead would detract from the success and pleasure of their journey.

Life is the same in this regard. If you are to make the best of the journey, you must know the nature of the challenge. You must know the nature of reality and what it demands and the nature of the field and terrain on which you will travel. You must have the facts.

Skills and Techniques

The second aspect of knowledge consists of skills and techniques. Some skills require practice in order to achieve mastery. These skills make it possible for people to excel, develop, grow, and advance. Like our African travelers, you must know the skills necessary to traverse the land and deal with the people you may encounter.

It's no different when hiking through the terrain of life. You need to develop certain skills and techniques to make your life a successful adventure.

Thinking

Finally, there is thinking. There is no question in our minds that some ways of thinking are more beneficial than others.

Ask a lot of kids the question, "How do you like your school?" and many times the answer is, "It stinks." Sound familiar? What kind of thinking and experience has led to that conclusion? Is this just kid talk?

Maybe so, but many adults go to work each day with that same attitude toward life. What is going on in their heads? After years of routinely getting up, going to work, coming home, and going to bed, many have come to the same conclusion: "Life stinks!"

In a world loaded with opportunity, conveniences, easy access to water, soft or hard beds of their choosing, good food, electronic marvels, and more, why are so many people unhappy with their lives? They just don't get it. They don't have a success system in place and only see the world from their own limited life stories. Failures see walls as obstacles. Successful people see walls to climb.

So, because we know stuff can and will happen, we must take control of that which we can control. That starts with designing a successful system for yourself.

Designing a System

Write this down and put it someplace in the back of the book:

> Every outcome is the result of a perfectly designed system for achieving that outcome.

You may not completely understand this statement now, but when you finish this book it will become very clear.

Take a chocolate-chip cookie recipe for instance. It's a system for putting ingredients together to get a great cookie. So think of life as a cookie. To have a great life, it's important to put together the right ingredients.

•

Ashley took his mother to the ophthalmologist. While he was sitting in the waiting room, the doctor came out and said, "I just want you to know that I think your mother is a remarkable woman." He then went on and on about how lovely, special, and wonderful he thought she was.

This wasn't the first time Ashley had heard this about his mother and wondered about what it was that she did that had so many people thinking she was so wonderful. To make so many people like her. In this case she had not spent a lot of time with this doctor. They never socialized outside the office. And this reaction was the same with just about every person she came in contact with. Ashley was perplexed. Was his mother operating on a system?

•

Ashley's mother did in fact have a system. But, like Ashley, she was probably not aware of what it was. She may have never taken note of the ingredients in her system. She may not have even thought of it as a system. It was "just her way."

You most likely have known people like this. If so, write down their names and make a list as to some possible elements of their system. Then compare your list to our list regarding Ashley's mother's system:

- She smiles a lot.
- She's appreciative and tells people how grateful she is.
- She's interested in the people she meets, wants to know about their lives, and finds out information in an innocent way without seeming nosy or intrusive.
- She compliments others on their achievements.
- She has a positive attitude and speaks of nothing that might be depressing.
- She is willing to listen and leans toward people in a friendly way.
- She says "thank you" and lets people know they are worthy of praise and respect.
- She makes small talk easily.

Make note of this list. It is a good system for drawing people to you and gaining their good will, admiration, and respect. These are the people you'll need to rally around you when stuff happens.

Once more: "Some get it. Some don't. Some will. Some won't. Those that do, do. Those that don't, don't." Are you going to be one of those who don't? Or one of those who do?

The fact that you are still with us means you are interested in improving your life. Keep reading, and we will show you how to get it!

Keep this in mind. As you gather knowledge, you will also gather many different feelings. There are a lot of times in life when you just won't feel like doing something you must do. As a matter of fact, you most likely won't feel like doing a lot of the things suggested in this book. If that's the case, highlight this:

> Not feeling like doing the right thing is no excuse for not doing the right thing.

Practice Makes Perfect

Okay. So you learn the right thing to do. What then? Practice what you've learned. Like learning how to walk, you not only have to learn — you have to practice. To learn how to play the piano, you have to practice. To learn how to do anything well, you have to practice. It's the same with your mind. To learn how to control your mind, you must practice. Designing the right system for yourself and living by it takes practice.

As we said before, there is a way of thinking that can cause you to bottom out, to feel defeated, to think of life as too depressing. Too many people say, "I can't do it. This won't work." There is a more powerful way of thinking that will help you focus your energy and make everything work. We'll discuss this technique later in Reality Rule #6 ("To Change You Life, Change Your Mind").

Yes, knowledge is power. However, ignorance is as powerful as knowledge, pulling you in the wrong direction. When we talk about knowledge, we also have to talk about common sense.

COMMON SENSE
The observation and application of those principles that tend to govern reality, the violation of which causes us to ask, "What the heck were you thinking?" When you make a bonehead mistake, ask yourself, "What the heck was I thinking?"

On Being an Oxymoron

Here's a bit of useful knowledge:

In order to be free, you must first be a slave.

This may seem to you like an oxymoron. How can you be free and also be a slave? Actually, it makes a lot of sense. In order to be free, you must be a slave to discipline. A slave to doing the right thing. Discipline is an enabling force.

Discipline will help you stay on course whenever stuff happens. Discipline will help you get through the deepest stuff imaginable.

The height of maturity is the ability to impose discipline over your impulses. How many of you procrastinate? How many of you give advice that you don't even take yourself? How many of you have ever gotten involved in an argument with someone and halfway through the argument figured out you were wrong but kept on arguing? If you answered "yes" to each of these questions, you are due for a change.

ONE MORE TIME
Just because I don't feel like doing the right thing is no excuse for not doing the right thing.

It should be obvious by now that this book is mostly about change. You should not be the same when you finish reading it. Think about this. Johnny comes to school and cannot read. By the time Johnny leaves school, what should he be able to do? Read. That's a change. Diane comes to school and can't do calculus. By the time she leaves school, what should she be able to do? Calculus. That's a change. You read this book. What should you be able to do? And don't say "read and calculus." You should be able to make a better life for yourself. Whenever stuff happens, you should be better equipped to fix it and get back on track.

Remember One Thing

Is this all getting to be too much for you? You don't have to remember everything you read here. But try for at least one thing. Work with that one thing. Put it together and practice. Remember that facts in and of themselves don't change people. Skills and techniques don't change you unless you use them and apply them. A recipe means nothing until you bake the cake.

And thinking alone doesn't do it. You have to be willing to do the work. Sometimes it's hard, and you will always be nervous taking that step from A to B, but you'll never get there unless you first stop balancing on the one leg and take that first step.

Easy? No. Impossible? No! Remember, never confuse that which is hard with that which is impossible. You will make mistakes. But catch yourself. And rewrite your story to fit a new you.

The only reason that this kind of book even exists is because we all make mistakes. Humanity is flawed. Stuff happens! We don't do the right things all the time. We put our foot in our mouths. We say stupid things when we shouldn't. We refuse to move ahead when we need to move ahead even if the opportunity is right there. The key word here is *change!*

Speaking of Change

On the television show *Friends,* all the main characters are close friends. Although they have their own little quirks, they all seem to have the same goals in life. They all want to be successful and happy. It's just make-believe of course, but this is actually where art imitates life. What has all this to do with you? Here's the lesson. If you want to change your story, start examining who *your* friends, mentors, and associates are.

> "I can tell more about a man, not by his speech, but by the company he keeps."
> Martin Luther King, Jr.

You see, like the cast of the television show, your friends and associates are the costars in your life's story, and they will shape your life from beginning to end.

There's an old saying that goes like this: "You can lie down with dogs, but if you do, you better believe that you will wake up with fleas." What this means is that whom you associate with will make a huge difference in how your life turns out. So pick the best.

Think about this. In sports the best players like to practice their sport against better players than themselves. They want the challenge. They need the challenge. They know this is how to become better players. Life is no different.

If you feel you're not up there where you think you belong, start looking around at who you hang out with. If you think that they may be holding you back, it's time to make a change, to start playing with people who are better than you are. Environment is a powerful motivating force. If you want to move out of that rut, you may have to start hanging out with a better crowd.

Write It Down

We're going to repeat this mantra throughout the book: To know what is really going on in your mind, it is essential to write things down. The words we write allow us to see how we think, to see what we are accomplishing as we gather knowledge.

Writing things down and looking at them is feedback. Later on we'll emphasize the importance of feedback to assist us in staying on track, remaining balanced, and moving forward.

Remember that today could be the first day of your new story; a whole new life for yourself. So start today by putting your thoughts on paper. If you don't, your mind will play tricks on you. You're going to forget some

MIND TRICKS
How many of you have been sitting in a meeting or school or some other learning situation, and your body was there but your mind was somewhere else? How many have gotten up and gone into a room and couldn't remember what you went in there for? How many of you have found a piece of paper with a telephone number on it and didn't know whose number it was?

pretty important stuff. It's a fact of reality that things un-recorded just seem to get lost.

Your mind will play tricks on you, and if you don't control your mind, somebody else will. Writing things down is all part of helping you understand how to operate yourself. And it's a great way to record how much you've changed, how close you are to your goal. It's all part of the overall plan: How to "fix it" when stuff happens!

REALITY RULE RECAP
Reality Rule #3

Knowledge Is Power

Some get it. Some don't. Some will. Some won't. Those that do, do. Those that don't, don't.

The fact that you are still here reading this book tells us that you're one of those who get it! You're seriously looking for the knowledge to fix it when stuff happens.

Knowledge consists of three things:

1. Facts.
   - To make dreams come true, you have to wake up.
   - You must know the nature of the terrain on which you travel.
   - You must know the facts.

2. Skills and techniques.
   - To achieve mastery in a skill requires practice.
   - Skills make it possible for people to excel, develop, grow, and advance.

3. Thinking.
   - Certain ways of thinking are more beneficial than others.
   - People who don't appreciate all the wonders of life don't get it.
   - Those who don't get it see walls as obstacles.
   - Those who get it see walls to climb.

Every outcome is the result of a perfectly designed system for achieving that outcome.

The Chocolate Chip Cookie System

- 2 1/4 c. all-purpose flour
- 1 tsp. baking soda
- 1/2 tsp. salt
- 1 c. butter
- 3/4 c. granulated sugar
- 3/4 c. light brown sugar
- 1 tsp. vanilla extract
- 2 eggs
- 2 c. milk chocolate chips

Heat oven to 375°. Sift together flour, baking soda, and salt. In a large bowl, beat butter, granulated sugar, brown sugar, and vanilla until creamy. Add eggs; beat well. Gradually add flour mixture, beating well. Stir in milk chocolate chips. Drop rounded teaspoonfuls onto ungreased cookie sheet. Bake 9 to 11 minutes. Result: 6 dozen cookies.

A recipe is nothing more than a successful system for putting ingredients together to get a specific outcome. Life is not unlike a cookie. It's important to put together the right ingredients.

Are you starting to get it? If not, go back to the beginning of this chapter and look at the ingredients in Ashley's mother's recipe-system. That should provide a good start for your system.

A recipe alone will not make a cookie. You have to take action. Discipline will help you stay on course whenever stuff happens. Discipline will help you get through the deepest stuff imaginable.

Remember at Least One Thing

- Facts, skills, and techniques won't change you unless you use them and apply them.
- A recipe means nothing until you bake the cookies.
- Thinking alone doesn't do it.
- You've got to be willing to do the work.

AND...

- Consider hanging out with a better crowd.
- Put your thoughts on paper.
- Control your mind or someone else will.

Some get it. Some don't. Some will. Some won't. Those that do, do. Those that don't, don't. Are you going to be one of those that do?

Still here? Good. Read on.

Reality Rule #4

Be Prepared

*Some stuff will happen for sure.
Sometimes it's to remind you of what you
take for granted.*

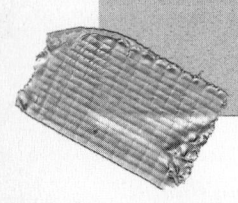

Prepare Yourself

Here's the number-one fact about reality: Life is hard. It's difficult. You struggle with it; you have your ups and your downs. You go up one step, back two. Sometimes stuff happens and you experience pain. It's going to rain sometimes, so get prepared for the rain. That's a fact in this game of life. But if you are prepared for it, you can overcome the problem and pull yourself back up.

•

A couple of old friends, one a priest and the other a rabbi, for years spent time together sharing observations about the

Some get it, some don't. Some will, some won't.

foibles of life, the passing of time, the misadventure of youth in popular culture, and the ways things were changing. They would go to plays, sporting events, and movies and would get together over coffee to discuss philosophy and current events. On one occasion they went to a boxing event, a prize fight. As they sat in the arena and watched two formidable fighters come into the boxing ring, the rabbi became fascinated by one of the fighter's prefight warm-up ritual. The fighter would bend, stretch, jump up and down, and ever so often stop, bend over on one knee, and using his right hand, cross himself.

The rabbi watched for a while and after the fighter had done this three times, turned to his friend and asked him, "What does it mean when that fighter does that?"

The priest looked at the fighter, then back to the rabbi and said, "It doesn't mean a darn thing if he can't fight!"

•

The moral: You must prepare. Not preparing for what you know will come is detrimental to your well-being in the face of reality. Were the fighter in the story to merely do stretching exercises and pray, regardless of his intentions, being ill prepared would get in his way of success. Preparation requires a systematic way of training. He needed to spar with other fighters, do the road work, have a coach, a trainer, a nutritionist, a physician, the right equipment, and an aptitude for fighting, and be guided every step into the appropriate workout routine in order to go for the gold.

Those that do, do. Those that don't, don't.

One thing we can say here for sure is that in life there are some inescapable facts of reality, things you can count on. For sure, water wets, fire burns, cold freezes, gravity works, you are here reading this material, and stuff happens.

With this in mind, there are things that we think are essential to know and act upon. Because we know that stuff can and will happen, what can we do for sure?

It is all balanced out as we put forth our effort and direct our energies supporting, encouraging, inspiring, and energizing each other to be the best and most decent human beings we can be and taking control of what we can control.

We start with preparation. If we know that some things are eventually going to happen or that something is more likely to happen in a given situation, and we fail to prepare for it, we are not doing what common sense dictates or what reality demands of us!

In other words, get ready by being prepared because there will be stuff that happens that you can count on happening. The only way to get ready is to prepare for it.

> For all thy days prepare
> And meet them
> ever alike.
> When you are the
> anvil, bear!
> When you are the
> hammer strike!
> *Edwin Marham*

Make Bad Stuff Work for You

When stuff happens, it demands work on your part to fix it. You can get hurt and heal. You can suffer loss and learn from it. What's really exciting about it is that you are alive. (Always be excited about being alive!) And you are growing from the stuff that's happening. Life is embodied in a universe of unlimited opportunities. Too many people don't get full enjoyment from their lives because they are always worried that something bad is going to happen to spoil everything. Toss out this negative approach right now! Reverse your thinking process. Instead of something bad happening to you, think about the possibility that something good could happen to you at any moment. The lottery is out there to be won. This is life. Relish it. When stuff happens, use it to grow.

●

Joanne is an actress. Of course, a lot of people in Hollywood call themselves actors. All it usually takes is a picture and a resume to qualify. But Joanne was an employed actress and had worked hard to get all those parts on television shows and network commercials. Hundreds of interviews and cattle calls had paid off. She had an agent and good casting-office contacts. The big break came when she landed an ongoing roll on an afternoon soap opera.

Yes, Joanne had made it. The nice paychecks kept on coming. There was the new Jag that whisked her nightly to her new house in the Hollywood Hills. She had a closet full of designer clothes to wear to all the "in" restaurants. During the fourth year of the show she even won an Emmy.

That was the good news. The bad news was that she won her Emmy for her flawless portrayal of a dying woman. The producers of the soap opera decided that the story called for her character to die. And although the character died in a blaze of glory, Joanne became another out-of-work actress.

Because Joanne was on the same show day after day for four years, she never actively kept up with what was going on outside her little world. All her previous show-business contacts had either moved on or out. Her agent had stopped calling long ago, and she now found herself out of the loop.

It didn't take long before there was no Jag and no house in the hills. Was it all just a mirage? What a shock to be a well-paid actress and then see it all dwindle down to nothing.

> "Failure is the opportunity to begin again more intelligently."
> Henry Ford

But Joanne was fortunate. She happened to be strong willed and was able to shake it off and get moving again. Instead of sitting around and complaining, she took advantage of what she had learned from this experience. It wasn't easy. It meant the daily grind of finding a new agent and going back on those awful cattle calls. But most important, she learned she must constantly keep up all her contacts, to stay in the loop.

After going to several auditions Joanne landed a small role in a small independent movie and got good reviews. Her phone started ringing again.

Joanne is now making regular television appearances, and her prospects for the future are bright. All she needed was to keep herself out there, to keep building momentum, and to use the skills she had accumulated on both the climb up the *ladder and the slide down. Joanne is on her way back up. Could the Jag and the little house in the hills be far behind?*

•

The moral of Joanne's story is that her first failure had actually helped her attitude. The possibility of failure is one part of living (stuff happens). You have to learn from it and use it to your advantage.

•

*To most people, **Itzhak Perlman** needs no introduction. His international reputation as an outstanding violinist of the twentieth and twenty-first centuries is well known. What is not so well known is that at the age of four he lost the use of his legs to polio. Although he has braces on both legs and walks with the aid of crutches, this has no effect on the brilliance of his performances.*

At first, it might be a little disconcerting to see him walk slowly and painfully across the stage to his chair, unhook his braces, and sit down. But any possible embarrassment on the audience's part quickly disappears the moment he picks up his violin and strikes his first note.

But according to reports, something happened during one concert at Lincoln Center in New York City that might have changed all that. It seems that after he played just a few bars, the audience heard a sharp, loud snap. One of Itzhak's strings had broken, and everything came to a complete halt.

The possibility that Itzhak would now have to repeat his torturous walk across the stage to find a replacement for the broken string sent a silent shudder through the audience. But Itzhak never wavered. He simply signaled the conductor to continue and picked up the music from where he had left off.

Everyone in the audience knew that the concerto couldn't be played with three strings. So what was he trying to do? Itzhak was doing the impossible. He was actually re-composing the music in his head, making adjustments, and even tuning the strings as he went along. He was determined to continue the piece with what he had left.

At the conclusion, the audience sat stunned in silence. But this lasted only a moment. In seconds they rose to their feet cheering, applauding, and shouting. This went on for almost five minutes before Itzhak raised his hand. The audience sat back in their seats and listened as he said, "Sometimes it is the artist's task to find out how much music you can still make with what you have left." The audience again rose to its feet and cheered until Itzhak left the stage.

●

In this story you'll note stuff happened twice. First, when Itzhak Perlman was struck, but not struck down, by polio at age four and lost the use of his legs. And second, when the string broke in the middle of his concert.

Itzhak Perlman prepared all his life to make music on a violin. Then, all of a sudden, in the middle of a concert, stuff happened, and he found himself with only three strings. No "Why me?" here. Itzhak Perlman could still make great music. He was prepared, and it paid off.

Of course, you don't have to be a musician to apply this lesson to your own life. In this fast-changing, sometimes bewildering world, we all have to make our life work, at first with all that we have and then, when that is no longer possible, with what we have left.

No More Excuses

Truth? Most stuff that happens to us is sudden, and we have no control over the situation. But we can be prepared. Certainly, there are earthquakes, tornadoes, some accidents, catastrophes, and other disruptions that can't be avoided. On the other hand, much of the stuff we have to deal with in our everyday relationships, we create ourselves. But we also have the ability to create the right or wrong ways we respond to this uncontrollable stuff.

Keep saying it. It's not what happens to you that's important—it's how you respond to what happens. We can choose to be responsible or not. It is a matter of choice.

Some people use the bad stuff that happens to them as an excuse for their failures in life. We call it SGV2 (Stuffgeneratingvictimitus).

> **SGV2 SYMPTOMS**
> One who is full of excuses, selfish, a braggart, a blamer, a talker who never listens and, most of all, a person who walks, talks, and looks like a victim.

•

Calvin attended college, graduated class of '67, and immediately moved to Los Angeles. He loved the fast lane, wine, women, and song. No doubt about it, he was fun, lovable,

and gregarious, always the one to find a party or create one.
Calvin loved to run the streets in search of another party. He
was noted for having a full-time job and being full-time
broke. When asked why, he said, "Hey, stuff happens!"

He was always in a hurry, yet he was always late. When
asked why, he said, "Hey stuff happens!"

Calvin eventually met a young lady and married her,
but he continued to keep late hours, leaving his wife alone.
One night he came home to find his apartment engulfed in
flames. Fortunately, his wife had escaped to safety. When
asked about where he was, he said, "I got tied up, you know,
stuff happens!" Finally, his wife said, "I've had enough!"
Tired of all the rumors, being left alone, and being called
paranoid, she left Calvin and filed for divorce. All Calvin
had to say afterward was, you guessed it, "Hey, stuff hap-
pens!"

●

When Calvin said, "Stuff happens," he was totally
abandoning, or ignoring, the idea that he was the one in
charge of Calvin, no one else. It is possible that Calvin
didn't know how to be any other way. Perhaps he lacked
the insight, wisdom, and skills required to get on a different track. In this case, lack of knowledge about what to do
was a problem. A problem that only Calvin could correct.

The first thing Calvin had to do was pay attention to
what was happening to him and accept the truth—to
change his attitude toward it. You have to change what

made things in past situations bad for you. You have to be-have in a new way. It is *your* conduct that *you* must change or control. You must accept responsibility.

Above all, don't be a victim. You too could come down with SGV2.

REALITY RULE RECAP
Reality Rule #4

Be Prepared

Some stuff will happen for sure. Sometimes it's to remind you of what you take for granted.

How to prepare for stuff:

- Acknowledge that you live in a universe of unlimited possibilities.
- Know that each of you is subject to the impact of any and all possibilities.
- Acknowledge that no problem is bigger than you are and that you have all you need to meet every challenge.
- Realize that you can handle any stuff that comes. It's just a question of balance.

Take a piece of paper and make a balance list consisting of two columns. On the left, write down what you consider to be your weaknesses. On the right, put down what you think are your strengths. And be honest with yourself. Nobody but you is going to see this list.

Weakness Examples	*Strength Examples*
• I'm not very good at my job.	• I'm a good learner
• I don't like criticism.	• I'm willing to work hard.

After you've made your list, start using your strengths to compensate for your weaknesses. It all becomes a question of balance.

Itzhak Perlman reached the balance by practicing to be the best at his profession. When his violin string broke in the middle of a concert, he called on his mastery of the violin, which had come from years of practice (his strength), to compensate for the weakness caused by the broken string. He then went on to finish to a standing ovation. Stuff happened, and he was able to fix it.

Don't expect too many standing ovations in your life, however. If you sweep floors for a living, your accomplishments are not going to be greeted by a roaring crowd. But that should never stop you from using your strengths to be the best floor sweeper you can be. If you're a waitress, win an award for being the best in the room. If you're the boss, make it a point to be a better boss. That's preparing for success.

When stuff happens, it usually leaves you little power over the situation. But when one of your strings breaks, you should at least be prepared to control what you can control. And never take your good life for granted. Don't wait for stuff to happen to appreciate what you already have.

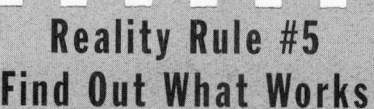

Reality Rule #5
Find Out What Works

Working Hard at What Doesn't Work Doesn't Work!

Reality only respects action. Ya gotta do something!

The Wrong Direction

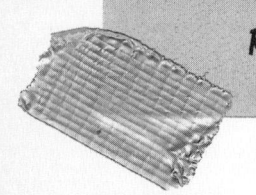

Still here? Good, you're getting further ahead in this game. Highlight this right now: What works works; what doesn't work doesn't work. Here's the clincher: Working hard at things that don't work will never make them work.

A man leaves Kansas for a vacation in Canada. Halfway there, he discovers he's headed for Mexico, the exact opposite direction. So what should he do? Drive faster? Does that work? No! Working hard at things that don't work will never EVER make them work. You have to find out what works.

Some get it, some don't. Some will, some won't.

•

Todd was 14. He was handsome, bright, and given the privilege of a private-school education. But he never seemed to be able to make friends and was easy prey for bullies and unfair teachers. His answer was to blame the school, the teachers, and the other students. To solve this problem his parents kept changing schools.

However, regardless of which school he was at (three in one year), the same stuff kept happening, and each time Todd always had someone else to blame. Although he was bright, he continued to get poor grades, he still couldn't make friends, and he was picked on. "It's not my fault" became his mantra. Todd did not realize that, like Calvin in Reality Rule #4, he was also suffering from SGV2 (Stuffgeneratingvictimitus).

It became obvious that continually changing schools wasn't working. Then one day in the schoolyard Todd saw a younger boy being picked on by a couple of bullies. For some reason he stepped in to help, and the bullies ran away. Instead of thanking him, the younger boy walked away, muttering over his shoulder, "It was their fault, not mine." It was then that Todd realized he was looking at himself. And what he saw was someone he didn't want to be.

For the first time he started looking at the other students, the popular ones who had lots of friends and got good grades. He studied them in order to find out what worked for them—why they were so well liked by the teachers and all the other kids. He found out that it wasn't the fact that they were good looking or wore cool clothes that made them

Those that do, do. Those that don't, don't.

popular. After all, he also wore cool clothes. It was their attitude. They listened when other kids spoke. This showed they were really interested. They walked like winners and took responsibility for their actions. Something clicked, and Todd decided to mimic the students he wanted to be.

It took a while, but eventually he saw his new Todd persona begin to work. Before long he was completely cured. He no longer had SGV2, he had lots of friends, and he graduated with honors. Todd managed to change his life.

●

What worked for Todd could work for you. You see, Todd finally got it. Got what? That you can't change all situations, conditions, or other people, but you can change yourself. And although things occur that may not be your fault, your response when stuff happens should be to accept some responsibility and make changes in yourself.

Todd used to ask "why" when he should have asked "what." "Why don't people like me?" instead of "What is my goal?" He was always thinking about what to say or do. He should have thought more about the response he wanted to get.

What can parents do to show kids like Todd that they have the ability and the responsibility to handle stuff that happens and to make changes in their own way of doing things? To stop doing things that don't work?

First, let them know that their feelings have been heard and respected and are being taken seriously. Todd admitted that he was picked on and that it hurt. People learn to deal with feelings more effectively when they don't have to defend, smother, or hide them.

Second, kids like Todd must have it made clear to them that they are adding to the situation by the way they respond to it. And they can only begin to change things by actively playing a new role. Study the achievers, the winners, the movers and shakers, and do what they do.

FACT

SGV2 (Stuffgeneratingvictimitus) is not limited to schoolyards. It happens in business, families, and anywhere people are trying to just get along. The cure is always the same.

Be What You Want to See

Always keep in mind that in changing your life routine, the magic is you. The control of you is inside. Know the role you must play in making things better, and then, like Todd, act the part. When you act the part, you become the part. In other words, act like a jerk and you'll not only refine the skill of being a jerk, you will generate a reputation for yourself as being someone nobody wants to be around. The act of mimicking people you want to be like is a great tool for making changes in your life.

Here's the drill. Look for people who are good at influencing other people and mimic their behavior. Act positive and you will become positive. Be what you want to see.

You want people to be patient? You be patient. You want people to be inquisitive? You be inquisitive. You want people to be considerate? You be considerate. Be what you want to see. You want people to listen to you? You listen to them.

We've all had bad days when stuff kept happening and wondered, "Oh no, what next?" Don't let it throw you off track. Just keep repeating the mantra you learned in this book: It's not what happens to me that's important—it's how I respond to what happens.

Sitting around and moping when stuff happens just doesn't work. And that is what this book is all about: finding out what works and moving forward. If it's working, you keep doing it. If it's not working, it's time to change. And the first thing you have to change is yourself.

Exercise: The Dance That Mom Taught Us

We keep using the word *change* like it is an easy thing to accomplish. It's hard. We've all been conditioned to follow certain rules in our lives. Mothers spend a lot of time convincing us to "get it." Get the knowledge, the facts, the religion, the habits, and the right thinking. They taught us that if we do X, Y, or Z, we maximize the odds of certain good things happening. But if we do 1, 2, or 3, we maximize the chances of certain bad things happening. Is this starting to sound familiar?

First, you're told to get an education. Then, get yourself a good job. Then, find someone you love and get married, and have children, and then for the rest of your life that is your story. And not only do you have your story, you create music to go with each story and dance to the music. You dance to the music of the story that you believe.

It goes like this: Get up, go to work, come home, go to bed. Get up, go to work, come home, go to bed. Come on, you know the steps. In case you're not the best of dancers, we've provided an easy diagram for you to follow.

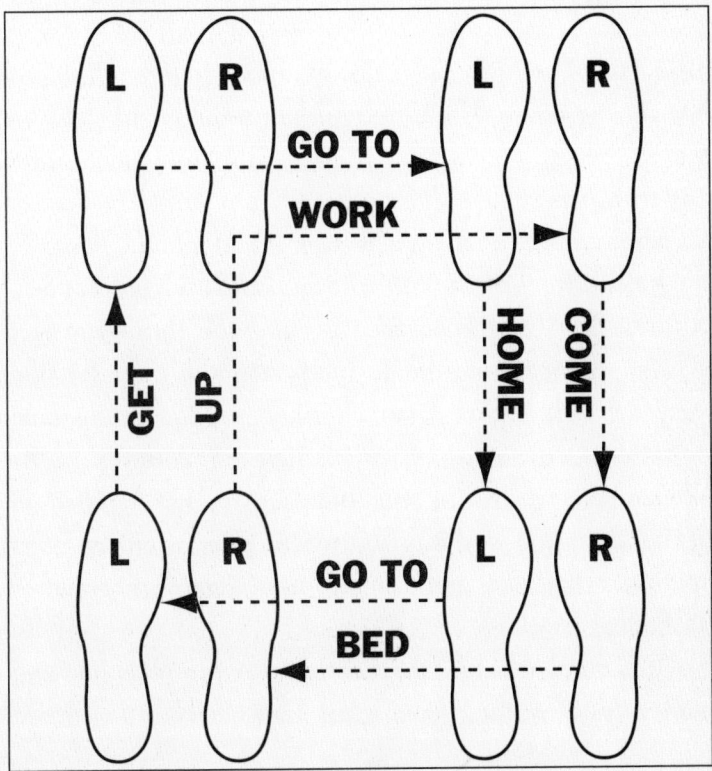

Got it? Okay, stand up and try it. Just follow the diagram. Just dance and sing along. One, two, three, four: "Get up, go to work, come home, go to bed. Get up, go to work, come home, go to bed."

Of course, if you are a mother, the dance is a little different. To do this, you add one step. "Get up, go to work, come home, *go to work,* go to bed." If you are doing this dance for real, do you consider yourself in a rut? Hey, change the dance.

•

Tom came home from work one afternoon to find total mayhem in his house. His three children were outside, still in their pajamas, playing in the mud, with empty food boxes and wrappers strewn all around the front yard. The door of his wife's car was open, as was the front door to the house.

Proceeding into the entry, he found an even bigger mess. A lamp had been knocked over, and the throw rug was wadded against one wall. In the front room the television was loudly blaring a cartoon channel, and the family room was strewn with toys and various items of clothing. In the kitchen dishes filled the sink, breakfast food was spilled on the counter, dog food was all over the floor, a broken glass lay under the table, and a small pile of sand was spread by the back door.

Tom quickly headed up the stairs, stepping over toys and more piles of clothes, looking for his wife. He was worried she may be ill or that something else serious had happened. He found her lounging in the bedroom, still curled in bed in her pajamas, reading a novel.

She looked up at him, smiled, and asked how his day went. Bewildered, he looked at her and asked, "What happened here today?" She smiled again and answered, "You know every day when you come home from work and ask me what in the world I did all day?" "Yes," was Tom's incredulous reply. "Well," she said, "today I didn't do it."

•

Tom's wife wanted to change her dance. You want to learn something? Just look around. You will see people doing their dances in many different ways. There are some people who come to work and are very uptight. They agonize over every step of the dance. Then, there are those who love to dance that dance. They're happy. They love their jobs. They feel lucky just to be alive. Leave them alone.

However, if that dance isn't working for you, it's time to make that change. Time to change your story. Change your dance. Take that first new step.

One way to do this is to first single out what's good about your job and concentrate on that. Forget those negative "Why me's?" and try and make your job interesting. If that doesn't work, then…well…. What works works. What doesn't work doesn't work. You have to stop working at things that don't work, take the next step (from A to B), and move on.

Before we continue too far in this "change" thing, you must start doing something right away. You must start organizing that very valuable time of yours. Begin by writing things down. Make notes to yourself. Keep a diary. Examine where you are now and where you were 10 years ago. Look at where you want to go, what you want your life to represent.

DAYTIME ONLY PLEASE

Go to a cemetery. Note that each gravestone has a name and a couple of dates, for example, "Charles Swindoll, 1840–1932," and between those two dates, there's that tiny little dash. That dash (–) is supposed to represent Charles Swindoll's entire life: 92 years. What a put-down. That infinitesimal dash says nothing about the people he helped and nurtured. It says nothing about the children Mr. Swindoll may have raised or sired. It tells nothing about how he lived his life, the kind of person he was. We want you to start right now thinking about what your dash will stand for.

The Do-It-Yourself Obit

Try this. Take out a piece of paper and write your own obituary. Gruesome? No way. This is life we're talking about here. Start out by listing the people you love and who love you. Note the accomplishments you've made in your life, no matter how small. Married? Raised kids? Jobs you've held. Charities you've worked on. Anything. Do you consider yourself a good person, a kind person? Write it down. If you feel your list is too short, add the things you want to accomplish in the rest of your life. Write it as if you have already done them. And then start doing them. If you want your dash to mean something, remember that reality only respects action.

REALITY RULE RECAP
Reality Rule #5

Working Hard at What Doesn't Work Doesn't Work!

Reality only respects change. Ya gotta do something!

Of all the reality rules, this one is most likely the one you will keep repeating long after you finish this book. If stuff keeps happening to you, it's time to analyze what you keep doing that isn't working. Todd's parents, for example, kept changing schools to solve his problems. That didn't work. Todd himself kept blaming others but soon found he was like the man who set out for Canada and headed for Mexico instead; driving faster just didn't work. Todd had to find out what worked.

Here's the drill: Write down all the things you are doing that aren't working for you. For example:

- I hate my job.
- I can't seem to make friends.
- I'm bored.
- I have no life.
- Nothing I do seems to work.

Beside this list, write down the names of people you know who fit the following:

- They love their job.
- They make friends easily.

- They never seem to be bored.
- They appear to have a great life.
- Everything they do seems to work.

Now start doing what they do. Study what makes them love their jobs, how they make friends so easily, and what makes their lives work. Then be what you want to see. The act of mimicking people whom you respect is a great tool for finding out what works.

In other words, if it ain't working, fix it!

Reality Rule #6

To Change Your Life, Change Your Mind

A positive attitude begins between your ears.

Getting a Grip on It

Remember your newly learned mantra: It's not what happens to you that's important—it's how you respond to what happens. One common response to stuff happening is anger. Anger sometimes is justified. But it is very important to get a grip on your angry impulses.

Feelings never tell us what to do; they are only messengers that tell us that something needs attention.

There's certainly enough going around these days to make one a little edgy, isn't there? When the economy slows down, a tragedy or some other unfortunate event oc-

Some get it, some don't. Some will, some won't.

curs, and people get laid off—not to mention the dot.com–to–dot.bomb mess—what's a normally rational person to do?

Frustration and stress have become almost the norm. Living in a universe of unlimited opportunity means that anything can happen at any given moment, both good stuff and bad stuff.

FIRST: It's important to be mindful that life is the time you have between birth and death. How you use your time defines and shapes your personal experiences.

•

*When Olympic athlete **Wilma Rudolph** was told as a child that she would never walk, her angry response was, "I'll show them!" Years later Wilma traded in the crutches, leg braces, and corrective shoes for running shoes and became the first American woman to win three Olympic gold medals in track. Known for breaking racial and gender barriers, Wilma positively used anger to achieve worldwide fame and respect. Stuff happened, and Wilma fixed it.*

•

Where we put our energy will make a difference in what we do. Before you speak out in anger, always consider what you want the response to be. Wilma refocused her energy. Can you focus your energy? You bet! But you have to do it mindfully. You have to be aware of what you are doing in the moment you are doing it.

All of us are entitled to and have access to the full

Those that do, do. Those that don't, don't.

range of human emotions. We have to remember that feelings never tell us what to do. They are only messengers, telling us that something needs attention.

Today there are plenty of reasons to be angry. Anger is a natural, emotional response to threat. Whether that threat is to our physical well-being, to some thing we value, or to our sense of self-respect, we've all experienced this powerful feeling. Pain, emotional hurt, deception, or betrayal can elicit anger as well.

Some of us have the ability to naturally channel anger into positive action; anger over poverty and blight drives some to move out of destitution. Others are immobilized, driven to violence, or defeated by anger. Then there are those who have cultivated and developed the ability to respond with grace and style.

Maintain Control

It's been said, "Those whom the gods would destroy, they first make angry!" In the workplace anger can be used to motivate and sustain an effort to achieve, or it can breed self-defeating attitudes that contribute to counter-productivity.

Regardless of whether we view anger as positive or negative, it's important to approach it as an attitude that can be controlled. Once anger is addressed from a new perspective, individuals can view it not merely as an uncontrollable, instinctual urge but as a chosen response to a stress-inducing situation when stuff happens.

Most people who react negatively to angry feelings are people who have simply never learned how to positively cope when stuff happens. Anger is one of the most powerful emotions.

Stay in the Present

When stuff happens, acknowledge what is happening at the moment it begins to happen. Be mindful of what you have tended to do and when. If it is a negative response, a potentially destructive one, you have to redirect it. Only you can do that.

Remain current with your emotions. Don't allow things to smolder and build up. Find someone to talk to before it gets to be too much for you to handle.

Take note of your feelings. There's no doubt that some events, conditions, or things that people do can bring out the worst in us. We all have a dark side that can throw us into an unpleasant place. Some of us have to consciously impose discipline on our impulses; others do it with greater ease because their threshold for frustration is higher. It's important to know when you are moving toward anger.

Be Productive

The key is not to be misled that you have to get it out by yelling, screaming, ranting, and raving. A lot of times "going off" just makes things worse. Getting it out or coping in a productive way might mean that you do one or more of the following:

- Talk it through with someone who will listen.
- Write out what's bothering you.
- Exercise to the point of exhaustion; run, walk, dance.
- Meditate to music.
- Find the humor in the situation.
- Move into a different environment. This means getting with people who are uplifting or finding a job or relationship where there is less frustration and greater ease of flow and movement.
- Use anything that can help you reframe your perspective and adjust your attitude. How do you know an attitude? You know it by what you say and what you do. Put a conscious watch over your mouth and your behavior.
- Think again, and reframe your perspective.

What does this mean in the grand scheme of things? Some things are worth getting angry about but not worth flying off and unthinkingly shooting from the hip. Too much of this, and you will be known as a person with a bad attitude.

A Good Attitude or Bust

> FACT
> No one likes to be around a person with a bad attitude!

Many times one of the most important changes a person must make in order to deal with life when stuff happens is a change in attitude. How many of you have heard the comment, "That person has an attitude problem"?

What do other people think about your attitude? It's easy to recognize a good or bad attitude in other people. But it's not so easy when it comes to judging yourself. This attitude-judging thing is very important. If you want to change your life, you must consider changing your attitude.

Your attitude is the ultimate weapon in the battle for strengthening relationships and gaining that competitive edge and getting back on track. To succeed in life and overcome difficulties, you must learn how to use your best attitude to influence other people in a positive way.

Think about it:

- A lawyer must influence the jury or the judge in a positive way. If not, an important case is lost and a client goes to jail. If you were on a jury, would you be influenced by a lawyer with an "attitude problem"?
- A bellhop must influence the hotel guest and a waiter the customer in order to get a good tip. How many of us judge the amount of a tip we give on the attitude of the person receiving the tip? Bad attitude: low tip. Good attitude: good tip. Great attitude: sky's the limit. We can all learn something from that bit of truth.
- The coach of your favorite team must influence the team to win. Coaches' attitudes as they talk to and

train the team are sometimes the only difference between winning and losing the game. Think of life as a game and you as the coach of your destiny. Are you going to be a winner or a loser?

- When you interview for a job, you must influence the interviewer to get that job. How does one usually get the job? The interviewer sees that the job seeker has a positive attitude. If the position is available and you go into the interview with a positive attitude, you'll have a good chance of getting the job. And keeping it.

On the other hand, a bad attitude can earn you the reputation as being hard to work with. This causes people to avoid you as much as possible. Why? Because unpleasant people are seldom surrounded by people who care. If you don't realize this and make a change in your attitude, you will be caught off guard when stuff happens and there will be no one there to help.

> People may forget what you said. People may forget what you did. But people never forget how you made them feel.
> *Source unknown*

How important is all this attitude stuff? Whether you are in your own business or work for someone else or just want to develop and improve your personal life, you are only as successful as your ability to create and maintain positive human relationships. The ability to manage your attitude not only is important to people you work with but is just as important to your own self development and personal advancement.

The fact is that when you help others you help yourself. A good attitude enables us to turn even the most difficult situations into constructive stepping-stones, helping us to handle the most demanding challenges. A positive attitude enlivens, uplifts, and moves us to pursue great things.

On the other hand, people with negative attitudes rarely advance in their jobs. They think of themselves as being right and entitled to success in spite of how they behave. They just can't understand why, when stuff happens, others move forward while they continually stay behind. These negative achievers usually succumb to (here it is again) SGV2 (Stuffgeneratingvictimitus).

> "People who need people are the luckiest people in the world."
> From the musical
> *Funny Girl*

They have all the symptoms. These "victims" blame others, or events, or bad luck for their failure, not realizing that their own negative attitude caused the situation. This attitude turns people off, and people need people to succeed.

Why? Because first of all, they frequently bring talents, skills, and resources that may be viable and essential to assisting you in achieving what you want.

Second, they may add to the ease with which you move through life when stuff happens and accomplish your goals. It is important to take note of what others think—and even more, how they behave in your pres-

ence: The goal is to influence people in a positive way.
Third, they just might be there when you most need them.

•

*Charles Plumb was a U.S. Navy jet pilot in Vietnam. After
75 combat missions, his plane was destroyed by a surface-to-
air missile. Plumb ejected and parachuted into enemy
hands. He was captured and spent six years in a communist
Vietnamese prison. As a motivational speaker, he now
shares his story to more than four thousand audiences
around the world.*

*One day, when Charles was sitting in a restaurant, a
man at another table came up and exclaimed, "You're
Plumb! You flew jet fighters in Vietnam from the aircraft
carrier Kitty Hawk. You were shot down!"*

*"How in the world did you know that?" asked Charles.
"I packed your parachute," the man replied. Plumb gasped
in surprise and gratitude. The man pumped his hand and
said, "I guess it worked!" Plumb assured him, "It sure did. If
your chute hadn't worked, I wouldn't be here today."*

*Charles couldn't sleep that night, thinking about that
man. Charles says, "I kept wondering what he might have
looked like in a navy uniform: a white hat, a bib in the back,
and bell-bottom trousers. I wonder how many times I might
have seen him and not even said, 'Good morning, how are
you?' or anything because, you see, I was a fighter pilot and
he was just a sailor."*

*Charles thought of the many hours the sailor had spent
at a long wooden table in the bowels of the ship, carefully*

weaving the shrouds and folding the silks of each chute, each time holding in his hands the fate of someone he didn't know. Today Charles Plumb is constantly thankful for all the people who continually pack his parachute.

•

People need people to back them up when stuff happens. And when people detect a positive attitude about you, they tend to move in your direction. They are prone to want to assist you. They are less inclined to avoid you and more inclined to work with you. A positive attitude will bring you friends and colleagues who will be there for you when stuff happens.

•

Diane was having lunch with a coworker. They were sitting at the diner counter close to other customers when her friend suddenly asked the unaskable question, "How old are you, Diane?" It suddenly got quiet, and all ears at the counter turned in their direction. Without so much as a batted eye, Diane proudly proclaimed, "I'm 51." Her friend said, "I can't believe it. You look so much younger." A young man sitting nearby leaned over and said, "If you'd take off a little weight, I think you'd even look better."

Everyone at the counter suddenly looked embarrassed, but Diane didn't wait a beat before she answered. With a big kind smile on her face she said, "Well, as far as I'm concerned, kid, what I think of myself certainly doesn't depend on what you seem to think. I know for a fact that there are those who consider me the most beautiful, sexy, wittiest, and loveliest person they've ever met. So your opinion doesn't matter to me at all!"

At *that point, the other customers broke out in applause.*

●

Question: Of the two people here, which one would you prefer to have as a friend or colleague? The young man who made the remark or Diane?

Isn't it a given that it's Diane you would like to know better? Like to be around? Of course it is. That's because she has a positive attitude, and this attitude comforts and inspires people around her. People draw from her resilience and confidence. She has a "winner's attitude."

The young man's comment might have been considered offensive, but Diane handled it using one of reality's rules.

HERE IT IS AGAIN. REALITY RULE #1
It's not what happens to you that's important—it's how you respond to what happens.

One—More—Time:

It's not what happens to you that's important—it's how you respond to what happens.

Shut Up and Listen for a Change

•

Frank and his wife, Liz, went out to dinner with one of their friends, Robert, a well-known actor. Rob, as he is called by his friends, is a person whose company they always enjoyed. The conversation for most of the meal was about things Frank and Liz had accomplished, or about Liz's job, or what the couple had done that day. It was a fun evening.

Later, after returning home, they realized that Rob didn't do very much talking about himself. Although they knew Rob had a lot of interesting stories to tell of his own, he had been listening so intently, was so interested in what Frank and Liz had to say, that they just kept rattling on. And because of this, Frank and Liz had a great time.

When they got home, the reality of it all finally dawned on them (Dah? Light bulb! Boing!). The reason the evening turned out so great was because Rob was genuinely interested in what they had to say. And he was LISTENING!

•

FACT

Most people like talking about themselves, especially if they have a good audience. And a person who listens is a person everyone likes to be around.

Because of this experience Frank and Liz formed a secret pact. From that moment on, whenever they entertain guests and one of them realizes the other is monopolizing the conversation, he or she will kick the other under the table. That is the signal to change the conversation to asking about their guest's day and start listening. Try it. It works every time.

> ### QUICK THOUGHT
> Wouldn't it be great if you could use this technique on some of your guests or business colleagues?

You see, Frank and Liz's movie-star friend clearly had the power to influence. His sincere interest in other people's lives endears them to him, and he clearly has them under his spell. A good, warm, and comforting spell, that is.

AN ASIDE

There's a story about a man in a friendly conversation who was going on and on and on, talking only about himself. Realizing this, he suddenly stopped. "Golly," he said. "There I go. Everything is about ME, ME, ME. Why don't we change the subject and talk about YOU for a change? (Short pause.) What do you think of ME?"

We've all been around someone who talks too much and never listens, right? Rarely does this person ask questions or really want to know how you're doing. Really boring.

Listening to others is an art and a very positive way to exude warmth and interest, to help people relax, and to build relationships. These traits are interpreted as positive attitudes and have real power in changing your life. It's nice to have people you can depend on when stuff happens.

Now all of this should be obvious, but unfortunately, some people just don't really care. This "Why should I care?" attitude is self-defeating and prevents one from building and improving human relationships. As we've already pointed out, people need people to succeed. By listening, smiling, looking at, and attending to other people, you lower the tension and can work more effectively with others. Without this, you can have no success, either in life or in your work. So start listening.

Exercise: Walking the Walk

No challenge has ever been met, no change ever adapted to, nor any success achieved without a positive attitude. We all know that contact with negative people can darken our day.

A down attitude can make or break a relationship...a church...a home...a family. On the other hand, a positive attitude can turn a job that is tedious, depressing, and laborious into one that is fulfilling and successful. You can't change the past or the fact that people will act in a certain way. But you can control your attitude. You can program yourself.

So get with the program. Put the book down, stand up, and walk THE WALK. Walk around like you're celebrating. It may seem silly at first, but just do it. Carry yourself like you're really glad to be alive. Move through the room as if what you are doing is the greatest experience in the world. Hold your head high and stick your chest out. And smile! One thing you are going to realize right away is that it is impossible to feel depressed while walking the walk.

Don't stop now. Just keep walking around the room. Act like you own it (you probably do). Hold that head high and keep smiling. Now, try to be depressed. You can't, can you? Okay, reverse the process. Hang your head and frown and walk with a slump. Already feeling depressed? See how your are in control of your own attitude? Isn't it great?

> ### WHAT DOESN'T WORK
> There's a story about a overzealous boss who kept berating his employees by constantly yelling, "I'm the boss and you're nothing." One day one of his employees answered, "Big deal! Boss over nothing!"

Yelling, constant criticism, gossiping, and humiliating just doesn't work. It actually creates an even more negative and intimidating environment. Moaning, groaning, and whining doesn't work either. The only way to affect change in others is to focus solely on your own behavior.... Period.

A Lesson in Attitude

•

William usually makes it a point to be at the airport one hour ahead of his flight departure. Today he was late.

It seemed that everything that could possibly occur to delay William even further was put in play by the Anti-Destination Society. The Anti-Destination Society consists of every person who, for whatever reason, prevents one from getting to where one wants to go in a timely way!

Well, today William got into his car, and the first thing he noticed was that he was low on gas. So he had to stop at the service station. He then raced to the indoor parking garage where he usually parked, and the shuttle—which is usually there and ready to go—was not there. He had to wait for it to return. When it finally arrived, five more people from the Anti-Destination Society arrived to be taken to their respective terminals as well! So William had to wait for them to board.

As a courtesy, the garage offers free coffee. One woman was determined to get coffee, and William's time continued to slip away. It was only 30 minutes before William's flight departed, and he still had to get through security and check-in, not to mention stopping at each terminal for each Anti-Destination Society member to be dropped off. William decided to be cool.

They got to the first stop, dropped the first passenger—it was now 25 minutes until William's flight departed. They stopped at the International Terminal and dropped off the coffee lady and man. Then finally, it was William's turn.

He had three bags. No time to check bags at the curb. It was only 15 minutes to departure time. William figured he'd get through security and check his bags when he checked in for his flight. But there was still security to deal with.

In the security line a dozen members of the Society were ahead of him. The line moved well, however, and he got through the security check with three bags. But on this day he just happened to meet the president of the Anti-Destination Society, and she pulled one of his bags for a random security check just 10 minutes before his flight. And he still had a long walk to the gate. This was the one she wanted to check.

With a certain amount of arrogance, William hoisted the bag up on the table, unzipping and opening the bag in a fit of frustration and a desire to have this over with. The clock was ticking—"I've got to go," William was saying to himself. She saw his arrogance and quickly responded by calling over a supervisor, all the while telling him, "He has an attitude" (referring to William, of course). William was a little perplexed. He hadn't said anything to her, but he was indeed annoyed, and she sensed it. She, of course, was just "doing her job."

After what seemed like forever (she really did take her time), she finished. William grabbed his bags, raced for the gate, and arrived with less than five minutes to go. The other passengers had boarded the plane; William was the last one.

He showed the gate agent his identification, and she asked the standard questions: "Have your bags been in your control at all times? Has anyone given you anything to carry on board?" Before William thought about what he was saying, he responded, "Only an attitude!" He then asked himself, "Now why did I say that?" After all, the only thing he really took on board was the attitude he had created. He was the one who was late this morning. It was William who didn't allow enough time for all the possible problems. Stuff happens, and you have to be prepared. William had developed an attitude that was partly responsible for his almost missing his plane and upsetting him for the rest of the day.

•

There's a lesson to be learned here regarding attitude. Planning ahead is essential, of course. Stuff happens! So do the best you can to plan ahead. And stay cool. William almost lost it when the security person saw he had an attitude. But she was right. However, she also had a bad attitude. Obviously, these are the moments that make her day. But these are also the moments that can disrupt the days of people like William, and his attitude did nothing to help. So once again, it's not what happens to you that's important. It's how you respond.

If you meet the Anti-Destination Society, here are some responses you might try:

- Correct your posture so you look sure of yourself. Don't look like a victim.

- Make eye contact, smile easily, and lean in and not away from people.
- Move toward challenges; be animated with a sense of hustle but with caring, kindness, and trustworthiness.
- Don't gossip, ridicule, judge, put down, bully, or threaten.

If you follow these suggestions, you will be more inclined to win people over rather than doing things that alienate or produce conflict.

> Focus on the response you want to get and not just on what you want to say.

The remarkable thing about all this is that we all have a choice. We can choose the attitude we will embrace for the day. You can start your day by thinking positively every time you speak to other people. Look for the good and point it out. Be encouraging. Be enthusiastic!

This is all part of developing the mental outlook needed for meeting challenges head on. An attitude adjustment or correction is a proven way to deal with life when stuff happens.

REALITY RULE RECAP
Reality Rule #6

To Change Your Life, Change Your Mind

A positive attitude begins between your ears.

Some things are worth getting angry over. Control is the key. But before you totally flip out, do the following:

- Make that obligatory count to 10.
- Carefully consider what you want as a response to your anger.

What you should want:

- Someone who listens.
- Intelligent answers.
- The problem solved.

People who react impulsively to anger by yelling and screaming have simply never learned how to cope positively when stuff happens. How to cope? Try these:

- Don't allow things to smolder and build up.
- Find a friend to talk to, even to yell at, before it gets to be too much for you to handle.

- Know that anger alone can anger others and prevent solutions.

The ability to handle stuff and produce a desired effect begins with changing your attitude. No one likes to be around a person with a bad attitude. But when people detect a positive attitude, they tend to move in your direction. You're going to need people to give you backup when stuff happens.

A person who listens is a person everyone likes to be around. When you feel you might be monopolizing a conversation, try the following:

- Have a friend who will kick you under the table.
- Or kick yourself.
- Then shut up and listen!

Is this all starting to depress you? WALK THE "WALK"! It is impossible to feel depressed while walking the walk:

- Strut around the room.
- Hold your head high.
- Stick your chest out.
- Wear a silly wide smile!

- Yell out "Why me?" while thinking about the good stuff that's happening to you.

Start every day by thinking positive thoughts:

- When you speak to other people, look for the good and point it out.
- Be encouraging.
- Be enthusiastic!

Reality rule #6 is a tool for adjusting your attitude to help meet challenges head on. An attitude adjustment is a proven way to deal with life when stuff happens. And it's all between your ears.

Gratitude Is the Most Powerful Attitude

Say "thank you" when you wake up in the morning.

Life Is a Gift—Don't Trash It!

Everything you have—skin, eyes, ears, taste buds, finger-nails (imagine trying to pick up a dime on a flat surface without fingernails)—is all part of life's gift. You're sitting there reading this book probably in the comfort of your own home while people in other parts of the world, Bosnia, Tibet, Rwanda, Iraq, are still trying to put it together just attempting to make people be civil to one another.

Life is hard. But if you will just look at it as a gift, you'll discover that life is a joy interspersed with highs and lows,

Some get it, some don't. Some will, some won't.

mysteries and revelations, miracles and tragedies, holding on and letting go, ebb and flow, up and down, back and forth. Life is bittersweet.

So act as if life is a gift and watch what happens. Even your enemies are a gift because you learn something very valuable from people you don't like! You learn how not to be.

Life is a gift—don't trash it. The sun rises and sets. The stars come out. Flowers bloom and give forth grand fragrances. Ants walk on earth. Man walks on the moon. Bees make honey. Birds fly and look beautiful. Tides come and go. And then there's the experience of flight, automobiles, modern medicine, and music from Schubert to James Brown, Mozart to Elvis, string quartets to the Beatles, Bach to Boyz to Men.

Then there are plays, novels, poetry, parties, fiestas, comedy, dancing, motion pictures, concerts, and all kinds of religious expression. And love, marriage, the birth of your children, and their first words. The list is so long that it would take another book bigger than this one to complete it.

Exercise: Blessings That Count

Okay, it's time for another exercise time out. We call it *Making Your Blessings Count.* Put the book down and pick up your pencil and paper (we hope by now you have learned to keep a pencil or pen and paper always ready).

Those that do, do. Those that don't, don't.

You're going to make a list, and you will have only two minutes to do it.

Quickly write down six things for which you are grateful.

Come on now. You shouldn't even need two whole minutes to do this. How about just being able to write? Or read? Or being alive? Then there are family and friends, love, freedom, nature's wonders, opportunity. If you're having trouble, go back to the last section and steal a few of ours. But if you really think about it (that's why we give you two minutes), you'll find you have so much to be thankful for, you won't need any outside suggestions.

You don't have to stop at six, you know. However, we suggest you start with six favorites for now and paste the list in the back of this book. Label it *Counting My Blessings* and keep it next to your new life story you have been writing while reading this book. Then, whenever you need your next high, take it out and look at it. We suggest that you keep the list open. As you continue your changed life, it is going to grow. That is, if you keep fertilizing it with all the stuff that is happening to you.

•

Author **Laura Hillenbrand** *came down with a disease so disabling that performing the normal basic routines of life, like walking or even turning over in bed, were almost impos-*

sible without suffering intense pain. The disease, for which there is very little treatment or cure, is called chronic fatigue syndrome. Despite this debilitating illness, she toiled night and day for over four years to write the story of a "rough-hewn, undersized horse with a sad little tail and knees that wouldn't straighten all the way. A big-hearted animal that "turned into a gentlemanly horse with a keen intelligence, awe-inspiring speed, and a ferocious competitive will."

Laura wrote, "Humans aren't the only creatures to seek mastery and rebel at being mastered." That horse went on to be one of the greatest racehorses of all time, and Laura, fueled by her own bounding will to win, also persevered. She didn't sit back and say, "Why me?" She took the stuff life dealt her and used it to identify with and write the best-seller Seabiscuit: An American Legend.

•

When you hear a story like Laura's, a person who had to surmount all kinds of stuff happening to her in order to further her writing, don't you wonder how she could keep from uttering the age-old lament "Why me?" Well, we've always wondered why people never say, "Why me?" when they have good things going on!

Here's another assignment for you. Try asking, "Why me?" when things are going well. "Why me?" when you wake up in the morning. "Why me?" when you feel good. Do it right now. Think of all the good things that have happened to you and walk around the room saying, "Why me?" If nothing else, it will make you feel pretty good. And besides that, with all the walking around the room we are suggesting, think about all that good exercise you're getting. Two birds with one stone and all that. And speaking of that….

Exercise: Storing Up Memories

When stuff happens to you, it can cause a big letdown, a feeling of depression. It can last for hours, days, and in extreme situations, weeks. At this point it is very hard to say "thank you." Well, when it does happen to you, here's a little exercise to help you fix it.

Close your eyes and think of a time when you were absolutely in charge, absolutely on top. Everything was clicking, and you were at the controls. Remember how good that feeling was. Think about how many times you have been in a low funk before and then got back up to that great feeling again. Remember that time of ecstasy, that uplifting moment and accomplishment when you were *with it*. You know from past experience you will be at that moment again. So, relive that past moment. Think how good it will feel again when you get over this present stuff and get back on top. Think, "This too shall pass, and I will be happy again."

"But what if I've never had such a moment of ecstasy?" you ask. Come on. Think! Think hard. Loved ones, boyfriends, girlfriends, achievements, music you've enjoyed, parties you've been to, classes you've passed, beautiful days riding your bike, skating, dancing, loving, swimming. The list can be as long as you live. Yes, you're alive. You're here. The opportunities are endless.

Put the book down, lean back (no walking is necessary), and try this exercise right now. "But things are going well right now," you say. "Why do it now?" Think about it. This is the best time to store up good memories—*before* that bad stuff happens. What you are doing is recording those good moments in your mind for future use. But go further with it. After you've locked a good past moment in your mind, write it down.

Put the bookmark in and do this exercise right this minute. The next chapter can wait.

REALITY RULE RECAP
Reality Rule #7

Gratitude Is the Most Powerful Attitude

Say "thank you" when you wake up in the morning.

This rule is a perfect follow-up to rule #6. Gratitude IS the most powerful attitude. Take a look at that list you made of the six things for which you should be grateful. And, if you haven't already, include these:

- Being alive (You might hum "Staying Alive" while making this list).
- Family.
- Friends.
- Love.
- Freedom.
- Birds that fly and look beautiful.
- Music you love.
- Books to read.
- Sports to watch and play.
- (fill in).
- (fill in).
- (fill in).
- (Keep going until you're smiling!)

Now repeat the storing-up-good-memories exercise:

- Close you eyes.
- Think back on a great moment in your life: marriage, graduation, a child's birth.

- Lock that moment in your mind.
- While it's there, memorize the feeling.
- Be thankful for it.
- Be aware that life always has its ups and downs.
- Tell yourself you'll soon be on your "up" and you'll have that feeling again.
- Say "thank you" that you are alive.

Life is a gift. Don't trash it.

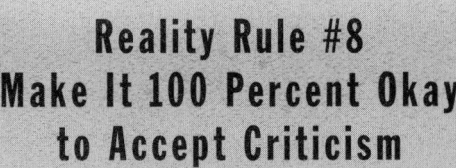

Reality Rule #8
Make It 100 Percent Okay
to Accept Criticism

Feedback... The Breakfast of Champions

The Value of Accepting Criticism

There's a chain of restaurants called Carol's Coco. One employee told us how she used to always get furious and lash out when somebody tried to give her criticism. However, one time when someone started to criticize her, she took a deep breath and for the first time in her life, held her tongue and listened. And according to her, she really learned some constructive things that changed her life.

What did this employee do? She did what most of us need to do more often: bite our tongues and listen. Too many people are so intent on being right and justifying

Some get it, some don't. Some will, some won't.

and getting defensive and trying to prove that they are so interesting that they never ever hear anyone else's opinion.

Most people love to learn, but they hate to be taught. You see, teaching includes criticism, and most people can't stand to be criticized. How about you? Do you dislike being criticized? If so, look at it this way. Being criticized gives you the information you need in order to self-correct. If you can't take criticism, how are you going to make things better? How are you going to learn? How are you going to grow? Here is a rule you can use for the rest of your life.

> Make it 100 percent okay to receive criticism.

Think of criticism as music to your ears. When some people hear it, they get moody. They get upset. Don't be so thin-skinned. Criticism doesn't mean that the critic is right. However, just take the time to listen and consider, "Hey, maybe I can make a little adjustment here, a little tuck there. Maybe I can set some higher goals for myself." Test it. We need the criticism. We need the input. Knowledge is power. And one way to get knowledge is feedback. Criticism is feedback. To succeed in life and get past all that stuff, you must receive criticism.

Need further proof? Read on. If you are health conscious, you probably weigh yourself. Are you aware that you are criticizing yourself? More so if you are overweight. If you have a problem with blood pressure, you have a doctor read it and give you feedback. When you are entering new territory, you use a map and look for signs and mile-

Those that do, do. Those that don't, don't.

stones to tell you where you are and how far along you've progressed. This is feedback. Men always get the bad rap that they never ask for directions. They think they don't need the feedback. Well, who ends up lost? You require feedback in life to tell you how you are growing, developing, and progressing (and where you are).

In creating this book we would each write passages and then pass them on to each other for feedback. We debated, made concessions, and after making the agreed changes, passed our work on to our editor, Matt Holt, at publisher John Wiley & Sons. After making more changes, we finally had a book. Without this input we could never have arrived at what we feel is a worthwhile book.

Now it is in your hands, and your feedback will help us in writing our next book. Our address is in the introduction. If you had stuff happen to you and figured out how to fix it, let us know. We just might use it in *Stuff Happens II*.

The truth is that feedback from others is generally welcome when it yields pleasure and generally unwelcome when it is unpleasant to hear. But suppose it were possible to know and analyze ahead of time what proper moves to make before you did something inappropriate, self-defeating, illegal, immoral, or displeasing. Suppose you could get a grip and avoid self-defeating behavior. What would it be worth to you to operate yourself more effectively? Wouldn't this be great? To be successful in life, you must accept criticism.

> HOW SUCCESSFUL CHEFS BECOME SUCCESSFUL
> When the world's great chefs are preparing a new dish, they engage in a certain activity to assure that the outcome is precisely what they want. Recipes are systems used for achieving outcome, so chefs are constantly engaging in getting feedback. They stand at the pot and they taste. They are criticizing their own work. Then these successful chefs have other people taste their results and await their reaction. Their criticism. This is how they learn how to prepare successful food. Criticism is the chef's key to success.

So, in order to really make your life work and have things you want to have and to be able to be what you want to be, to have success and do what you want to do, to prepare yourself for when stuff happens, you have to be feedback dependent. You have to get fat on the knowledge that comes from feedback. All systems require feedback in order for the participant to adapt, adjust, grow, develop, and change. Like the chef, you have to taste your recipe a thousand times a day.

We have to constantly ask ourselves and others, "How are we doing; how are we moving along?"

Another example: Most companies today are constantly surveying their clients, their customers, to find out how they are doing. Many stores have surveys. "How did we do?" they ask. They want the feedback.

If you looked in the mirror this morning, you got feedback. Why do we do this? We need feedback in order to assure ourselves that we are on course. That's what criticism is. After checking your scale's criticism, you might not go on an instant diet, but you might take a moment to consider cutting back on your next meal. You are, therefore, not only accepting criticism, but you are also making changes. And change is what this book is all about.

Exercise: Unlocking Your Body

Let's try a little feedback experiment now. Put down the book and stand up for a moment. Empty your hands. First, prop the book up so you can follow the instructions. We're now going to get rid of Body Lock (for those of you who feel a little uptight). To get rid of Body Lock, you take one leg and shake it.

Make sure that it shakes all the way up to that glue that's holding your body tight—really get it shaking. Now put that leg down and do the same thing with the other leg. Shake it a little bit, then shake it a lot. You can hold on to things if you need to.

Now take your right hand and shake it. Let your hands move up and let your fingers hang loose. Move until your fingers are like udders on a running cow. How's that for a visual? Got it going? All right, good. . . . Now make those udders float up and then bring them down. All right, do the same thing with your left hand. Now bring both hands down and bring your shoulders up to your ears and hold them tight. Then let go. Take a nice deep breath, hold it, and then let it out.

Now stand on one leg without the benefit of holding on to anything. Great. Don't hurt yourself. Now put that foot down, close your eyes, and attempt to stand on that one leg. You can sit down now and start reading again.

How many found that when you attempted to stand on one leg with your eyes closed, you were a little shaky, you felt a little off balance? Here's why. You weren't getting any feedback. We rely on our senses to give us feedback in order to stay balanced.

This is a graphic example of how we all need feedback. You not only need the feedback from other people, you need the feedback that your body gives you. You need the feedback that your mind gives you.

We use our senses: taste, touch, sight, sound, smell, and one of the senses they don't talk about but you just experienced—balance. Remember gravity? We need a sense of balance in our lives. And we need feedback to achieve that balance. If you want to find out how your relationship is going, ask questions, get feedback. If you wonder how you are doing at work, get feedback. You want your life to get better? Start asking yourself questions. Ask other people. Write it down, be honest, and accept whatever criticism comes your way.

REALITY RULE RECAP
Reality Rule #8

Feedback...The Breakfast of Champions

Make it 100 percent okay to accept criticism.

When people give you honest constructive criticism, don't be so thin-skinned. If the word *criticism* bothers you, call it *feedback*.

Consider this: "Hey, maybe I can make a little adjustment here, a little tuck there. Maybe I could start setting some higher goals for myself." To be successful you need input from others.

Here's what feedback can do:

- Give you the information you need to self-correct.
- Let you know and analyze ahead of time what proper moves to make before you do something inappropriate, self-defeating, illegal, immoral, or displeasing.
- Let you get a grip on your life and avoid self-defeating behavior.
- Help educate you to what changes you might make for improving your chances for success and happiness.
- Give you the power of self-knowledge.
- Give you another tool to "fix it" when stuff happens.

You want your life to get better? Want to find out how a relationship is going? How you are doing in work? Take the feedback test. The next time someone starts to criticize you, try the following:

- Take a deep breath.
- Hold your tongue.
- Listen.
- Be honest and accept what comes your way.
- Think of it as beneficial feedback.
- Think of it as music to your ears.
- Write it down.
- Act on it.

Reality Rule #9
Choose

The Power to Choose Is Within

You have freedom of choice but never freedom from consequences.

Taking Control of Your Vessel

This is our final rule and probably the most important. How you deal with stuff that happens depends solely on how you live your life every day.

When we are born, stuff starts happening right away. We are launched in a boat on the sea of life. We can't control the wind, the storms that throw us off course. We can't control the depths of the ocean or the currents. All we can do is do our best in controlling the vessel we're in.

If we are to understand how to make it in life, we have to understand certain basic things. There are difficult peo-

Some get it, some don't. Some will, some won't.

ple to work with, challenges to meet, and hard decisions to make. Sometimes we're torn by having to make ethical decisions. A part of making it all work is acknowledging that there are rules and principles that when followed, make a positive difference in how we manage stuff.

In life there are some things you can always count on. You can count on change. Change is one of the most pronounced features of life and is reflected in growth.

You can also count on people of character and integrity because they operate with a set of principles. They embrace virtues that collectively reflect the essence of character.

Try this: Make a list of the most dependable, responsible people you know. These should be people that you know personally, people you can count on to be fair, trustworthy, honest, civil, and considerate, people who accept the rules of the game, work hard, and know the principles of what is good, right, and decent. Take a break right now and make your list.

How many people did you come up with? Now think! Here's the real test. If all of the people on your list were to make their own list, would you be on it? Would they trust you with their children, their money, their pets, their most-prized material possessions? If you have any doubts, it's time for a change in your life.

Can you do it? Can you really change? Of course you can. Remember, life has affirmed your viability. You fought to get here. You came with all the things you re-

Those that do, do. Those that don't, don't.

quire to meet challenges, deal with change, and take advantage of opportunities.

But to make these changes, to make it in this vessel called your life, you must use your rudder. Yes, you do have a rudder, and holding on to it will enable you to shift and change your direction at will. Your rudder is called choice.

CHOICE

Most of us lucky people live in a time and place where we can do just about anything we want to. You can talk anyway you want. You can dress anyway you want. You can pierce anything you want. You can tattoo anything you want. You can grow stuff on your face. You don't have to go to work. You can work 24 hours a day, 7 days a week. You can have many girlfriends or boyfriends, or no girlfriends or boyfriends. You can live anywhere you want. You don't have to bathe. You can wear the same underwear for nine months if you choose to. You have freedom of choice. But highlight this: ALTHOUGH YOU HAVE FREEDOM OF CHOICE, YOU WILL NEVER IN YOUR LIFE HAVE FREEDOM FROM CONSEQUENCE.

Choice—that is your rudder. Yes! No! Right! Wrong! Good! Bad! Decent! Indecent! Choose! Some people get more than their share of bad stuff because they just don't get it. They make the wrong choices, and stuff happens.

The world discriminates against those who don't get it and who are ignorant, uninformed in the ways of life, the principles governing reality, human nature, and the human condition.

In order to thrive and survive the wind, the rain, and the underwater currents of life, you not only have to have a rudder but you have to make the *right* choices. And to help guide you, you need a compass.

Compass Points to Lead You

To help you chart your direction in life, you have to have a compass. As we've said before and will keep repeating until you get it: Although you have freedom of choice, you will never in your life have freedom from consequence.

Each of us makes choices daily: to work or not to work, to bathe or not to bathe, to eat or not to eat. We decide how we want to be at any given moment. We decide how we will respond to things.

We have been given free will and freedom of choice. If choice is the rudder in our boat, the compass allows us to set a specific course. And with a course set and holding on to the rudder, we can increase our odds of getting to where it is we want to go.

Compasses normally have four points, but in this book you will find a compass that has five points (four just isn't enough). Five compass points to help you have a better life.

Compass Point #1

Life is a Gift. Don't trash it!

Because we consider this first compass point to be the guiding principle behind everything in this book, we have already discussed it in Reality Rule #7. But it is a rule that should be repeated over and over…and over.

Go back to the exercise in Reality Rule #7, "Blessings That Count," and look over the list you made of things for which you should feel grateful. If you followed directions, you labeled your list "Counting My Blessings" and pasted it to the back of this book. Stop and check your list now. See if you can add to it now, that you are nearing the end of the book. The longer the list, the greater the realization that life truly is a gift and something for which to be very thankful.

Compass Point #2

Of all the gifts you possess, the greatest gift of all is your mind.

Your mind will enable you to meet challenges, solve problems, and take advantage of opportunities.

For years you have been filling your head with stories about yourself. Stories that keep you from going forward.

You may think you are not good enough. Perhaps you don't think you have enough education to have a happy, successful life. These stories are not true, and as far as you are concerned they are lies you keep telling yourself.

But, as we know with the tooth fairy and Santa Claus, a lie is as powerful as the truth if you can get anyone to believe it. But don't you believe those bad stories you've written about yourself. You have everything you need inside of you to make your life work. It comes with the package.

Your mind is the greatest thing you have. You just have to develop it, ask questions, and write things down. Make a list about your life, with "pro" on one side and "con" on the other. Write all the pros and cons about your life and look at them. Analyze them and start getting rid of the cons. Write out a new story about how you want your life to be.

Don't wait. The clock is ticking. Your mind is the greatest gift you have. Don't waste it. Put it to work. You're here. You were born. You are already ahead of the game.

Compass Point #3

Develop your talents and give them back to the world.

There are those who say, "You are what you do." We prefer, "You do what you are." In other words, find out what you are good at, then do it, develop it, improve it, and give it back.

Some of you are good at talking to people. Some of you are good at planning, teaching, homemaking, writing, or sports. Whatever you are good at, pass it on. Show others how to do it and maybe they will also pass it on. This could be your legacy. This could be what that dash (–) on your tombstone will stand for. It's a great way to live, and it will give you a lot to be thankful for. It will give you many pleasures to fall back on when stuff happens. Prepare yourself and do it. Do it before your time runs out. Say over and over again, "If it's to be, it's up to me."

•

George *was 15 years old. One of his favorite pastimes was sitting by the edge of the lake watching water-skiers skim over water. He was always completely awed by the skiers' uncanny ability to glide over what looked like a glass-topped table. He secretly yearned for the thrill of doing something like this but never told anybody about his dream.*

Then one day the phone rang. It was a friend of his father, an attorney named Tom. "George" he said, "I JUST BOUGHT A BOAT, and I'm taking some kids water-skiing tomorrow. Want to come along?"

True to his word, Tom arrived early the next morning. He was driving a motor home (a first experience for George), and soon George found himself at the lake waist deep in warm water with several of the other boys. Tom and his girlfriend were up front in his brand-new boat. She would be doing the driving. George would never forget the smell of the outboard motor fumes and water—a smell that would bring back the wonderful memory of this exhilarating experience for the rest of his life.

Tom looked back and asked, "Okay, who's first?" George jumped at the opportunity. He nervously put on the skis as Tom threw him the towline. "Okay, keep your arms straight, your knees bent, and stay behind the boat," Tom said as they started the engine. George took the towline handle and sat in the water with the ski tips up as he was instructed. He nervously said, "Hit it," and the boat took off. George was jerked up, flipped over flat on his face, and dragged through the water. Stuff happened! However, the only thing hurt was his ego.

It happened for five more attempts. Tom then got out of the boat, came back with another pair of skis for himself and an extra towline, and sat down next to George in the water. "Now remember what I said. Keep your arms straight, your knees bent, and stay behind the boat."

Tom yelled out, "Hit it!" Again, George attempted to get up, but this time Tom was skiing right next to him and reached out with his hand to hold George's upper arm straight out. Tom kept saying again and again, actually yelling at George, to keep his arms straight, arms straight. Over and over and over he said it.

George began to get it. He had locked it in his mind. "Arms straight, knees bent," and he was up. He was in a squatting position, but he was on the surface of the water with Tom next to him still holding his arm and encouraging him to get up into an upright position. He did. He got it. He kept his arms straight. He flexed his legs. Tom let go, and *there he was, alone and literally flying over the water as Tom yelled, "Stay behind the boat!"*

Oh what a joy. He was now just like the guys he had watched and dreamed about. It was then that he realized what he had always wanted. He wanted to ski. But he had needed a teacher who would pass on his skills. And a teacher had appeared.

Ten years later George BOUGHT A BOAT. And guess what? He got some kids together who wanted to learn how to water-ski, took them out on the boat, and told them the same thing Tom had told him: "Okay, keep your arms straight, your knees bent, and stay behind the boat." It was funny how the same scenario repeated itself. The new kids all flopped and splashed, but George knew exactly what to do.

He got out of the boat with an extra pair of skis and sat down next to each kid one at a time and said, "Now remember, keep your arms straight, your knees bent, and stay behind the boat." He would take each kid's arm, hold it out straight, and together they would rise up onto the surface. Everyone he ever took water-skiing learned how to do it and never forgot this great experience.

Proof? Ten year later, George got a call from one of his successful water-skiing kids, who was now grown. "Guess what?" she said, " I JUST BOUGHT A BOAT!"

•

This story is not just a great example of developing your talents and giving them back to the world. It is also an excellent metaphor of how to fix it when stuff happens in your life. When you keep falling down, "Keep your arms straight, knees bent, and stay behind the boat." This means that in coping with the stuff of life, there are times when you have to be resolute and firm. You have to keep your arms straight. Then there are times when you have to be flexible enough to bend when life becomes too choppy to remain upright. In all cases you have to remain behind what drives you or, in this instance, pulls you along. It is your vision and your values that fuel your desire to move forward.

Like a water-skier, you can jump to the side from time to time, and it can be very smooth. But you can never get too far ahead of yourself. And remember, each of us needs other people to succeed. Tom learned to ski and taught George. George learned and taught someone else. And that person continued the legacy.

So when stuff happens, remember: "Keep your arms straight, your knees bent, and stay behind the boat." And when you learn how to do it, give it back to the world.

Compass Point #4

Be the most decent person you can be.

When things are broken, let's get together and fix them. When things are dirty, clean them up. If you see somebody suffering, reach out to help. If you see an injustice, stand up and fight to make it right. It takes courage. Ethics is not for wimps. You have to stand and hold the line and take a position.

●

In 1973 high school graduate **John Naber** *was competing for a spot on the world-championship swim team. He was a favorite to win in the 100-meter backstroke and knew that if he won here, he'd most likely win a medal at the World Championships. He won the race, but he was cited by an official for an infraction. The judge said that she didn't see him touch the wall of the pool at the end of one of his laps. He thought he had, but then some doubt started to creep in. Maybe, just maybe, he hadn't. John could have protested and fought it just to get the title, but he knew how this self-doubt would follow him for the rest of his life.*

John knew what was at stake, but his upbringing didn't allow for cheaters. It would have been so easy to cry foul, which is what many of his friends were insisting he do. But the truth was, and he was beginning to realize it more and more, that he had broken the rules and had to be held accountable. Being a person of character is not just about following the rules, of course. He could have fought — he had a right to fight — but it would have been the wrong thing to do because now he knew that he hadn't touched the wall. Adhering to what is allowable is one thing; doing what is right is something else.

●

By the way, John Naber didn't make the 1973 World Championship team for the 100-meter race, but he did qualify for the 200-meter backstroke and won a bronze medal in Belgrade, Yugoslavia. At the Olympic games in Montreal he earned four gold medals and set a world record.

There are principles of civility that can work for us but when violated create more stuff for people to deal with. It is a fact that some of the worst pains some of us have had to endure have been the result of people using words in a hurtful way. Unwarranted criticism done in a deprecating way, betrayal of secrets, sarcasm, public humiliation, malicious gossip, and unabated anger have power to hurt others. Knowing what is good, appropriate, and right and doing it are part of the formula for integrity and character. Speaking unfairly of others violates a principle of civility and decency. The admonition "If you can't say something good about a person, don't say anything!" is a principle worth observing. Applying this principle keeps a lot of unnecessary stuff from happening.

Exercise: What's in a Name?

This is your last exercise before the end of the book. So put down your book, take up the pen and paper, and play "What's in a Name?" First, write down your name. Next to each letter, assign a virtue to that letter. Call it your decency alphabet.

Virtue (vur'choo), n. 1. moral excellence; goodness;
righteousness, decency. 2. conformity of one's life
and conduct to moral and ethical principles.
Webster's Encyclopedic Dictionary

Take John, for example:

J = Joyful

O = Open

H = Honest

N = Nice

You'll find that some letters are difficult to match, like
"Y" or "X." If that's the case, just substitute any letter you
like. When you are finished, put it in the book alongside
your *Counting My Blessings* list. And then...LIVE UP TO
YOUR NAME!

•

Montel *took his two children to the county fair. The admission price was $10.00 for adults and children over six. Montel's son Jason is 11 and La Tonya is 7 years old. When Montel paid the admission, he paid for three adults. The ticket seller asked, "How old is your little girl?" Montel told him she was seven. The ticket seller replied, "Hey, bud, you know, you could have saved ten dollars by telling me she was six, and I wouldn't have known the difference."*

Montel responded, "Yes, I guess I could have done that, but you know what?" as he stood looking at his two children, Jason and La Tonya, "They would have known!"

•

In coping and using a guidance system, Montel had taught his kids a lesson and, we hope, reminded the ticket seller of what was the right thing to do!

Montel was principled enough to embrace the virtue of honesty. He could have easily lied about the age of his children, but in the process what would he have been teaching them, and in turn, set into motion for the future?

Compass Point #5

Remember, in this particular game there is no guarantee on time.

How many of you know someone who did not live to be 35 years old? Frank was 17. He stepped out of a store, and somebody put a knife in his chest. That was it—17 years gone. Finished. You never know.

●

Sam *opened his wife's underwear drawer and picked up a silk-paper–wrapped package. "This," he said," isn't any ordinary package." He unwrapped the box and stared at both the silk paper and the box. "She got this the first time we went to New York, eight or nine years ago. She never put it on. Was saving it for a special occasion. Well, I guess this is it," he said as he walked to the bed and placed the gift box next to the other clothing he was taking to the funeral home. Sam's wife had just died. He mused, "Never save something for a special occasion. Every day in your life is a special occasion."*

●

In closing this book, keep in mind this thought: The alternative to stuff happening is nothing happening. You can fix it when stuff happens. But nothing is nothing. Just like the grass in the yard, we all need a little stuff now and then to grow.

It is our belief that *living well,* prospering, and growing in awareness are the best revenge for stuff that happens.

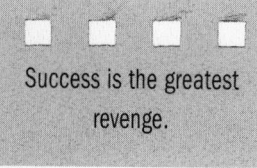

Success is the greatest revenge.

Life gets better as you get better. What matters is not so much whether you have been hurt, oppressed, denied, set back, discriminated against, failed, separated, or victimized by disease or disorder in the past. None of that can be undone. But if you are alive and conscious of the truth, aware of the story you use to describe your condition, you can change your experience of things.

Final Story as Told by John Alston

•

My aunt Lois taught at UCLA and for three years in a row was voted the number-one professor by her students. I used to go and see her when I had problems in my life and was trying to sort things out. She was a young woman. I had been on the road, and I came home to a message on my machine. It was my mother's voice saying, "Lois is in the hospital. They don't expect her to live another 24 hours."

I got in my car and raced to the hospital. Security directed me to a physician's parking space. After bumbling my way through the hospital, I found her room. There in the bed lay the body of a woman that if she weighed 60 pounds she weighed a pound. I'll never forget the breathing.

I remember that I took her hand, and I held it and said, "Lois." I squeezed her hand, and I swear that though she never regained consciousness, she seemed to squeeze back. Do you know that it was then that I said "thank you"? Do you know it was then that I told her how much I loved and cared about her? Do you know it was then I kept saying, "Why her?" We have people out there who are stealing, killing, and tearing up people's lives; why this good woman? And then she was gone.

Ladies and gentlemen, there are people in your life whom you love and who care about you. There is so much for which you should be grateful. I never leave my house even going to the store for 10 minutes without hugging and kissing my wife and daughter goodbye. We don't know, so love them now. Say "thank you" now.

●

REALITY RULE RECAP
Reality Rule #9

The Power to Choose Is Within

You have freedom of choice but never freedom from consequences.

In this vessel called life you have a rudder—something you can hold on to for shifting and changing direction. This rudder is called choice. You can steer yourself in any direction you choose. But remember, although you always have freedom of choice in life, you never have freedom from the consequences.

Therefore, for you to thrive, you have to make the right choices. For this, you need a compass. Ours has five points.

1. Life is a gift. Don't trash it!
    *   Say "thank you" when you get up in the morning.
    *   Say "Why me?" when good things happen.

2. Of all the gifts you possess, the greatest gift of all is your mind. Some of you have been filling your heads with stories that keep you from going forward. They are lies. Try this:
    *   Put a rubber band around your wrist.
    *   Every time that inner voice tells you a lie, snap the band hard.
    *   Feel the pain.
    *   Remember the pain.

After a while you won't need the rubber band any-more. Remembering the pain associated with the lie will be enough to remind you it is a lie.

3. Develop your talents and give them back to the world. Hint: Buy a boat and show a kid how to water-ski, or teach someone how to fish or how to read. It has been said that if you give a person a fish you feed him for one day. Teach a person to fish and you feed him for a life-time.

4. Be the most decent person you can be. Knowing what is good, appropriate, and right and then doing it are a part of the formula for dealing with life's problems.

5. Remember, in this particular game there is no guaran-tee on time. You have to get going.

> Keep this thought in mind: The alternative to stuff happening is nothing happening. You can fix it when stuff happens. But nothing is nothing. You're here. You're something. You're alive. And just like the grass in the yard, we all need a little stuff now and then to help us grow.

Epilogue

Okay, let's try to sum this up. You made it to the egg first. Then you had your first experience of stuff happening: You were born (evicted, you might say).

You came into this world a babbling, helpless infant. When stuff happened, you cried and people came to your rescue.

You grew, learned to take that first step, fell down, and learned how to get back up. But that caused more stuff you had to deal with. You learned that life is both the result of what happens to you and how you respond. At one point you were told, "Okay, baby, stop crying and get to work."

Some get it, some don't. Some will, some won't.

Moaning, groaning, crying, and complaining not only are unattractive and display a poor attitude; they do nothing to enable you to manage stuff. Stuff will always happen, even when things are good and going well. You have to know how to respond to what life deals you.

Some get it. Some don't. But to thrive and survive, you have to stop doing what doesn't work and figure out a system that works.

When it doesn't work, it just means more stuff to deal with. That is the consequence of not having a good system that works and messing up when either natural consequences prevail or you fail to accept criticism that could help steer you back in the right direction.

But even when you are clipping along with everything working, like Harry, the dot.com bomber, stuff can still happen. It may be happenstance, bad luck, idiot boneheads, acts of God, criminals, or people in your life that come along and screw up. Regardless, you have to have a system for handling the screwup, the consequence of things not working. You have to take control of your stuff, or someone else will. You have to be in control of your responses to bad things happening.

Stuff that happens may not be your fault. It could be bad or poor parents, bad schools or teachers, or a physical handicap. Think of Roger Crawford, who fixed it by becoming a tennis pro, and Laura Hillenbrand, who became a successful novelist. One thing we have to get is that we have to handle what comes. Each one of us can have a sys-

Those that do, do. Those that don't, don't.

tem to cope. We have to gather the knowledge to develop that system. But first, acknowledge that you are here now and appreciate what is happening now. Say "thank you" now.

To get it you must have knowledge. Knowledge is power. Within that knowledge is something that works. If there is a solution to a problem, then you have no problem. If not, look for and create a solution. Some get it. Some don't. Get what? That the solution is in the body of knowledge. You must always be aware that anything can happen at any given moment and that you must be prepared.

Yes, you are here, you have ability, and you have resources. So get off your butt. You will be nervous, but you have to take action. You have to do something. Right or wrong, do something. If it works, good. Less stuff to deal with.

Some get it. Some don't. Some will. Some won't. Those that do, do. Those that don't, don't.

And that's what it's all about.

Say "Thank you," when you wake up in the morning.

End Message from John and Lloyd

It is our hope that after you finish reading *Stuff Happens*, you won't just put it back on the shelf and forget about it. We made it short enough that you could take it out from time to time and reread the parts you might need to help you overcome any recent bad stuff. In the meantime here's a suggestion. As soon as you finish the last page, sit down and write a personal affirmation for yourself.

An affirmation, as opposed to a negation, is an affirming and positive self-pledge, a personal mission-in-life statement consisting of encouraging words and phrases that support, uplift, direct, and remind you of what is im-

Some get it, some don't. Some will, some won't.

portant for you to do and that is designed to fuel your immediate actions. Negative thoughts, like "I am insignificant, life is too hard, it's not fair, I can't handle this, I am all alone," are not allowed.

Take your time. You don't have to do it all at once. After all, this is something you are going to live with and, we hope, act on for the rest of your life. This exercise will be a beginning. You can work on it at your own pace, but at least work on it.

This last assignment is designed to enhance your effort to deal with stuff. Isn't that why you bought the book in the first place? If you're stuck as to how to begin, we've included the following example to assist you. You most likely will have other ideas, but this affirmation is ours, and you are welcome to use it to help you write yours.

Affirmation

I am somebody, and I was not put here to fail. In fact, it is my intention to achieve more and to be better today than yesterday. I have ability, I have resources, and I am committed to using both. I have the capacity to be what I want to be, to do what I want to do, and to have what I want to have. And I know I must work hard to get it.

I know that life is bittersweet, and I will minimize my tendency to whine, cry, moan, groan, and complain about things over which I have no control. I can choose to get

Those that do, do. Those that don't, don't.

better at solving my problems, or I can choose to wither and die on the vine. I choose to live.

I will make allowances for other people's shortcomings and will take care to know my own and correct them. I will use my strengths to compensate for my weaknesses, and because I have learned that respect is valued more when it is earned, I will work hard to gain that respect.

I know the greatest battle I fight is the one within. It is the ongoing struggle between what I should do and what I feel like doing. With this in mind, I will strive to consciously control my impulses, direct my instincts, and accomplish my goals in an honorable way.

I know that if it is to be, it is up to me, but with the realization that no one achieves anything alone.

Finally, I have come to the realization that life is a gift, and I will say "thank you" when I wake up each morning.

This is my affirmation. May my vision remain clear and my actions immediate, honorable, and strong!

Okay, stuff....I'm ready.

Happen!

OK Stuff. . .
I'm ready.
HAPPEN!

Appendix

A Few Bits of Reality to Stick on the Fridge and Help You Stay on Course

- Life is a gift. Don't trash it.
- Some get it. Some don't. Some will. Some won't. Those that do, do. Those that don't, don't.
- Remember, the greatest gift you have is your mind. Use it and your life experiences to grow.
- Know the goal. Find out what you're good at, develop it, and give it back to the world. The world is waiting for your contribution.
- Always be the most decent human being that you can be, and DON'T WASTE YOUR TIME!
- First rule of life's game: Show up.

Some get it, some don't. Some will, some won't.

- When you were born, you showed up. You're 1 in 200 million.
- Shout "Why me?" when good things happen and shut up and listen for a change.
- Always remember to say "thank you" when you wake up in the morning. After all, if you woke up, you're still alive and in the game!
- You're constantly writing the story of your life, so make it count.
- When bad stuff happens, think of it as fertilizer. It will help you grow.
- Adjust your attitude and move on. Don't waste your time.
- The only thing between birth and death is time. How you use your time will define your life.
- Write your story down. You're writing the recipe that you will cook with for the rest of your life.
- Whom you associate with is going to make a big difference in your life. So pick the best.
- Take control of your mind. If you don't, somebody else will.
- Get prepared for the rain.
- Gravity works. When you were born, you couldn't walk without falling down.
- In order to get from A to B you have to take that first step. You have to learn that that's when you are most vulnerable to being knocked down.
- People who do stupid things are trying to defy gravity.

Those that do, do. Those that don't, don't.

- Not feeling like doing the right thing is no excuse for not doing the right thing.
- Knowledge is power.
- We are all feedback dependent.
- Make it 100 percent okay to receive criticism.
- Attitude is everything. It is how you influence other people.
- You can be only as successful as your ability to create, maintain, and influence positive human relationships. People need people.
- No one likes to be around a person with a negative attitude.
- People with negative attitudes rarely advance in their jobs.
- It's not what happens to you that's important. It's how you respond to what happens.
- A positive attitude uplifts the spirit.
- In order to get people to like being around you, to influence other people, you just have to shut up and listen for a change.
- The magic is you. The control of your attitude is inside.
- Know the role you must play in making things better, and then act the part.
- Be what you want to see.
- Practice training your mind. Practice gathering knowledge. Look for people who are good at influencing other people and mimic their behavior.

- Be a slave to discipline. Discipline will help you get through it when bad stuff happens.
- What works works. What doesn't work doesn't work. Working hard at things that don't work will never make them work. Stop working at things that don't work.
- Get up, go to work, come home, go to bed. Boring? To change the story of your life, change your mind.
- Move through life like it is the greatest experience in the world.
- It is impossible to feel depressed when you hold your head up and smile.
- Recognize the difference between a problem and an inconvenience.
- Respect, like prosperity, is valued more when it is earned.
- Life is an ongoing struggle between that which you know you should do and that which you feel like doing.
- Although you have freedom of choice, you will never in your life have freedom from consequence.
- To navigate in life we not only need a rudder; we need compass points to guide us.
- Remember, there is no guarantee on time. Don't waste it.